WE ARE NOT SAINTS

THE PRIEST

WE ARE NO✝ SAINTS

THE PRIEST

H. LES BROWN

Gibson-Brown Media, Palm Springs, 92262

© 2021 H. Les Brown
All rights reserved. Published 2021

Printed in the United States of America

ISBN: 978-0-9798668-8-3

Dedication

To my faithful husband, Craig, who, for over a quarter of a century has helped make God's promises come true beyond our wildest imaginings; and to those LGBTQ+ priests, ministers, rabbis, mullahs, and consecrated religious who have provided God and his people lifetimes of faithful service, despite the frequent darkness and loneliness of the ecclesiastical closet.

Acknowledgements

The author wishes to acknowledge the contributions of his readers, Steve Black, David Todd, and the late Nye Willden whose comments, corrections, and suggestions have been invaluable, as well as his editor, Michelle Barker from Darling Axe, and Stephan Smith of Smith Creative Group for his creative advice and original artwork. Most importantly he owes a huge debt of gratitude to his husband, Craig Gibson, whose editing skills, encouragement, and patience helped keep the spirit of creativity alive.

Preface

I hope that the characters in this story come to life for you, since we live shoulder-to-shoulder with people like these. Each of them is attempting to find his or her way in a world of moral ambiguity. Nonetheless, please know that this story is entirely fictional. None of the characters is based on myself or anyone I have ever known. The events are also fictional and, even though some settings may be real, to my knowledge, nothing like what is described here ever happened there.

The world of the Catholic clergy can seem esoteric and mysterious, regardless of one's religious background. To assist my readers, I've provided a glossary at the back of this book, to clarify some of the terminology that may be either unfamiliar or unclear. I hope you will find it useful.

The fact that many of these characters are Roman Catholic clergy involves an additional layer of complexity to the story. These are men and women who have committed themselves publicly to Christian values and thus have invited us to judge them by our own expectations of what that means.

Some readers may see these clergy as failures. Others may see them as hypocrites. What they are meant to be in fact is a group of fallible human beings trying to give flesh to a complex spiritual life to the best of their abilities. As in real life, some have more success than others. My hope is that you will see these people as neither better nor worse than we. Moral ambiguity remains forever the warp and woof of the fabric of our humanity.

Chapter 1

Deacon Jared Röhrbach stood at the window of his fifth-floor dorm room looking out across the rooftops of Rome. In front of him, the dome of Saint Peter's was brilliantly illuminated, glowing like a jewel against the inky blackness of the pre-dawn sky. The view from his window was awe-inspiring—one of the best in the city—and it never failed to fill him with a sense of wonder. In so many ways, Saint Peter's was the center of the city and the center of his world. There was concentrated the spiritual power and authority that had given meaning and direction to his life since he was a boy, and it drew him even now.

Nights were still chilly this early in June, but he had his window partially open to enjoy the cool breeze. Like New York, Rome is a city that never sleeps. But it does take the occasional cat nap, like now. The only sounds floating in on the morning breeze were the rustling of the leaves in the cloister courtyard beneath his window: a moment of heavenly calm before the city erupts in a maelstrom of the traffic for which it is so justly famous.

Jared was annoyed. He wanted to feel as quiet and serene inside as the world outside his window, but he couldn't. He hadn't slept well. The dream that had been playing out its strange performance just before he awoke was still haunting him. He still had the image in mind of himself standing in front of his father and his deceased mother. It made him feel small and vulnerable. But why? Were they judging him? He didn't care anymore about pleasing his father and he could never know whether or not his mother was pleased with him from wherever she was in the Great Beyond. So, why did it matter? Yet, despite all his brave self-talk, deep down, it did. He hated that feeling. He wanted to feel something else—*anything*.

His gaze drifted down from the heights of Saint Peter's to the seminary chapel that formed the far wall of the cloister. All the stained glass in the building was dark. It looked as though the chapel was asleep. But Jared knew that Paul was in there somewhere. He could feel a tug at his heart. Paul was his ...his *what?* What was Paul to him? A paramour? A spouse? That question hung like a sticky cobweb in the back of his mind. As often as he brushed it away, it always kept returning. His *Paul.* As close as they had been for so many years, it still felt like they were on opposite sides: he in his bedroom staring across an open space at Paul in the chapel.

The whole scene was imbued with loneliness. The residence was nearly empty. Students and seminary staff had left for summer assignments or gone on to be ordained somewhere else. The silence of the empty building weighed on him. It left him too much time to think and to feel things— uncomfortable things. Their ordination wasn't for several more hours. The waiting was getting to him. He wanted it over. He wanted to experience kneeling beside Paul and feeling the weight of the cardinal's hands imposed on his head.

Enough! He crossed the room and flipped on the light. *Time to shower.* No need to rush, but he couldn't daydream too long, either. He grabbed the thin, threadbare faded blue robe from its hook on the back of the door and slid it on over his arms. He almost did without it, but he didn't want old Father Rinaldi to come out of his room and be suddenly faced with six-foot-two, two hundred pounds of naked flesh. *God knows if he'd survive the shock!* Jared laughed out loud at the thought. He grabbed his towel and, as he went for the doorknob, he couldn't avoid the temptation to check himself out in the mirror on the back of the door. He had crafted himself into a well-built young man and wasn't beyond grabbing an admiring glance at his handiwork in the mirror. That's why he'd put it there, after all!

He headed out and down the corridor toward the communal showers at the end of the hall, his bare feet slapping softly against the cold tile floor. This early in the morning, the corridor was lit only by a series of dim night lights on the walls at ankle height, alternating from one side to the other the whole length. The hall was also lined on both sides with identical doors, all standing open, showing the dark, empty dorm rooms within. Just one door was closed and, as Jared passed it, he paused. He could see through the transom that the light was on. *Jeff's still here.*

He knocked on Jeff's door. The mumbled response from inside was unintelligible. When Jeff opened the door, the tall, handsome young man was dressed only in boxer shorts and a t-shirt. He looked fresh-scrubbed and smelled of Safeguard soap. "Well, this is a surprise," he said with a smile, "seeing Jared Röhrbach up before the sun. To what do I owe this honor?"

"Nothing. I was on my way to the showers and saw your light on. I thought I'd see what you were up to. Going down for some breakfast?"

"Not right away. I'm getting some last-minute packing done."

Jared could see beyond Jeff into the chaos that had once been a neat and tidy room. "So, I see. What's the hurry? You are coming to the reception this afternoon, aren't you? The cardinal will be there."

"I know. Paul invited me, but he said it was going to be his immediate family, and I didn't want to be the odd man out."

"I'm sorry to hear that. I just assumed that was the reason you stayed behind here."

"I thought about going. That's what I wanted to do at first, but I changed my mind."

"We'll miss you,' Jared lied. He was relieved that he wouldn't have to watch Jeff fawning over Paul. "I'd better get going," he said, nodding toward the half-finished packing. "I don't want to hold you up. See you at the ordination, then." Jared turned to leave.

"I'm not going."

"What," Jared said, turning back. He hadn't expected that. "Why not?"

"It's just something personal," Jeff said, avoiding Jared's gaze. "I thought I could do it, but I just can't."

It was obvious how emotional Jeff was. It told Jared all he needed to know about Jeff's lingering feelings for Paul. *Okay, Buddy, you can fool yourself, but you can't fool me.* He decided to keep playing the role of unsuspecting spouse. "Paul will be so disappointed ...and so will I." He knit his brows. "Have you told him? He hasn't said anything to me."

"Not yet. In fact, I was going to go look for him as soon as I get some clothes on. Have you seen him this morning?"

Not since he left my room. "No, but, knowing him, he's probably in the chapel already."

"That's what I thought." Jeff hesitated for a second, then gave Jared a warm smile. "I guess this is goodbye, then. Congratulations in advance on your ordination. I know it'll be awesome." He took a step forward. "I'm going to miss you." He wrapped his arms around Jared and gave him a warm hug. "Hope we'll see each other again soon. Stranger things have happened!"

Jared returned the embrace and said, "Yeah, me too." Then he continued on his way to the showers.

It wasn't long before he rinsed off, shut off the water and, grabbing his towel, stepped out of the shower and started drying himself. He was still too preoccupied with his own thoughts to take much notice of what he was doing. As he started back to his room, he wasn't even aware he had neglected to put his robe on but carried it with his towel draped across one arm. Yet, he wasn't preoccupied enough to miss seeing the door to Jeff's dorm room standing ajar. He approached it and pushed it open. The room was dark with only the shaft of light from the hallway lighting up the interior, but there was just enough light to see that the room was piled with luggage and boxes but was otherwise unoccupied.

Jeff's out looking for Paul. Overcome with curiosity, he slipped through the empty doorway. All year, Jeff's dorm room had reminded Jared of some rural midwestern high school kid's bedroom. He had posters of some rock and movie stars on the walls, and he even kept a couple of his track and field trophies on his desk. Jared thought it was all a little much, even for

4

a boy from Racine, Wisconsin.

All that was gone now, and the walls were bare. Even in the dim light from the hall, Jared could see that Jeff was in the last stages of packing. As he wandered about the room letting his curiosity get the best of him, Jared leafed idly though the various piles of clothing and sundries. He wasn't looking for anything in particular. He found nothing lying around in the organized chaos of the room that interested him. At that point, he was just being nosey.

On his way out, Jared passed Jeff's desk and noticed his briefcase lying there. *Oho! This oughta be interesting.* He gave the top of it a flip with two fingers. The case must have been unlocked because it came right open. With one hand, he reached inside and shuffled the papers around. He was almost disappointed that it was all the usual stuff they all carried when they travelled: airline ticket, passport, visa, school documents, even some cash. None of it interested him. In the top of the case, there was a large pocket that was bulging in the middle. Slipping his hand inside, he pulled out a stack of envelopes with a rubber band around them. He recognized the envelopes as the stationery imprinted with the school logo for the students. He recognized something else: Paul's handwriting.

He shuffled through the stack with his thumb. They were all the same, except the postmarks were from different dates. He slid one of the envelopes out from the middle of the stack. He didn't want to disturb the ones on the top or bottom. Jeff might notice if one of those went missing. But he might never catch on that one was missing from the *middle*. He grabbed his robe and shoved his arms though, sliding the envelope into a side pocket with one hand while he replaced the stack in its hiding place and shut the briefcase. He stepped to the door and peered into the hall, even though he knew no one was there. He would have heard someone coming into the dorm long ago. Part of him enjoyed playing the sleuth, especially if it led to the uncovering of some juicy secrets!

He padded back to his room, almost tiptoeing with his bare feet. He tossed his damp towel and dop kit on the bed and sat down, fishing his piece of

5

"evidence" out of his pocket. The postmark was from Rome and dated the fifteenth of July last year. The return address was Saint Patrick's Church on the Via Boncompagni where Paul had served his last summer assignment. The letter was addressed to Jeff at his parents' home in Racine. Even though Jared had expected as much as soon as he saw the letters, he felt his anger welling up inside him, overshadowing the nervous excitement he had first felt at his "discovery." He slid the pages—there were four—out of the envelope and spread them out. He started to read. What he read confirmed everything he had suspected, and more so. The letter was so explicitly erotic that he was taken aback. Even though he was alone in the room, he impulsively covered himself up with the folds of his robe.

He had seen enough. He didn't need to read the whole thing. He refolded the pages and slipped them back into the envelope. His insides were in turmoil. At first, he was tempted to unleash the rage that was boiling inside. *No. Bad idea.* After all, this relationship was hardly a surprise. Although nothing was ever said, Paul was bad at hiding his feelings and so, not surprisingly, he was a terrible liar. Jared never let on that he had deduced the truth. *Besides, I don't own Paul.* That's the story he had told himself all that summer when he suspected the affair was ongoing. Paul must have put an end to it that fall after they had all returned to school, but Jared now figured that Jeff hadn't been able to let go quite so easily. First, there was the lingering behind at school for so long after his term had ended, and now there were Paul's letters that he had held onto this whole time. He guessed with some bitterness that they were being kept as relics of a failed love affair.

It didn't take long, once he had thought it all over, for Jared to calm down. For an instant, he even considered returning the letter, but he decided against it. God only knows what situations the three of them were going to be getting themselves into once they got back home. Furthermore, it was anybody's guess whether Paul and Jeff were that done with each other. He would keep the letter. *After all, he'll never miss just one letter.*

He got up, took his mother's picture from where he had left it on his desk and slid both it and the letter back under the clothes in his suitcase. He heard footsteps in the hall outside and Jeff's door closing, adding an "amen" to his reflections. He nodded to himself with satisfaction. *Well done. Made it and in the clear!* With that, he glanced up at the clock and saw the time. If he was going to have any hope at all of grabbing a cup of coffee and something to eat, he'd better get himself down to the dining hall *now*. He threw on a pair of black slacks, black loafers, and a clerical shirt and hurried out the door, locking it behind him.

Chapter 2

Deacon Paul Fortis sat on a hard wooden pew in the loft of the darkened chapel staring into the gloom—a void broken only by the flickering ruby flame of the sanctuary lamp. Although he was bathed in a column of light from a small fixture in the ceiling, it made him feel even more alone: an alien in his sacred surroundings. The chapel that had always been a source of solace and joy for him today felt cold and empty.

His divine office prayer book rested on his lap, open but unread. Today was the day he had been working for, for almost as long as he could remember. It was supposed to be the most memorable and important day in his young life. He needed to focus his spiritual energies on the step he was about to take in a few hours; he would need to rely most on the God who had supported him this far. He craved the strength and courage that came to him in prayer, yet he could not pray.

Paul had been sitting in this lonely spot since he'd left Jared's room, but the more he tried to focus, the more distracted he became. His mind kept returning to the memory of Jared asleep by his side, snoring gently. He could still feel Jared's arm draped across him. When he sniffed at his own arm, he found the all-too-familiar scent of Jared's body. He had delayed showering on purpose.

After more than a decade of life with Jared, Paul was finding it increasingly difficult to cope with the contradiction between his feelings for his partner and the expectations he was about to assume with his upcoming ministry in the church. His feelings for Jared were as much a gift of God as his vocation to the ministry. Yet, the life of service they were both dedicating themselves to demanded that they not only forsake one another but also renounce any hope for a committed life together.

As he sat in the darkened room listening to his own breathing, Paul realized everything he had experienced so far, everything he'd been taught, had been little more than theory and speculation. When he presented himself for ordination to the priesthood later that morning, theory would give way to practice. He would be splitting himself in two, driving a wedge between the person he was at the core of his being and the person he would commit to being from then on. It was no longer question of loving Jared versus loving the church. The differences would be irreconcilable.

He looked down at the book in his lap. Should he ask for the strength to forget Jared? He couldn't believe that walking away from Jared was what God wanted. *He* didn't want it. Should he pray for the courage to abandon his calling to the priesthood? It would mean abandoning his faith community—the very community Jared, too, would be promising to serve today. He couldn't do that, either.

He sighed and closed the book. He knew what he had to pray for: the knowledge of God's will for him and the strength to do the right thing. He got down on his knees to ask for that miracle and lost himself in prayer.

The glow of the first morning light sent bright colors from the stained-glass windows across the chapel floor, awakening it from the dull gray of its nightly slumber. Paul sensed he was not alone. Lifting his head, he looked around, but the loft appeared empty.

"I'm behind you," said a soft voice.

Paul twisted around, half-kneeling, half-sitting on the pew. Jeff Hensen sat behind him, elbows on his knees. The light from the ceiling highlighted the candy blond spikes of his hair and cast deep shadows across his lean frame. Most of his face was in shadow, but Paul could make out the look of deep concern in his piercing blue eyes.

"How long have you been there?" he asked.

"A while," said Jeff. "I saw you were deeply into it, and I didn't want to disturb you. Is everything okay?"

Paul heaved a sigh and pulled himself the rest of the way onto the bench.

He hung his elbows over the back of the pew and cradled his chin in his hands. "I guess so," he said. "Just premarital jitters." He managed a weak smile. "What brings you here so early? Weren't you out celebrating last night?"

"I ran into Jared. He said you'd probably be here."

Paul tensed up but tried not to show it. He didn't think Jeff would do anything stupid, like telling Jared about their relationship. He never had, but there was no guarantee. "Jared's awake? That's not like him. He doesn't do early mornings."

"Yes, he's up. But I'm glad I found you alone. I wanted a little time for just you and me."

Paul looked away. "Listen, if this is about last summer, I..."

"No, no. That's all behind us. I get it. We're good."

Paul tried his best not to stare at Jeff. He still found it way too easy to get lost in his friend's welcoming blue eyes. He hated being reminded about what had happened between them. It shouldn't have happened. It had been a moment of weakness—well, several moments, if Paul was being honest. But it was long over, and he'd already promised himself nothing like it would ever happen again. Not that Jared had been entirely faithful himself, but Jared didn't know about Jeff, and he never would. If he found out, who knew what he'd do? Jared was reckless, and he had a vengeful streak that was concerning.

Jeff cleared his throat. "I need to tell you something important and I wanted you to hear it from me." He shifted in his seat. "I'm not coming back next year."

"What? Why?" This was not something Paul had ever expected to hear from Jeff. "You've always seemed happy here. And you've only got a year to go until you're ordained a deacon."

The chapel door opened below them. Paul put a finger to his lips and watched as a stooped figure in a long black robe shuffled up the aisle and disappeared into the sacristy. "It's just Father Rinaldi," Paul murmured. "He must be coming to get something for this morning's Mass."

Jeff nodded and went on, this time in a whisper. "That's just it, Paul. I already know what the future will be like. This whole year has convinced me this life isn't for me."

Paul hung his head. "If it's because of me, I'm so sorry. I never meant to make things difficult for you."

"No." Jeff grabbed his arms. "It's not at all because of you."

Paul tilted his head. "I don't believe you."

"It's true." Jeff's face broke out in a shy smile. "Well...it has *almost* nothing to do with you."

Paul smiled back.

"Our time together..." He winced. "It only confirmed what I already suspected about myself." He tightened his grip on Paul's arms. "But that's only part of it. Much as I love it, the whole direction my life's been taking just feels wrong for me." He let go of Paul and sat back in his seat. "They tell us these years in the seminary are supposed to be years of discernment. That's what they've been for me. People like you and Jared knew what you wanted to do years before you got here. The rest of us were never that sure. But I knew I'd never be at peace with myself unless I gave it my best try. So, that's what I did. I gave it my best. Now I don't have to wonder any more. I can get on with the rest of my life knowing I'll be on the right track—or at least, knowing I won't be on the wrong one."

Paul's neck was tensing up. *Something else to feel guilty about.* "But what'll you do? Are you going back home?"

"Maybe for a few weeks, just to see everybody. It feels like I've been in Rome forever. But then I'm headed out to the West Coast. My uncle Roger is an attorney in San Luis Obispo, and he's offered me a summer job as his paralegal. I think I'll enjoy working for him and, if I do well, Roger said he'd give me a hand getting into law school. I'll look into it, at least." His smile broadened. "You know what they say: 'When God closes one door, he opens another.' That's how I'm looking at it, anyway."

Despite his best intentions, that old admiration and attraction to this charming, handsome man welled up inside Paul. "I wish you all the best. Whatever you wind up doing, you'll be great at it. You're still one of my favorite people and, you know, under other circumstances..."

Jeff threw up his hands in mock horror. "No. Don't even think of it."

Paul giggled. "When will you be leaving Rome? You're staying the night, right? We're expecting you at the reception dinner."

"I'm afraid not, my friend. My plane leaves this afternoon, and I have to be at Fiumicino in an hour or so. I'm almost packed. All I have to do is catch a cab."

Paul was stung. "You're not coming to the ordination?"

Jeff stood and laid his hands on Paul's shoulders. "Don't take it personally. Seeing the two of you ordained is just something I don't want to put myself through right now. It's not about you; I have enough going on. I hope you understand that my love and prayers will be with you the whole way."

Paul swallowed the lump in his throat. Another piece of the life he was giving up would now slip farther away. "Will you at least keep in touch? I don't want to lose you." Realizing what he'd said, he added, "As a friend."

Jeff smiled. "We'll see."

Paul raised himself up on his knees and reached over the back of the pew, wrapping his arms around Jeff's waist and pulling him to himself. Jeff bent down to kiss Paul on his cheek, but Paul turned his head and met Jeff's lips full-on. He knew he was kissing Jeff goodbye, and he wasn't going to be shy about it now. Jeff's eyes grew wide, and he almost drew back but didn't. Paul didn't want to let go, but Jeff broke the kiss and straightened himself up. He stared for a moment into Paul's eyes, and then he turned and was gone.

Paul realized he was kneeling backwards on the pew with his back to the sanctuary and the altar. He turned himself around and thudded onto the seat. He hadn't been awake an hour yet and already he was exhausted. Picking up his abandoned prayer book, he stood and rested one hand on the balcony railing to steady himself. It was nearly full-on dawn. He looked around the chapel as if recording the moment for posterity. He was, in effect, saying goodbye: goodbye to Jeff and the chapel, goodbye to the seminary and his studies, goodbye to the life he had lived up until that moment. Though he had no clear idea what he was getting himself into, he knew that when he left the chapel this time, there would be no coming back.

Brushing at his eyes, he turned and walked up the set of low risers that led to the back of the loft and the heavy oak doors leading out. He heaved the doors open and let them swing closed behind him.

Chapter 3

Saturday, June 11, 2011

The frosted glass doors to the refectory dining hall were still dark. It was rare for Jared to beat Paul down to breakfast. As a matter of fact, it was rare for him to beat anyone down to breakfast. Paul must have been up in the chapel praying up a storm. Dignitaries' portraits lined the walls of the corridor: former rectors, dour-faced bishops, and even a few cardinals dressed in their scarlet and ermine finery. Jared imagined his own portrait up there. *One day.* One day he would be bishop. Maybe then, his father would respect him.

He pushed through the refectory doors and flipped on the lights. The large room was lined with rows of long, plain wooden tables and chairs—enough to accommodate well over a hundred students and a dozen or more faculty. There was nothing fancy or even charming about it. In fact, it was quite plain. It had fluorescent lights and plenty of hard surfaces that reflected the noise. When it was full of students, you could barely hear yourself talk. Now, devoid of bodies and voices, it looked and sounded hollow and abandoned.

Jared's first stop was the espresso machine, and, in no time, the room filled with the sounds and smells of brewing coffee and the cheerful clink of dishes and flatware as he set a place for himself. He was about to grab his coffee and sit when he realized Paul would be coming down soon. Secretly pleased that he'd thought of someone else for a change, he set another place next to himself for Paul.

Long minutes passed in silence as he sipped his coffee. He felt content and focused. The sun was almost up, and the early morning light poured through the tall windows lining the opposite side of the room. But still, there was no sign of Paul. Jared didn't want to wait and have to rush to get ready later, so he decided to go ahead and eat. If Paul was going to take his time coming down for breakfast, Jared wasn't going to stay hungry waiting for him.

With the dorm empty, there was no longer any kitchen staff on duty to make him a hot breakfast. Nonetheless, someone had been kind enough to provide trays of fresh fruits and pastries. He loaded his plate with a little of everything and carried it back to the table. He bit into a large ripe peach, almost too pretty to eat, and the juice ran down his chin and onto his napkin. Why did food always taste better in Italy? The fruit, the pastries, the pasta, the meats, the fish—everything. It was part of the charm of Rome that he never got tired of.

"Couldn't wait for me, hey?" Paul strode into the refectory. He wasn't as tall as Jared, but he outweighed him. Even though he didn't look rotund, his round face and thinning hair accentuated his size.

"I don't need to ask what took you so long," Jared said. "Just look at you."

Paul wore crisply tailored black pants, spit-polished black shoes, and black socks. His pure white formal shirt was starched and pressed with simple pleats, double cuffs, and plain gold cufflinks, but collarless to accommodate the clerical collar he'd need to put on later.

"I thought I was making an effort." Jared nodded to his slacks. They were a big improvement over his usual breakfast attire of flip-flops, sweatpants, and T-shirt. "You make me look like a slob."

"The truth hurts." Paul jabbed him in the side on the way to the espresso machine. He filled his cup, his back to Jared. "You feeling okay?" he asked when the machine had stopped hissing.

Jared straightened. "Yeah. Why?"

Paul turned, stirring his coffee. "You were a bit drunk last night. You fell asleep on top of me. To be honest, you still look a little rough around the edges."

Jared gripped the side of his chair to keep his temper in check. Was Paul going to criticize his drinking again? "On the contrary, I slept great last night and I'm feeling great this morning, thank you very much." He gave a little snort. "And I wasn't drunk. I just fell asleep."

Paul shot him a sideways glance.

"What?"

"Nothing," Paul said. "Not important." He carried his coffee over to the table, settled himself next to Jared, and took a sip. "Can I share some of your goodies?"

"Sure." Jared held out his still-stacked plate. "Help yourself." When he set the plate back down, he took a bite of a Danish. "Are you going to see your folks this morning before the ordination?"

Jared liked Bruce and Yvette Fortis. They were so normal compared to his parents, and they had always treated him like another son.

"No, they're having breakfast at the hotel, and I've arranged for a car to pick them up and take them to the church. We probably won't get to talk to them until the dinner this afternoon." Paul took a big bite out of his pastry. "But don't worry, you'll have plenty of time with them. They'll see to that." He gave Jared a wry smile. "Sometimes I think they love you more than me."

Jared raised his eyebrows. "I can see why. Look what God gave them to work with." Paul slugged him on the arm. "Ow! That hurt." Jared rubbed the sore spot, giving it much more attention than it deserved. "Are you guys still planning to do some sightseeing for a few days before heading home?"

"Absolutely. I promised to take them down the Amalfi Coast." Paul swiveled in his chair. "Are you still staying in Rome 'till Wednesday?"

"Yeah. Why?"

"I was just thinking...if you're not doing anything important, why don't you spend a few days travelling with us? We've rented an SUV, and there'll be plenty of room. The folks would love to have you come with us—and so would I."

As much as he liked Paul's family, being cooped up with them on vacation didn't sound like something he'd enjoy. "Sorry, Bro," he said. "I'd love to, but there are some things I need to do in the city that I can't get out of."

Paul's look said, *Like what?* but Jared chose to ignore it.

"Okay." Paul scowled. "You may not miss me, but I'll certainly miss you. God only knows how long it'll be before we see each other again."

"I know." Jared rested his hand over Paul's. "We'll find a way to spend some time together. We'll have a few weeks at least before we start our assignments. Did the bishop give you any clues as to where you'll be going?"

"None. How about you?"

"Nope." He took his hand away. "I thought you had an in with him."

"*Al contrario, amico mio.* And here I thought you had an in with the cardinal."

"Wrong again." Jared laughed. *I wish.* "I guess we'll both have to wait and see."

The doors to the refectory opened and in came Father Rinaldi. Giuseppe Rinaldi was a tall, thin, elderly priest whose stooped bearing was accentuated by a shock of snow-white hair that covered his head like a halo. He always wore the same clerical garb at home or abroad: a simple black cassock and sash. His smile was so warm and genuine that the seminarians had adopted him as their surrogate grandfather.

"Good morning, my boys," he said.

"Good morning, Father," they intoned in school-child unison.

"You were both up very early this morning, weren't you? I heard you two in the chapel when I went to get the vestments for the ordination."

Paul's cheeks reddened. Jared hadn't been there with him, but he could guess who was. He looked at Paul, but Paul turned away with a nervous laugh.

"It was just me, Father," he said. "I was up in the choir loft praying."

"Oh? It sounded like whispering. Are you nervous about today?"

"Not at all. I just wanted to start this day off right."

"I'm sure you did." Jared glared at him, not even caring if Father Rinaldi saw. Paul's face was a mixture of confusion and alarm.

"You boys have a nice breakfast and remember to straighten up. There's no one here to clean up after you anymore." He took Jared's empty cup and put it in the dirty dishes rack. "You have plenty of time, but don't dawdle too long. I'm taking the vestments over to San Sergio now. I want to have everything set up over there before everyone arrives. I'll see you there." He smiled at both and started to leave, but then turned back to look at Paul. "Don't worry, son. Everything will work out just fine. God's got everything under control."

"Thanks, Father." Paul looked down. "I'm counting on it."

Father Rinaldi gave him his broadest grandfatherly simile and left the room. The silence that followed grew uncomfortable.

"So," Jared said. "You have something you want to talk about?"

"As a matter of fact, I do." Paul looked him in the eye. "I haven't wanted to bring this up, knowing how sensitive you are about it, but it's been on my mind."

"And...?" Jared took tried to sip his coffee, but realized the cup was empty. He'd intended to force a confession out of Paul, but now he wondered if Paul was even referring to his affair with Jeff.

"I was wondering if maybe you'd changed your mind about inviting your father to the ordination. You know how much it would mean to him."

He set the cup down with a clatter. "You know how I feel about this, Paul. Why would you even ask?"

"I just thought..."

"You thought what? That I'd forget about everything they did to me and just welcome him and his concubine with open arms? What do you expect me to say? 'Sure Dad, come to Rome and be sure to bring that miserable old sow you married.'" Anger boiled up inside him and it was all he could do to keep it at bay. "I'll tell you right now, it's not going to happen. You might want me to handle this differently, but it's not your decision."

Paul drew back from him, almost cowering. "No, of course not. I don't want to change your mind. It's just that I was thinking... What would you do if they showed up anyway—you know, to surprise you?"

Paul was hiding something. Jared could see it all over him. "Is there something I should know?"

"No. Nothing like that."

"Because if there's something I ought to know that you're not telling me, you're going to be one sorry little man."

Paul blushed scarlet. "No. I promise. There's nothing."

Jared sat back in his chair and stared at Paul. Once Paul got his teeth into something, he'd never let it go. Nobody in the world knew more about Jared's past than he did, but he was still on this kick about Jared's father. Jared stood and went to make himself more coffee, his anger settling to a low simmer. When he sat down again, he said, "I'm not sure what I would do if he showed up here today with—with that woman."

Paul pulled his chair closer and laid his hand on Jared's arm. Jared couldn't help but notice the earnestness in Paul's eyes. "Look," he said, "I wish I had met your mother. She must have been an amazing woman. That's obvious from the way she brought up you and your brother."

Jared winced at the mention of his twin brother, Justin.

"You're such an incredible person," Paul said, "and you know I'd do literally anything for you."

Jared shifted in his chair. As often as he'd heard Paul go on about this subject, and as much as it irked him, he felt an obligation to hear him out. "I know you would. You already have."

"I'm not in your shoes," Paul said, "but aren't you still letting Hannah run your life?"

Jared clenched his jaw but thought it best to say nothing.

"If it weren't for Hannah, you'd have your father here with you today. I know how much you loved Kurt. You always said he was the best dad ever. You still love him; I know you do."

Jared scowled. He'd been over this with Paul a thousand times. What wasn't he getting? "He married her!" He slammed his open palm down on the table. "That changed everything. He made her my stepmother, for God's sake."

"I know," Paul said. "You've told me all the things she did to you when I wasn't around. But aren't you still letting her control you by allowing her to drive a wedge between you and your father?"

"No," Jared snapped. "He had choices. This is his fault, not mine."

Paul's brows narrowed. "We have no idea what things were like in Austria during the war. Your parents know stuff about Hannah we'll never understand. They believed they were doing the right thing when they brought her back with them."

Jared shook his head. "It doesn't mean my father had to marry her." And not long after his mother had died either. He hated to be reminded of how close he and his father had once been. If only it was as simple as Paul was making it out to be. "You want to know what I'll do if Pop shows up here uninvited?" He gave Paul a sardonic smile. "I'll ignore him, turn my back on him like he turned his back on me."

Paul met Jared's gaze. "Isn't that unfair? Doesn't he have a right to be happy? Just because he married Hannah doesn't mean he rejected you."

Jared took a sip of his fresh coffee and burned his mouth. "Is that what you think, even after all this time? He married the woman he knew tried to destroy me—to destroy both of us."

Paul looked puzzled. "What do you mean she tried to destroy you?"

"*Us*, Paul. She tried to destroy us." For a moment, Jared felt conflicted. He'd never wanted Paul to know this part of the story. He let out a big sigh. "If it had been up to her, neither of us would be here today."

"How? What could she have done?"

"You want to know?"

Paul nodded.

"Maybe you'll get where I'm coming from. It was during our senior year at Catholic U, after Kurt told Hannah I'd been accepted to the seminary here in Rome. For God knows what reason, Hannah hates the Catholic Church with everything in her. She forbade me to become a priest, and I think she was determined to punish me for my disobedience." He put the last word in air quotes. "So, she wrote a letter to the bishop. She told him he shouldn't accept me because I was 'temperamentally unsuited for the priesthood.' Those were her exact words. The reason she gave him was that I was a homosexual and in a relationship with you."

"Oh, my God! She did that?"

"She sure did. The bishop called me in, and we had a little chat. I don't even remember what I said. All I know is he came *this* far from kicking both of us out." He brought his thumb and forefinger half an inch apart.

"Why didn't he?"

"I called Father Spencer back at Catholic U. Do you remember him?"

Paul stared at him.

"He's the Jesuit who got us the invitation to that Vatican embassy reception where we met Cardinal Romero. After I had a talk with him, Father Spencer must have put in a good word for us to the cardinal and, before I knew it, the bishop had changed his mind."

21

"What did you tell Father Spencer?"

"It's not important. The upshot is that you and I are getting ordained today, despite Hannah Schümer—or whatever she calls herself now."

Paul's mouth hung open. "Why didn't you tell me this before?"

"There wasn't anything you could have done. The gun was aimed at me. You were collateral damage. It would only have upset you and thrown your family into a panic. We would have had to come out to everyone, and that could have ended badly."

"So, Bishop Mickleson knows about you and me?"

"I assume so."

"And he's okay with...us?"

"He hasn't said anything more to me about it." He looked into Paul's eyes. "I've leveled with you about Hannah, right?"

Paul nodded.

"So, I have a favor to ask of you, okay?"

"Okay." Paul clasped his hands in front of him.

"Seriously...no surprises today, right?"

Paul looked away. "No."

It annoyed him that Paul was so transparent, but he was tired of the hide and seek. He hoped that whatever Paul was hiding, it wasn't what (or who) he thought it was.

Chapter 4

Saturday, June 11, 2011

Paul fiddled with his cufflinks, twisting them round and round as he and Jared sat in the backseat of the black Audi. The streets and people of Rome passed by outside the window. He'd made a huge mistake letting Jared's father know the time and place of their ordination. Maybe Kurt hadn't had time to make reservations. But he was a wealthy man and used to getting his way. If he wanted to come, he'd be there. *Damn!* Why hadn't Jared said something about Hannah's letter sooner? But why hadn't he listened to Jared from the beginning? He always had to be the hero. And now he'd gone and screwed up the most important day of their lives.

Jared reached over and took his hand. "You look like you're on your way to the guillotine."

Paul tried to laugh, but it came out as a nervous giggle. "I'm fine." No way could he tell Jared the truth. Besides, maybe Kurt wouldn't even be there. Or maybe he'd come without Hannah. When he looked at Jared, his stomach did a flip-flop. Jared's features were fine and chiseled— movie-star quality—with a lock of wavy black hair that hung over his forehead like Superman. And he had crystal blue eyes that Paul got lost in every time he looked into them. It only made him feel worse. Tears welled up in his eyes.

"Hey!" Jared gave Paul's hand a reassuring squeeze. "Everything's going to be fine. I'll be right beside you all the way. What are you scared of?"

"I don't know." Paul laughed, trying to turn it into something light and unimportant, which it wasn't. "I mean, it's only the rest of lives. No big deal, right?"

Jared smiled. "I thought you answered that question a long time ago. You can do this. You know the whole ceremony by heart. Take a deep breath and put it all in God's hands." He nodded toward the car window. "Look—we're almost there."

Paul followed his gaze, his stomach tightening with nerves.

"Once we're inside you won't have time to be nervous. Okay?"

"Yeah." Paul took a deep breath. He didn't feel okay, but Jared was right: he had no choice but to trust God and put one foot in front of the other.

They turned the corner and entered the Piazza della Madonna dei Monte, passed the fountain in the center of the square, and pulled up in front of the church of Santi Sergio e Bacco. It was a small church by Roman standards. Even the classical façade was unremarkable; although, when Paul squinted, he could imagine he was looking at the ruins of Petra.

He gave Jared's hand one final squeeze as the car pulled alongside the curb and stopped. Paul gathered up his vestments, opened the door and stepped out. Jared climbed out from the opposite side, his long white alb folded over his arm. Paul took a moment to rearrange his so he wouldn't look quite so messy alongside his fastidious partner. Looking sophisticated came easily to Jared, but it was a skill Paul had to work hard at, and he feared it would forever elude him.

The church was built in the form of a Greek cross—four wings of equal length meeting at the center—with the sanctuary at the rear and a chapel at either side. To the left was a chapel dedicated to the Virgin Mary; to the right, one dedicated to the Roman soldier-martyrs Sergius and Bacchus. It was appropriate they would be ordained in the church dedicated to two male saints. They may even have been a couple. Legend had it that Bacchus had appeared to Sergius in a dream, and said, "Be courageous in facing death, for your reward in heaven will be me!"

Paul and Jared entered the sacristy at the back of the church through a small door beside the Sergius and Bacchus shrine. The walls of the high-ceilinged room were pierced by small windows near the ceiling, allowing shafts of morning sunlight to dapple the polished marble floors. Along the wall opposite the door were two walnut vesting tables. On one was laid out an ornate white chasuble with gold embroidery and a matching bishop's miter for the cardinal. On the other were matching vestments for the two concelebrants. A half-dozen young men in black cassocks and white surplices milled about the room making final preparations. As Paul and Jared entered, Father Rinaldi raised his gaunt head and looked up from the large red leather-bound tome he was studying. He smiled. "Good morning, again, boys."

"Hey, Father." Paul looked around at all the preparations. "Looks like you've been busy this morning." The priest just smiled.

Jared wasted no time getting vested in his alb and tying the rope cincture around his waist. Father Rinaldi helped him put on his stole, worn as a deacon: diagonally over his left shoulder and held in place under his right arm at his waist by the cincture. Paul slipped his own alb over his head and fastened his cincture. Jared came over and held Paul's stole out to him, and Paul draped it over his shoulder. Jared then drew one end behind Paul's back as he pulled the other end across his chest. He slipped both ends into Paul's cincture on his right side, adjusting it so the ends were even and lay flat against Paul's hip. Paul was overcome by emotion. This would be the last time the two of them would wear their stoles like this.

At the sound of familiar voices, Paul turned to see Father Peter Duncan coming through the door. Peter was a former classmate of theirs who'd graduated a couple of years ahead of them. Like them, he had been mentored by Cardinal Romero who brought him into the Vatican to work with him and so Peter had risen quickly through the ranks. He was a striking man in his own right. He was tall, and the military-style flat-top haircut he always wore played up his height and lent him a no-nonsense, professional air. His hair was light brown with a sprinkle of gray on either side. He carried himself with casual dignity, yet his eyes worked a room ceaselessly, never missing a detail. He was engaged in a lively conversation and obviously distracted as he entered the room.

The other party to this conversation was Julio Cardinal Romero himself.

Ever since Paul had met the cardinal back in Washington, he'd been impressed by his oversized presence. The cardinal was Argentinian by birth and had the bearing of Spanish aristocracy. His dark hair was tinged with gray, which emphasized his noble features. A slightly olive complexion gave him the look of an outdoorsman, but the delicacy of his skin made him look far younger than his sixty-something years. He had a powerful presence and deep, mysterious brown eyes that captivated whatever audience was treated to an encounter with him. His smile never left his face, regardless of the situation, but those who knew him well could discern his real feelings in his eyes. As he walked in, the room fell silent.

The cardinal was a cool and astute strategist underneath all the warmth and good cheer. Paul knew he hadn't become prefect of the Sacred Congregation for Bishops on his looks and charm alone. As such, he had a great deal of say in the selection of church leadership worldwide. People whom he mentored tended to find themselves in positions of authority in the church. Paul was still in awe that he and Jared could count themselves among that select group.

The moment he spotted Paul and Jared, he left his conversation with Peter, crossed the room, and gave each of them a big embrace.

"Good morning, gentlemen," he said. "I must say I've been looking forward to this day for some time. Are you ready?"

"As much as we can be, your Eminence," said Paul with a nervous smile.

Jared gave Paul a curious look. "Yes, we're ready."

It took only about ten minutes for the cardinal and the other two concelebrants (Father Rinaldi and Father Peter) to finish vesting. Cardinal Romero looked every bit the prince of the church in his brocade chasuble and matching miter, crosier in hand. At a signal from the master of ceremonies, the church bells began to peal, and the little procession made its way out toward the street and reentered the church through the main doors. Paul and Jared walked side by side, with the concelebrants and the cardinal right behind them. The whole panorama felt like a dream. Though

Paul was aware of everything going on around him, he felt like he was above it all, watching it happen to someone else.

Paul was conscious of Jared's body next to his as they proceeded into the church and down the main aisle with triumphal choir and organ accompaniment. He was shaking inside. Jared stole glances at him, and he threw him a furtive smile. He couldn't have asked for anything more from this day than to know that, in this rite of passage, he and Jared were beginning this new life side by side. As the procession entered the sanctuary and the various ministers took their places, Paul and Jared stepped to the side and stood in front of their seats facing the altar. Paul's family sat together in the front pew, but Paul's gaze rested on the two empty places beside them. Catching his father's eye, he raised an eyebrow as if to say, *What happened?* His father shrugged. Paul gave an audible sigh of relief. Meanwhile, the cardinal climbed the altar steps and, at the top, turned to face the congregation. Signing himself with the sign of the cross, the cardinal began the Ordination Mass.

"The Lord said to Moses, 'Assemble for me seventy of the elders of Israel, men you know for true elders and authorities among the people and bring them to the meeting tent.'"

Paul's mind raced. Here he was, twenty-six years old. What kind of elder could he hope to be? What kind of authority could he have, not even ten years out of high school?

"I will take some of the spirit that is on you and I will give it to them."

His only hope of making a success of the life he was beginning today was to trust that God wouldn't fail him, no matter how things turned out.

"I plead with you as a prisoner for the Lord, to live a life worthy of the calling you have received, with perfect humility, meekness and patience, bearing with one another lovingly."

Wasn't humility seeing himself as God saw him and acting accordingly? Wasn't being here this morning a supreme act of arrogance? *What am I doing here?* He took a deep breath.

"Jesus called his disciples together and said, 'You know how those who exercise authority among the Gentiles lord it over them; their great ones make their importance felt. It cannot be like that with you. Anyone among you who aspires to greatness must serve the rest, and whoever wants to rank first among you must serve the needs of all.'"

His thoughts began to calm themselves. *Yes, that I can do.* Maybe, for him, it would be enough just to see what needed to be done and do it. Maybe that was as perfect as he would get to be. He looked up and realized the cardinal was preaching. He hoped one of his family members was recording this, because he'd already missed most of what the prelate had said.

"...Let us ask our Heavenly Father to pour His grace richly upon these young men who present themselves before us for priestly ordination this morning," the cardinal said, "that they may grow in the virtues of faith, hope, and love, and may serve Our Lord in his Church worthily, all the days of their lives. In the name of the Father, and of the Son, and of the Holy Spirit. Amen."

"Amen," said Paul, and he meant it with all his heart.

After asking the candidates to declare publicly their intention to undertake the ministry, the cardinal invited all present to pray. He then turned to face the altar and knelt. This was the awesome moment that Paul had imagined for himself all his life. He and Jared prostrated themselves face down on the sanctuary floor, foreheads resting on their folded arms as the choir intoned the Litany of the Saints.

"Lord have mercy. Lord have mercy.

Christ have mercy. Christ have mercy.

Christ hear us. Christ graciously hear us."

Paul forced himself to breathe: in, out, in, out. He felt his body relax and his heartbeat slow. It would be all right. The moment was here, and there was nothing left to do but surrender to it.

"Holy Mary, pray for us. Holy Mother of God, pray for us."

Yes, indeed. Pray for me.

"From every evil, Lord save your people. From every sin, Lord save your people."

If need be, Lord, save me from myself.

"Lord have mercy."

And the prayer was over. Paul and Jared raised themselves onto their knees next to each other. The cardinal, too, rose and stepped down from his seat before the altar, stood before the men and, in silence, laid his hands first on Paul's head and then on Jared's, pressing his fingers firmly into Paul's scalp. In their turn, Father Rinaldi gently laid his hands on Paul, then Father Peter. The three clerics stood on the altar steps side by side above the two ordinands, their right hands outstretched while the cardinal prayed the ordination prayer.

"Almighty Father, grant to these servants of yours the dignity of the priesthood. Renew within them the Spirit of holiness... We ask this through our Lord Jesus Christ your Son, who lives and reigns with you and the Holy Spirit, one God, for ever and ever. Amen."

And it was done. The years of preparation were over. They were priests.

Paul stood, and Father Rinaldi came over to him, unfastened the stole from his hip and crossed it over his right shoulder so that it hung evenly in front of him around his neck: it was the symbol of priestly dignity and authority. Father Peter was doing the same for Jared. Then the two the priests assisted them in putting on their chasubles for the first time—the vestments they would use to celebrate the Eucharist.

From that point on, the liturgy was a blur. Paul and Jared stood on either side of the cardinal to recite the Eucharistic Prayer with him. When it came Jared's turn to recite one of the prayers, Paul couldn't take his eyes off him. This man whom he knew better than his own brother and sister was being transformed right in front of him into a priest offering Mass. He was

29

still the same Jared, but he seemed to be a very different person. It all went by so quickly and, almost before he was aware of it, Paul was beside Jared at the foot of the altar steps giving Communion to the congregation: first his beaming mother, then his father, then his brother Dennis, his sister Fran, and Al, her husband. Face after face—some familiar, many not—approached them to receive Communion. Some came to Jared, some to him. To each one, they offered, "The Body of Christ." All the while, Paul scanned the crowd for a pair of faces he hoped weren't there.

The liturgy concluded, and moments later Paul found himself with Jared back in the sacristy. He couldn't believe his good fortune: they had gotten through the entire ceremony without a mishap. He had scarcely come through the door when the cardinal took off his bishop's mitre and got down on his knees.

"Father, your blessing, please," he said.

For a moment, Paul was taken aback. He'd been called Father before, but this was the first time he was given that title for real. It gave him chills. Of course, he felt the pride of his accomplishment, but he also felt the sheer weight of that word: Father. It humbled him. Sensing his hesitation, the cardinal looked up at him and smiled. Paul prayed, making the sign of the cross over the prelate. Then he laid his hands on the cardinal's head. Jared stood at Paul's elbow, and when Paul was finished, the cardinal turned to Jared with the same request.

When the cardinal rose from his knees, Jared then knelt before Paul. He looked down on the man he loved and blessed him, reaffirming the bond between them with a new depth. Then he, in his turn, knelt to receive Jared's blessing. Jared's hands on his head radiated an intense heat. Then, one after another, all the participants in the ceremony lined up to receive their blessings. Before long, Father Rinaldi came up to Paul and tugged on his sleeve. "Your fans are waiting at the altar for your blessing, Fathers," he said, grinning.

Paul tapped Jared on the shoulder. "Come on. We need to get back to the sanctuary. We're holding everyone up." They left the cardinal and the rest of the dignitaries behind and reemerged in the sanctuary to one side of the main altar. It seemed as though everyone who had come to see the ordination had already lined up down the center aisle to wait for them. Paul took his place with Jared beside him. Paul's parents were at the head of the line and, as Paul blessed them, they stepped aside to receive Jared's blessing as well. Paul glanced over at his friend; he'd never seen Jared so happy. Next, he blessed his brother and his sister and then her husband— and then he couldn't breathe. There was Kurt.

Kurt went directly to Jared. Jared's eyes grew wide and filled with tears. Instinctively, he grabbed his father and embraced him. Then his smile vanished, and every trace of kindness left his face. His whole body tensed up and he stepped away from the startled man in front of him and barked, "No!" There, right beside Jared's father, stood Hannah, looking as fierce and defiant as ever. Jared spun around and looked at Paul, his stare cold and terrible.

"Jared!" Kurt's shoulders slumped and his face grew pale. His eyes were filled with hurt and confusion. Paul wanted to say something, anything to diffuse the situation, but by the time he turned back to speak to Jared, he was gone.

Paul stood there, not knowing what to do next. He wanted to run after Jared and drag him back, but he knew he was no match for Jared's ire. He was painfully aware of the line of well-wishers standing in front of him, all of whom were confused by what had just happened and were still looking to him for their blessing. He couldn't bring himself to abandon them just to run after Jared. So, trembling, he stepped over to Kurt and took up his and Hannah's hands and then prayed over them the prayer of blessing. Then he hugged them both.

Chapter 5

Saturday, June 11, 2011

Julio Cardinal Romero sat alone in the backseat of his black, late-model Peugeot while Father Peter, his personal secretary, drove with old Father Rinaldi beside him. He was now wearing a plain black suit and clerical collar, indistinguishable from hundreds of other priests in Rome, except for a tiny tab of scarlet under the white of his collar that someone would have to look closely to see. "So, what do you think, Peter?"

"About what, Eminence?" Peter looked back at him in the rear-view mirror with a mischievous grin.

"About our two boys. Do you think they'll amount to anything...or have I made a mistake this time?" He loved teasing the young priest.

"Eminence, I've never known you to make that kind of mistake. Your protégés have always been the best of the best, and Jared and Paul are no exception."

"I know," said the cardinal. "I just wanted to hear it from you."

"Besides, look how I turned out."

"That's what I'm afraid of." Romero toyed with the small silver cross that hung by a fine chain around his neck. "I hope this dinner won't be too big. You know how much I hate these affairs." He'd been to enough grand celebrations to last him several lifetimes.

"No," Peter said. "I think it'll only be the boys' immediate families and the three of us."

"Perfect." With a small gathering, there was a good chance he'd get to enjoy himself. He had met Bruce and Yvette Fortis and Paul's siblings several times and he enjoyed them. But so far, he'd never met anyone from Jared's family. There must have been a reason for that, and sooner or later he'd find out what it was. *Chances are, within a few minutes of meeting them, I'll know*. He didn't like secrets. Secrets had a way of causing trouble.

The car pulled up to the curb and stopped. The cardinal waited in the back seat for Father Rinaldi to get out and open the door for him. As soon as he did, the cardinal grabbed the handle over the door and pulled himself up and out. Although he didn't consider himself old, he still found the handle a welcome assist. They were parked in front of one of his favorite restaurants in the city, the Ristorante Antico Arco in the Piazzale Aurelio. It was an intimate place with thick, rough-stuccoed walls that evoked the sophistication of a bygone era. He was pleased. The boys' families could have chosen one of the bigger, glossier, and more commercial establishments, but for him, this was a much more suitable choice.

Father Peter went ahead of them to the entrance, opened the door, and held it for them. A cloud of delicious aromas enveloped them: the scents of roasting savory meats intertwined with an ever-changing potpourri of spices. It was places like this that kept the cardinal from getting homesick—the Roman restaurants eclipsed even those in Buenos Aires.

No sooner had he stepped through the door when the maître d' ran up to him, beaming with pride. "*Bienvenuto, Eminenza*. Welcome back to Antico Arco," he said with a little bow. "Your company is awaiting you right through here. Please. Follow me." He led the cardinal and the others between the tables of a main dining room buzzing with conversation. Every table was filled. They passed through one of two narrow openings into a smaller private dining room that seated perhaps a dozen guests.

As they entered the room, Paul's father, Bruce Fortis stood and rushed to greet them, shaking hands first with the cardinal, then with the other two priests. Bruce was a balding man with a roundish face, on the waning side of his forties. Looking at him, the cardinal could see what his son might look like in twenty years. The other guests rose to their feet as soon as he entered. Mr. Fortis introduced him to his wife, Yvette, a petite woman beautifully dressed to set off her sparkling blue eyes, and the rest of the family. Paul sat at the foot of the table and stood to greet the cardinal.

Finally, Bruce introduced the couple seated on the opposite side of the table: Kurt and Hannah Röhrbach.

"Why Mr. and Mrs. Röhrbach, how nice to meet you at last." The cardinal shook Kurt's hand warmly but, always finely attuned to proper protocol, he merely bowed to Hannah since she hadn't extended her hand to him. "I've waited entirely too long for this pleasure." Kurt beamed back at him while Hannah fidgeted. "I don't remember seeing you in the family pew for the Mass this morning. How did I miss you?"

Kurt avoided direct eye contact. "Ach, Eminence," he said with a distinctive German accent, "my wife, Hannah, was not well this morning. We were barely able to get here this afternoon."

"My poor dear." The cardinal turned to Hannah. "I hope it was nothing serious."

She gave Kurt a withering look.

Ah. Here's where the difficulties lie.

Hannah crossed her arms at her chest. "Nothing serious. Nothing serious at all."

She turned to leave, but the cardinal wouldn't let the conversation end so quickly. "It's tragic that you missed seeing your son ordained. I am heartsick for you. Are you feeling better now?"

"Yes." She glowered at him. "*Danke*, I am fine."

He allowed the conversation to drop with just a smile, and she went to sit down. He was curious about this abrasive woman. She was not at all what he expected to encounter at this otherwise joyful celebration. Although her clothes were well-tailored—an elegant gown of turquoise silk set off by a double string of pearls—they did not suit her. Underneath it all, she seemed like a typical German *hausfrau*. Life had taken a heavy toll on her and her deeply lined features made her appear much older than she evidently was.

The cardinal looked around the table. "Please. Everyone sit. Father Jared and Father Paul have become very dear to me these past few years, and this is a special opportunity for me to get to know you all a little better."

Bruce ushered the cardinal to his place at the head of the table, with Father Peter and Father Rinaldi to his right, between him and the Röhrbachs. As soon as the cardinal had taken his seat, everyone at the table sat.

An older gentleman in a tailored suit stood by the doorway.

The cardinal beamed. "My friends," he said, "this is Alberto, the proud owner of this fine restaurant. He will make certain that your dining experience here this afternoon will be memorable."

"Thank you, Eminence," he replied, his face coloring. "In honor of the newly ordained priests, I would like to offer you all an aperitif of your choosing, with my compliments."

The cardinal ordered Campari for himself and his two associates. As Alberto went through the room taking the orders, the cardinal's eyes scanned the table. "But where is Father Jared?"

"I don't know, Your Eminence," Bruce replied. "He left the church before we did." He turned to his son. "Have you seen him, Paul?"

Paul reddened. "No, I assumed he went back to the residence for something."

Turning to Father Peter, the cardinal said, "Why don't you take the car back to the residence and see what's holding him up?" He smiled. "In any case, I'm sure he'll appreciate the ride."

"Certainly, Eminence," said the priest. With that, he left the room.

"Cardinal," said Kurt, "I do hope my son was not a lot of trouble for you. He can be a strong-willed boy."

"Like his father," said Hannah through pursed lips and not entirely under her breath.

He laughed. "Not at all. He got into no more trouble than any of his classmates. In fact, he was an exceptional student. You should be proud of his accomplishments." He turned to Bruce and Yvette. "All of you. I'm pleased to say both of these young men excelled at their classes."

Paul's parents beamed at him. He, in turn, reddened even more. His brother, Dennis, smacked him on the arm. "Show-off."

Alberto returned with the aperitifs. When everyone had been served, the cardinal was about to raise his glass when he remembered Jared still hadn't arrived. "Drink, please," he said to everyone. "We'll wait for our other guest of honor to arrive before we do a toast."

Hannah remained silent and sullen, but the cardinal wasn't about to let this opportunity pass him by. "Pardon me for noticing, but I hear a slight accent in your voice. Where are you from originally?"

"We are both Austrian," said Kurt, "but I was born in Hungary. Still, I've lived most of my life in California."

"You were born in Hungary? How interesting."

"Yes. My father was a professor at the University of Salzburg and when Hitler came to power, he saw trouble. He and my mother left to join friends in Sopron, Hungary. I was born there just before it was bombed. After the war, we were going to return to Salzburg, but my father was offered a position at UCLA, so we left Europe and became Americans."

"What about you, Mrs. Röhrbach? Were you born in Austria?"

He had hoped to draw Hannah into the conversation, but it was Kurt who answered. "My dear Hannah was born in Salzburg just before the war."

Hannah's lips were pursed, and her jaw was tight, but Kurt continued as though he didn't notice. "The war took a terrible toll on her. She is my late wife's cousin, but we lost track of her for a long time. When at last we found her, about twenty-five years ago, we brought her here to live with us. When Lilly died, she stayed on to help me look after the children. After several years, she consented to marry me a couple of years ago." Hannah's gaze never left her husband.

The cardinal decided to take another approach. "And you have become a very successful businessman," he said to Kurt. "You've had articles written about you. I understand you're an inventor?"

Kurt looked at his plate. "Yes, I did make some improvements to the shipping industry."

"Some improvements? Kurt is being too modest," Paul chimed in from the other end of the table. "He practically invented shipping containers. He built them by the thousands and leased them to all the major shipping companies worldwide. He revolutionized how commercial shipping operates. Just about everything that moves in the world today goes in one of his containers."

The cardinal smiled. "That's very impressive indeed, Mr. Röhrbach. I hadn't realized how extensive your business was. Do you still own the company?"

"Oh, no, Your Eminence." Kurt laughed. "I sold it when I retired."

The conversation on the other side of the table had waned, and Fran picked up from where Paul had left off. "It was quite a notable sale," she said.

"It was in all the papers," Dennis said, his voice rising. "It was worth almost a billion dollars."

"Son," said Bruce with a frown. "That's not something we discuss."

"That is, indeed, an impressive achievement," said the cardinal.

Kurt shook his head. "Yes, yes, I know. But how much do two old people need? We have a roof over our head and food on the table. We are grateful to God for all of it. All the rest is quite a bother, more than anything else. For my son, I've tried to be prudent. I want him to be able to manage wisely, so I've given him a small fund. So far, he's done well with it. I'm proud of my boy. That's why we're here: to show him our love and support."

Alberto returned to the table. "*Signore e signori,* shall I serve the antipasti?"

"Is everyone hungry?" The cardinal glanced around the table at a half dozen smiling faces. "Yes, Alberto, I believe so." Then, turning back to the guests, he said, "We can nibble on something while we wait for Father Jared."

"Very good," said Alberto.

"Cardinal?" said Paul's brother-in-law, Al, who had been silent until now. "May I ask you a question?"

"Of course, Allan. Ask me anything." The cardinal looked the man over. What hair he had left was graying, and his dark-framed glasses emphasized his aging features. He was likely younger than he looked. His comportment suggested a no-nonsense businessman for whom religion in general and the Church in particular held little interest.

"What do people study when they come here?" Al glanced at Paul. "Why did you have to come to Rome?"

The cardinal nodded at Paul.

"I guess it's a lot like studying to become a doctor," Paul said. "My undergraduate work at Catholic U was like pre-med, except instead of science courses I studied liberal arts and philosophy."

"That sounds useful," said young Dennis without any attempt to hide his sarcasm.

"It is," Paul said. "It teaches critical thinking." He grinned at Dennis. "Something you don't know anything about."

Dennis rolled his eyes.

"So, then, you came to Rome to study what? Religion?" asked Al.

"Sort of," replied Paul. "We do postgrad work in stuff like scripture, church history, theology, and church law."

"His courses are offered at one of the universities here in the city," added the cardinal, "while the seminary residence where he stays is in charge of training him in spirituality and preparing him to provide spiritual direction. The purpose of the seminary is to prepare our students for life as priests."

"Our last year at the seminary is like a medical residency," Paul said. "We've been doing pastoral work out in the community since we were ordained deacons last summer."

"Okay," said Al. "That makes more sense to me now. Sounds like the Church goes to a lot of trouble trying to make professionals out of you."

The waiter arrived and set out serving dishes loaded with salami, capicola, prosciutto, mortadella, and bresaola, along with chunks of Parmigiano-Reggiano cheese, marinated olives, roasted peppers, and focaccia bread. The guests helped themselves.

Bruce turned to the cardinal. "Would you care to say Grace, Your Eminence?"

A few of the less observant guests lowered their forks when they realized they were the only ones eating.

The cardinal glanced at his watch. "I was going to suggest Grace and a toast to our guests of honor, but I thought perhaps we should wait until they're both here." When he spied Father Peter walking into the room, he was about to comment on his providential timing—until he realized Father Peter was alone.

"Where's Jared?" asked Paul.

"I'm sorry," replied the priest. "He's gone."

The cardinal noticed the look of alarm on Paul's face.

"What do you mean, gone?" the cardinal said. "Gone where?"

"I don't know. His room is empty. The porter at the residence said he called a taxi to Fiumicino. I assume he caught this afternoon's flight back to Los Angeles."

"Oh my God." Paul's fork clattered onto his plate.

Yvette glared at him. "Honey—please."

"I'm so sorry, Kurt," said Bruce.

Kurt stared at Jared's empty place at the table.

"What did I tell you?" Hannah said, her chin jutting out. "We shouldn't have come. Maybe someday you'll listen to me."

Kurt straightened his jacket and swallowed hard before turning to the cardinal. "Please, sir. Do let's go on."

The cardinal sighed in resignation. "Benedic, Domine, nos et haec tua dona quae de tua largitate sumus sumpturi..." All heads bowed as he made the sign of the cross, blessing the table, "In nomini Patris, et Filius, et Spiritus Sanctus. Amen."

Bruce lifted his glass and said solemnly, "To the new priests."

The cardinal noticed that all the guests at the table raised their glasses and repeated, "To the new priests." All but Hannah.

Chapter 6

Sunday, June 12, 2011

Tony Keating perched on his regular bar stool with his back to the bar, swishing the ice in his vodka tonic in lazy circles. The bar afforded him an unobstructed view of the club's graceful curves and polished edges. Under-counter lights made the litter-strewn floor beneath his barstool glow. Behind him, a top-lighted mirror brought a thousand bottles of liquid alive, flickering behind the servers in their skin-tight tank tops or less.

The ceiling of the club was lit with countless brilliant flares that leapt from wall to wall, floor to ceiling, catching a piece of face here, a hank of hair there, a hat, a spangled vest, a tattooed arm, a bare chest—instantaneous images, here and gone. Through it all hung the pungent odor of sweaty bodies. Now and again, the acrid scents of amyl and alcohol cut through it, or the tell-tale smell of cannabis.

Where is he?

Tony looked out across the dancefloor at the organized chaos of bodies. The throbbing bass from the dance floor reverberated through his gut. Nobody listened to this stuff anyway. You just felt it. That was all that mattered.

"Hey there," a man dressed in neon said, tipping his head toward Tony and making no secret of checking him out.

Tony was showing off. He enjoyed the attention. He'd chosen his clothes to accentuate his broad shoulders and chest, narrow waist, and well-developed glutes and legs, and to give the illusion that he was taller than just five-foot-nine. He was more than a fixture at the bar. He was a feature. They could have used him in advertisements for the club, but they didn't need to. Word of mouth more than sufficed.

But the man in neon wasn't *him.*

41

Tony's eyes moved across the faces on the dance floor as the random dots of bright color lit them for an instant. If he wasn't careful, they could all become a featureless blur—not good for business. Every once in a while, he saw a face he recognized: a regular, a client he'd had God-knows-when, a drunk or druggie or dealer. Sooner or later, they all ended up here.

Where is he? He—the one Tony was looking for—was the guy that could get him off his barstool. Every night, he looked for the same guy. He'd be a stranger. He wouldn't be sucked onto the dancefloor, wouldn't be in a rush. He would move deliberately. He'd know what he was looking for just as certainly as Tony did.

He was out there in the crowd somewhere. He always was.

At the other end of the bar, a fight was shaping up. Tony knew the moves by heart: one of the men jumped drunkenly off the barstool, lunging forward, hackles up like a cornered dog, fists clenched, teeth bared, a vacant but crazed look in his eyes. Then came the shouting and the "Motherfucker this" and "Motherfucker that" until Bob and Steve appeared from the front of the house. There was a scuffle, and the two drunks were escorted out of the building, and the line that snaked around the corner got a little shorter. There was a line every night outside the door: a never-ending stream of fresh prospects.

Before Tony could resume his vantage point, somebody brushed up behind him. He didn't like anyone in his space. He spun around and came eye to eye with one of the most stunning men he'd ever seen: steel gray eyes, square jaw, and the cutest little Superman curl hanging down in the center of his forehead. "Where did you come from?"

"Rome," said Superman.

As soon as he heard the voice and the deep, quiet way he said that one word, Tony knew this was the man he'd been waiting for. Well-dressed. Nice quality; not overdone. Expensive shoes (you could always tell by the shoes). No jewelry. No ring tan line. Didn't look like a rebound. Then Tony noticed that the bar in front of the guy was empty. "Just got here?"

"Yup," he said.

"Want a drink?"

"You might say that."

The guy's confidence was making him a bit uncomfortable. "What'll you have?"

"What are you drinking?"

"Vodka tonic." He didn't mention it was just a little vodka and a whole lot of tonic. "Want one?"

"That'll do. Make it Stoli."

"Cody!" he called to a handsome blond bartender in a tight white tank. "A Stoli tonic for my new friend here." He gave Cody a wink, but Cody didn't move. Instead, he stared at Tony's new friend with a puzzled look on his face.

"Jared, right?"

"Right," said the guy.

Jared.

Tony suddenly felt off his game.

"How the hell are you, man?" said Cody. "Haven't seen you here in ages. Where've you been?"

"Rome," said Jared. "How've you been?"

"Still here." Cody grinned. "How about you?"

"I've been better, but I'll get over it." He glanced at Tony.

Cody plunked down the vodka tonic in front of Jared. He seemed about to launch into more conversation when a sloppy drunk from farther down the bar hollered for a bartender. "Gotta run, man. Busy night. Great to see you again." And he headed off.

Tony wasn't letting this one get away. "So, I guess your name is Jared and you've been here before. Mine's Tony." He held out his hand. "How come I've never seen you here?"

"Like I told you," said Jared, taking his hand, "I've been away."

"Right." He took a swig from his drink. "What do you do that takes you to Rome?"

"Sales," said Jared.

Jared's drink was half gone. Not good for business.

"And what do you do, Tony?"

There was something in the way Jared said his name that made him wonder if he was for real. It didn't matter. He was going for it. If Jared was playing him, time would tell.

"Well?" asked Jared.

Tony realized he hadn't answered. "I guess we have a lot in common. I'm a businessman."

"What kind of business?"

"I supply what my customers need."

Jared's eyebrows rose. "You're a pusher?"

"Hell no. I don't fuck with that shit. Messes with the head. Bad for business. I've seen too many guys get into it and wind up doing time. I smoke a little sometimes, but I draw the line there. No, man, my clients have other needs."

Jared set his empty glass down on the bar. That was fast. Either he was a bottomless pit, or he was escaping something.

Tony signaled Cody who came right over. "Give Jared another one, okay?" He gave Cody a wink—his signal not to spare the alcohol. *Let's see how this dude rolls.*

"Sure thing." Cody grabbed the empty glass from Jared and returned with a full one in less than a minute.

"Thanks," said Jared. "So, Mr. Businessman, where's your office?"

"That table over there." Tony pointed to a little café table for two in the corner with a prominent "Reserved" sign on it. "Why don't we go to my office? It's more private there."

"Sounds good." Jared picked up his drink. For the first time that night, he smiled.

Tony grabbed what was left of the drink he'd been nursing and led the way. "Have a seat." He motioned to the empty chair.

Jared set his already-empty glass down on the table and took the seat.

"Dude, you might want to let up a little," Tony said. "I don't do unconscious."

"I'll be fine," said Jared.

Tony's "office" was the one spot in the whole club where it was just quiet enough to have a conversation without shouting over the music. Thank God for bad acoustics. Jared got settled in his seat and waved to Cody for a refill. *I might be in trouble.* He couldn't look away from those piercing gray eyes. Still, he did his best to stay casual. "So, Mr. Salesman, what's a guy like you doing in a place like this?"

"Looking for a guy like you," Jared said in a silky voice that made Tony's mouth go dry. "Tell me, what would it take for someone like me to do business with you?"

"It depends," Tony said.

"On what?"

"On who you work for."

Cody ran by, dropping off yet another drink for Jared.

"I work for myself."

"All right then," said Tony. "If someone wanted to purchase my services, it'd set them back a hundred fifty an hour. I work the whole night for two-fifty. But, for you, I might be willing to negotiate a deal."

"What kind of deal did you have in mind?" He took a deep swallow of his drink.

"Why don't we head over to your place and we can discuss it on the way?"

As they stood, Jared said, "I gotta get my tab."

Tony slipped one arm around Jared's waist and waved at Cody. "Relax," he said. "I've got this." He steered Jared through the packed dancefloor, holding him tightly against himself, enjoying the undulating ripples of his body maybe a little too much.

Once they were out on the street, it took a couple of minutes to stop a cab. Tony slid into the seat first, with Jared close behind.

"The Andaz, please," said Jared, and the cab was away.

"No less." Tony appraised his conquest. "Sales must be good."

"Could be worse," said Jared. "Now, what were you saying about a deal?"

"Not here, man. Don't worry—I'll make it worth the wait."

"I'm counting on it," said Jared, squeezing against him.

The cab lurched through downtown traffic, but Tony paid little attention to their progress. The heat from Jared's body was already making him sweat. He was getting nervous. This shit didn't happen. Not to him. But this guy had something. Tony wasn't sure what it was, but without saying much of anything, he was already seeping around Tony's walls.

They stopped in front of the hotel and Jared slipped the driver a twenty. This time, it was Jared's turn to wrap an arm around Tony's waist as they walked across the vacant lobby and into the elevator. Jared used his key card and pressed the button for the private suite level.

As soon as the door had closed, Jared put both his arms around Tony and drew him close. The kiss made Tony weak in the knees. He needed out of there now, but his feet wouldn't move. He couldn't breathe. If he kept going, he'd be in uncharted territory with this guy.

The elevator door opened, and they broke their kiss. Jared guided him into the hall. He used his key card, and the two men stepped into the suite. Tony had been in almost every hotel in LA and most of the suburbs, but this was his first time in an Andaz suite. A glass wall, with a patio just outside, stretched the entire length of the room. Beyond that, the lights of the city extended as far as he could see.

"Can we go out?" Tony asked. When he turned around, Jared was stark naked, his clothes already arranged across the back of a chair. Tony gasped. Every muscle on Jared's lean body was visible and well-defined: his square pecs, his smooth ripped six-pack, his finely-veined biceps and forearms, his powerful hips and thighs, his sculpted calves and feet, and a hefty penis, standing straight out from Jared's groin. Tony took a step back and leaned against the cold glass. "Dude," was all he could manage.

"So, Mr. Businessman, what's the bottom line?"

He croaked out, "Tonight's on the house."

"Then, let's get rid of these." In two steps, Jared was on him, unbuttoning his shirt and loosening his belt so that his pants fell around his ankles. Jared hefted him out of his shoes and ripped off his socks. Tony was naked and hard and engulfed in the heat of this guy who had some kind of strange power to overwhelm him. Jared wrapped his arms around Tony, pressed his mouth to his, and whisked him off his feet, carrying him into the bedroom.

As soon as he felt the end of the king bed against the back of his legs, Tony scooched himself backward and up on the bed. He was about to ask Jared "the question," but Jared was already sheathing his rigid penis in latex and applying lube. "How do you want me?" asked Tony. "This is your treat."

"Just like that," said Jared. "I want to look you in the eyes." With that, Jared climbed up on the bed between Tony's raised knees.

Tony felt the amazing warm pressure inside him as Jared lowered himself on him, resting on his arms on either side of Tony's head. *Oh, my God. This guy is incredible.* He felt all of Jared's quiet power, but with an unexpected gentleness that allowed Tony to open himself to him. Jared stared into his eyes as if he were looking into Tony's heart. Despite the drinks, Despite everything, Tony surrendered. It seemed like half the night had passed before their union took him over and, before he could help himself, he began spasming, pouring himself out. He gripped the bedsheets and hung on. Jared was taking his time, but almost too soon he groaned, and his body tensed. The waves between them flowed on and on, vibrating back and forth.

Jared collapsed onto him and, without breaking their embrace, reached beyond the bed and turned out the light. Tony breathed in the scent of him. It was so foreign, yet somehow familiar. He felt enfolded. He felt owned. For the first time, he knew where he belonged, and it scared him to death.

Chapter 7

Jared opened his eyes. He felt the warmth of Tony's naked body against him. Tony was snoring contentedly. The hotel room was still dark, but the first dim glow of dawn came through the unshaded window and bathed their pillows in soft light. He turned on his side. He could see Tony's face, as innocent as a child's, topped with a chaotic mop of jet-black hair. In every respect, this guy was just his type: young, handsome, slender but well-built, street-smart but not yet hardened. There was something he liked about Tony. Maybe it was how easy it had been to win him over, or how anxious he was to please. Whatever it was, Jared wanted it. And what Jared wanted, he got.

He slipped out of the bed and padded barefoot to the john where he let loose a heavy stream of recycled booze. He didn't flush, not wanting the sleeping boy to wake yet. He passed into the sitting area, got himself a glass and fished a few half-melted ice cubes out of the bucket. Over the ice, he poured a healthy portion of Chivas. Then he opened one of the sliders, crossed the patio to the railing and looked down. The cool spring breeze at the top of the hotel caressed his naked skin and he gave a little shiver.

The scotch warmed him from the inside. What would it take to keep Tony around? He was a businessman all right but giving up the goods for free like he did last night wouldn't keep him in business very long. He didn't care that Tony turned tricks for cash. He wouldn't get in the guy's way in that regard. But wouldn't it be nice if Tony could be there waiting for him in LA whenever he came into town? The idea more than intrigued him.

"I suppose I ought to be going now," said a voice from over his shoulder.

Jared spun around. There stood Tony in the first light of dawn, as naked as he was, but a lot more awkward. "No, no," said Jared. "Please. Stay.

49

You don't have anything important to do this morning, do you? At least have some breakfast with me. I'd like that."

Tony beamed. "That'd be great."

"I know what I'd like for breakfast." Jared stared into Tony's eyes. "Come here."

Tony was across the patio and wrapped around Jared in an instant. "I was hoping you'd want that. Look what I've got for you." He sheathed Jared in a condom. Thank God Tony was a lithe little guy and Jared could lift him up. They kissed, clinging to each other until Jared was able to settle his conquest down and enter him. Tony leaned back, wrapped his legs around Jared's back, and flexed and released his thighs, alternating raising up and impaling himself on Jared. They continued this soundless dance until Jared began to tire. Tony, sensing his fatigue, doubled his efforts until both were grunting and squirming in release.

Jared set him down on his feet on the patio deck, both men panting and glistening with sweat. Jared unsheathed and tossed the condom over the railing.

"C'mon." He grabbed Tony's hand, pulling him inside. At the desk he found menus and passed one to Tony. "What do you want for breakfast?" Without waiting for Tony to look, he said, "How about bacon, eggs, hash browns, toast, juice, and coffee?"

"Uh, that would be great, I guess," stammered Tony.

"Or do you like sausage better? Are you a sausage guy?"

Tony looked down at Jared. "What do you think?" He tossed the menu back. "Get me whatever you're having."

Jared picked up the phone and ordered them both breakfast. When he was done, he said, "Listen, Stud, you got me all hot and sweaty out there. I'm going to take a quick shower, okay?"

Tony nodded.

"If the breakfast comes before I'm out, you'll let them in?"

Tony nodded again.

Jared ducked into the bathroom and turned on the shower. It was glass-enclosed, floor-to-ceiling, with polished granite walls and tiled floor. There were enough shower heads to soak six people. He stuck his head back out into the room and said, "Don't go anywhere."

The water was already hot, and Jared stepped in and soaped up. Sure, it would be fun to have Tony around when he wanted him, but it could also get complicated. Taking this time away to blow off steam in LA was one thing. Starting out a whole new ministry with Paul in the diocese and Tony in LA? That would be crazy. Then again, it wouldn't be the first crazy thing he'd done. Jared rinsed off, stepped out of the enclosure, and grabbed a towel. He was drying himself as he stepped out of the bathroom. "Breakfast here yet?"

Tony sat in one of the armchairs staring at him.

Jared stopped in his tracks. "What's wrong?"

"Nothing," said Tony. "It's just this." He held up a boarding pass.

"And? I told you I came from Rome."

"You're Jared *Röhrbach*?"

"Yeah. So what?"

"The son of Kurt Röhrbach, who started CalTainer?"

Jared took a step backward. The air on his still-wet skin chilled him. "How would you know that?"

"I told you. I'm a businessman. I read a lot, especially about local guys who are worth three quarters of a billion dollars."

Jared took a careful breath. He hadn't expected the guy to be this savvy. "I think we'd better chat over breakfast. Maybe we've underestimated each other."

"Maybe so," said Tony.

There was a knock at the door and Jared threw a towel around himself and went to open it. The server wheeled the cart in and set everything up. When he finished, Jared signed the bill, and the server bid the gentlemen good morning and slipped out of the room. Jared poured two cups of coffee. "How do you take yours?"

"Black," said Tony.

Jared took a sip and made a face. "That's the one thing I'm going to miss about Italy—the coffee." They started in on the food. "Okay, so you know who my father is. You want to know about the money?"

Tony nodded. "Mm-hmm."

"It's all Papa's. I don't get to touch any of it. He thought I needed something of my own, so he made me trustee of a little trust fund."

"How little?" asked Tony with a mischievous grin. He took a sip of coffee.

"Ten million."

Tony choked.

"So far, I've lived off the interest. I haven't had to spend any of the principal." He looked at Tony. "Do you understand what that means?"

"Of course." Tony sopped up some egg yolk with a hunk of toast. "You think this is my only gig? I satisfy customers of all sorts."

"What do you mean? I thought you told me you didn't deal."

"I don't deal drugs. It's bad for business. I deal in property. I'm a land broker. I do my business by cell phone during the day and, since I'm at the club every night, they let me reserve that table. I give them a little something for their trouble. Google 'Keating Enterprises.' That's me. Tony Keating."

"Damn, boy. You're something else." Jared laughed.

"So are you."

"Listen, Tony." Jared nibbled the end of a strip of bacon. "I'm going to be here for a week or ten days. What would you say to hanging out here with me? I'll make it worth your while." He picked up the pot. "More coffee?"

Tony stroked his chin. "Let's see...hanging out for a week at the best hotel in LA with the hottest millionaire in town who's going to pay me to do it?" He scowled. "I don't know." Then his face broke into a broad grin. "Sure! Why the hell not?"

"Awesome." Jared paused. "I'd like you to do something else for me, Stud."

"I thought I already did." Tony smirked. "What else do you have in mind?"

"Now that I'm back in the States, I need a car. Would you shower up and come shopping with me?"

"Man, you're killing me." Tony laughed. "Give me a minute." The bathroom door closed behind him and Jared heard the water running.

Jared dressed in fresh jeans and a polo shirt and slipped his feet into a pair of comfortable brown loafers. He readjusted the contents of the suitcase to make sure his clerical clothes were buried under stacks of street clothes. Tony had found out quite enough about him for one day. Maybe someday he'd tell him who he was, but not today. He opened the armoire and punched the code into the keypad on the safe door. Then he took out his checkbook and passport and closed the safe, resetting the code.

A few minutes later, Tony came out of the bathroom, toweling his hair.

"Yum!" Jared said. "Too bad you have to cover all that up."

Tony laughed and stepped into his slacks. "The car. Remember? Where are we headed?"

Jared slipped his hands into his pockets. "I kind of lied to you."

Tony stopped fastening his belt, his eyebrows raised.

"We're not going shopping." He pulled out his checkbook. "I've already ordered the car. We're just going over to the dealer to pick it up and pay them the balance."

"What are you getting?" Tony laced up his running shoes.

"A Porsche," Jared said as they headed out the door. "It's a little red 911 convertible. I'm kind of psyched about it."

They rode down in the elevator and got out in the lobby, now bright with sunlight and filled with guests checking out and tourist types getting ready to see the town. Cabs were lined up outside the door. Jared chose one and opened the door for Tony, then slid in himself. "Downtown Porsche on Figuroa, please." The cab took off, headed for the 10.

"Where do you live when you're not in the bar?"

Tony laughed, though he looked a little tense. "Getting kind of personal, aren't we? That's information I don't share with clients."

"I'm not a client, remember? Humor me. I'm thinking about something."

"I'll bet you are. I guess I deserve it, asking personal questions about your money." He crossed his arms at his chest. "To answer your question, I'm for rent, not for sale."

It was Jared's turn to laugh. "No, man, that's not what I was thinking. I'm going to be in LA pretty often once I'm settled in, and it would be nice to have a place I could leave some stuff and crash when I'm in town. Maybe I could rent something in your building."

"Good thought, dude, but you can't."

"You don't want me to hang with you?"

"It's not that." Tony looked a little embarrassed. "It's just...I don't have a place. I either stay with customers for the night or crash with a couple of buddies who don't mind having me around. I'm saving my money."

Jared thought for a moment. "Well, then, what would you say to doing it the other way around? I can rent a place, and you can stay there and pay me something—whatever works for you."

"What's the catch?"

"You *might* want to entertain me when I'm in town," Jared said with a wink. "Could you manage that, do you think?"

"It would be tough, but I think I could accommodate you," said Tony with mock seriousness. "Having my own place would be good for business, and I could move my office out of the bar. I'd rather pay you than them, anyway." He looked at Jared with a challenging stare. "This doesn't mean you'll own me, you know. No restrictions on how I conduct my business in this place?"

"None," said Jared.

Tony relaxed.

"Then it's a deal?" Jared extended his hand.

Tony's face lit up as he shook Jared's hand. "Deal."

"Let's hurry up with the car. I can't think of a thing I'd rather do today than go apartment-hunting in a brand-new Porsche."

Chapter 8

Bishop Clarence Mickleson, first bishop of the diocese of San Luis Obispo, sat behind a heavy mahogany desk that was elegant in its simplicity. As he sorted through stacks of manila personnel folders, he grew concerned. Maybe he'd overlooked some opportunity, but it seemed every time he checked the folders, nothing inside them had miraculously changed. He glanced at his watch. The two new priests would be here any second.

Sure enough, there was a knock on his door, and Monsignor David Yates, Vicar General of the diocese, stuck his head in. Monsignor Yates was the consummate manager, perfect for tackling the day-to-day chores of an active diocese. In his mid-fifties, he even looked the part: from his full head of dark hair, graying at the temples, through his tailored suit with its starched white clerical collar, down to the military polish on his black dress shoes, he projected the image of a man in charge.

"Pardon me, Bishop," said the monsignor, "but Father Fortis is here."

"Send him in."

The bishop closed the file folder, stood, and came around his desk to greet the young man. Paul came through the door looking fresh and every bit like the newly minted priest that he was.

Bishop Mickleson smiled and shook his hand. "Come in, Paul. Have a seat." He gestured toward the couch. "Would you like something to drink?"

"No, thanks, Bishop," said Paul. "I'm good."

"I'm sorry I couldn't make it to Rome for your ordination." He lowered himself into one of the club chairs. "I know you were in good hands with Cardinal Romero. When did you get back?"

"Just a couple of days ago."

"And where is Jared? I expected you two might travel together."

"Not this time. I stayed over there to do some touring with my family. Jared left right after the ordination. I haven't heard from him since. We had a kind of falling out. I've been trying to call him since I got back, but he hasn't returned my calls."

The bishop stifled a groan. "I'm sorry to hear that. I need the two of you to work together."

There was a knock on the door and Monsignor Yates appeared with Jared by his side. "Come in, Jared," the bishop said. "We've been waiting for you." He extended his hand and welcomed Jared. He couldn't help but notice that the young man looked somewhat more haggard than the last time he'd seen him: something about his eyes. He gestured toward the couch where Paul was sitting. "Sit down. Can I get you anything?"

"No, thanks, Bishop," said Jared. "I just finished a bottle of water." He walked over to the couch, ignoring Paul, and sat at the opposite end.

Mickleson sighed. They were acting like school children. "Paul said he hasn't heard from you since the ordination. Is everything all right?"

"Just fine, thanks, Bishop." But there was an unmistakable edge to his voice.

"So, you didn't spend any time in Europe?" asked the bishop.

"No," said Jared. "I needed to come back to Los Angeles to get some things in order."

Paul shot him a look of alarm that Jared ignored.

This was not a good sign. "You know I've been in close contact with the cardinal about you two almost from the time he met you back in Washington at Catholic U. You've both done well in your studies and have the highest recommendation from the seminary. He and I are very proud of you. The cardinal has great hopes for both of you, and you know he's a man who can make things happen. I share his enthusiasm, and I want you to know right off that I'll do what I can to help you succeed."

Paul gave Jared a questioning look, but he was staring at a set of mirror-backed glass shelving that displayed mementos of the bishop's life and work: from his parents' wedding photo to pictures of himself at prep school and seminary, priestly ordination pictures from the American Seminary in Rome, and of his installation as bishop. Many of the pictures featured him alongside a variety of notables but, most prominently, Julio Cardinal Romero.

The way Jared was looking at the photos made the bishop uneasy, but he shook it off and returned to the matter at hand. "I want to impress one thing on you," he said. "All this depends on you both keeping your noses clean. We expect excellence from all our priests, but you two have to go the extra mile. We gave you some leeway with your behavior while you were in formation, but that's over. You must avoid even the suggestion of a scandal. I'm happy to be your mentor, but, more importantly, I am your bishop. If you mess up, I can't help you and, even worse, the cardinal won't want anything more to do with you. Do I make myself clear?" He stared intently at both young priests.

"Absolutely." Paul looked at Jared, and his face reddened.

"Jared?" asked the bishop.

"Sure. Okay," he said.

Once again, Paul frowned at him.

The bishop went on. "I have your assignments. I'm not happy with either one, but they're the best I can do for you for now. Remember that this isn't forever. I'm going to need you both to do your best in these situations. I wish I could have assigned you to some pastor who knew how to mentor you through your learning curve, but that's not possible. As I told you, I'll help you as much as I can. I wouldn't give you these responsibilities if I didn't think you could handle them.

"We'll do our best, Bishop," said Paul, smiling.

Jared sat slumped in his seat, silent and stony-faced.

"Jared," said the bishop, "you're starting to worry me. I don't know what's going on here, but whatever it is, you'll have to fix it. We can talk about it later if you want. I need to impress upon you that these assignments will be challenging. I'll need you to support each other in ways that I can't. Am I clear?"

Jared looked down at the floor. "Yes, Bishop."

"Now let me explain to each of you what I need you to do. You first, Paul." He turned to face the young priest. "I've been without a secretary for months. To be honest, I've kept the position open all this time because I need someone with your skills here at the chancery with me. Monsignor Yates and Sister Margaret have been helping out as much as they can, but now that you're available, I want you here. I have to do all my own scheduling, and it's not working out very well. You'll probably feel lost for the first few months, and my time for explaining things to you will be very limited. Monsignor Yates and Sister Margaret will do what they can to help guide you. I'm sure you'll catch on quickly. Will you do this for me?"

"Certainly, Bishop," said Paul. "I'd be honored."

Jared glared at him.

"I'm meeting with Roger Spellman, our diocesan attorney, on Wednesday afternoon and I'd like you to sit in. I want you to get to know him."

Paul pulled out his iPhone. "I'll put it on my calendar."

"There's an empty bedroom at the cathedral rectory, if you want it. Or you can find an apartment for yourself. Just keep the costs down. If you take an apartment, we'll give you an extra stipend for rent and food, but you'll have to provide your own furnishings. Which would you prefer?"

"I'll take the apartment. That would be wonderful."

"Good. That's settled, then." *Well, that was easy.* "Now you, Jared. I'm afraid that your situation will be a little more...challenging. My choice would be to bring you here to the chancery, too—and we will, as soon as we can—but that's not possible right now." He took a deep breath. "There's a serious pastoral situation that needs to be addressed, and I need someone on-site whom I can trust. It could be a rough assignment, but I think you're capable of handling it. I won't force you to accept it though, if you don't think you're up to it."

Jared straightened, obviously intrigued. "What's the assignment?"

"Are you familiar with Monsignor Sullivan at Our Lady of Perpetual Help parish in Tres Robles?"

"No," said Jared. "I've never heard of him."

"I'm not surprised. He was already a pastor there when I was installed as bishop six years ago. I sort of inherited him. He's...how can I say this charitably? Independent. I've assigned associates there before—even some rather seasoned men—and he's managed to get them all to request a transfer, usually in just a few months."

"Sounds like he wants to be left alone," said Jared. "Why does he need an associate?"

The bishop leaned forward, resting his forearms on his thighs. "From what I can tell, the parish is suffering. It's the smallest parish in the diocese, only a couple of hundred families. Attendance is very low. It's also the poorest parish we have. The diocese has to send them extra support every month just so they can meet their expenses. I've been advised to close the parish, but I don't want to. It's rural, and it would be a real hardship for many of the parishioners to travel somewhere else."

"What would you want me to do?"

"I sense that something isn't right there. There are a number of wealthy parishioners who run some large farming operations there. From what I can gather, the people are more than capable of supporting the parish. Maybe they're holding back because of the monsignor. Nobody has been able to fill me in on what's going on."

"So, you want me to keep an eye on him?"

"Possibly. But even more, I'd like you to find out from the people what they need. See if you can bring some fresh ideas to that parish to get people more involved. I'm sure you'll get a lot of resistance from the monsignor. When you do, come straight to me and I'll back you. He's old school; I don't think he'd dare refuse me. What do you think? Would you agree to take this on?"

"I'm willing to give it a try." Jared's face showed more interest than at any time since he had arrived. It intrigued the bishop. Father Jared appeared to be someone who liked a good challenge.

"There's one more thing I want you to understand before we go any farther," he said to Jared. "In this job, you're going to confront something that has crippled men and women in the ministry with a lot more experience than you: isolation. I'm warning you: if you don't have the support of people who understand what you're going through, it can break you. I can give you some support, but if you're going to succeed at this, you'll need Paul." He turned to Paul. "I know you've been close friends a long time. I'm serious when I tell you that Jared will need a confidant that he can trust, and I'll be counting on you to do whatever's necessary to support him. Do I have both of your promises to support each other?"

He wondered, for a moment, if it was wise to have these two depend on each other in such a close relationship given their history, but he decided to give them the benefit of the doubt. The closeness would work in their favor.

"Absolutely." Paul beamed at Jared, even though Jared's 'yes' was unenthusiastic, and he still avoided making eye contact with Paul.

"I'm proud of you both." The bishop stood, signaling that the interview was over. "I'll give Monsignor Yates instructions to process your assignments. Please report there tomorrow morning. Paul, see Monsignor Yates on your way out and let him know you'll be looking for an apartment. I'll work out the details with him later. Welcome to the ministry, boys."

Bishop Mickleson watched them leave his office, hoping he hadn't made a terrible mistake.

Chapter 9

Monday, June 27, 2011

"Jared, wait!" Paul had to run down the steps of the chancery office to catch him. He grabbed him by the arm. "Listen to me. Please."

Jared spun around. "What could I possibly want to hear from you?" His icy stare cut right through Paul.

"I'm sorry. I messed up."

"Good for you. You think you can just apologize, and everything will be okay? That was my ordination you ruined, not some kid's game. I don't know what the hell you were thinking, or why, but you know what? I don't want to know. Just get out of my life, will you?"

"Jared, please." Paul glanced around and his voice dropped to a hoarse whisper. "Just listen to me for five minutes—that's all."

"I don't give a damn about your excuses."

A barely perceptible softening in Jared's glare gave Paul enough encouragement to press on. "Listen, man: I care about you. I would never do anything deliberately to hurt you. Ever."

"You have a strange way of showing it. I never expected anything like that—and from you, of all people."

Paul looked away. "I had no idea Hannah was trying to sabotage us. You didn't tell me that until just before the ordination. Your father was already in Rome. There was nothing I could do."

"Right, asshole. You could have warned me." The mention of Hannah's name brought bitterness back into Jared's voice.

"I know you. You would have bolted, wouldn't you? Be honest."

"I don't know, but you never gave me the choice. Besides, you knew how I felt. If you knew they were coming, why didn't you try to stop them? You knew what that would do to me."

"I wanted to tell you, but..." Paul sighed. "Look, your dad has been writing me ever since we went away to school in DC."

Jared straightened and took a step back, but Paul put a gentle hand on his arm. "He's been concerned about you. He loves you so much, and he feels guilty about what happened to you as a kid. He asked me not to tell you he was writing."

"He should feel guilty." Jared's voice was softer.

"He knew the ordination was coming up, and he wanted more than anything to show you he was there for you. He knew you weren't going to invite him, but he asked me point blank when it would be. He told me if I didn't tell him he would write the seminary rector and find out. Jared, he was going to find out anyway."

"So, you told him?" said Jared, much calmer now.

"Yes. I'm so sorry. I never meant to hurt you." Paul couldn't hold back the tears any longer. "I love you so much."

"All right, man." It was Jared's turn to sigh. "Maybe we should go somewhere a little more private to continue this conversation."

The sidewalk was empty, but there was a lot of traffic on the street. Paul wiped his cheeks with the back of his hand, embarrassed that someone might have seen him standing there in his clerical collar, crying.

"There's a café nearby," said Jared. "You can treat me to lunch."

Paul followed him the couple of blocks in silence. When they reached the café, Jared chose a table on the outdoor patio, and they settled in and ordered drinks. The warm California sun made Paul feel better.

Jared leaned across the table. "We used to tell each other everything. I guess that's not true anymore. You had your reasons, I get that, but still..."

Paul tilted his head. "You kept a secret from me, too. You never told me what your stepmother did. I would have tried so much harder to keep them away if I'd known."

"You're right." Jared sat back. "Maybe you're not the only one who messed up."

The server set their drinks down on the table and took their order.

"So," said Paul once he was gone, "do you forgive me? Are we good?"

"I don't know," said Jared. A smile broke through. "I guess I can't stay mad at you for too long. After all, you *are* my only friend." He winked at him. "Besides, the bishop made you promise to support me."

"Hey, hey, now. As I recall, he made us promise to support each other."

"Okay, then. I promise to be true to you," said Jared. "In good times and in bad, in sickness and in health..."

"Don't be an ass," Paul said. "At least let me help you out next time. It sounds like you'll need it, from what the bishop said. Can we at least talk about how we can support each other?"

"I guess it wouldn't hurt," Jared replied with a smirk. "What were you thinking?"

"Before I tell you, you never said you forgave me. Do you?"

"Yes." Jared rolled his eyes. "I forgive you."

Paul grinned. "I forgive you, too."

"Dork," said Jared, just as the server arrived with their plates of food. He set the plates down and walked away without a word.

"Nice," said Paul. Jared burst out laughing.

"Still love me?" asked Paul.

"As much as ever," said Jared.

Paul's demeanor turned serious, and he shook his head. "Damn. I thought I'd lost you this time."

"Almost," said Jared.

"Let's not do that again." Paul took a bite of his sandwich and noticed Jared's beer mug was empty. "Want another beer?"

Jared nodded. "Have you ever heard of Tres Robles?"

"Isn't it up by Monterrey? Two-hour drive from here." Paul caught the server's eye and signaled for a refill.

"It will make coming here more than a little inconvenient," said Jared.

"Look, the bishop's giving me the stipend for rent and food. He won't care if the apartment costs more than the allowance, as long as the diocese isn't paying for it. If you're willing to help me out with the rent, I can get a bigger apartment—say, two bedrooms—and, when things get to you and you need to get out of town, you can drive down here and stay with me. Anyway, we've got some catching up to do." He gave Jared an exaggerated wink just as the waiter appeared with their drink refills.

"Would you gentlemen like anything else?"

Jared shook his head and pointed to Paul. "Give him the check, okay?"

"Right," said Paul. "Make the poor guy pay."

Jared laughed. "You asked for it, dude."

"I guess I did." Paul laid a hand on Jared's forearm. "What do you think of my idea? Want to get an apartment together in town?"

"Sure," said Jared. "Why not?"

"What about the drive? You won't mind?"

Jared smiled. "I just bought myself a brand-new Porsche."

"Awesome!" said Paul. "Where is it?"

"Back at the chancery."

"Can I see it?"

"Of course." His eyes narrowed. "But, as for commuting, I have another idea that might work out even better than driving."

"What's that?"

"Wait and see, my friend," said Jared. "Wait and see."

The waiter dropped the billfold with the check in front of Paul. Although they had smoothed over this rough spot, something had shifted in their relationship. The easy openness he'd always felt with Jared was gone. Something in Jared's tone made Paul think this wouldn't be the last time he'd be paying for lunch.

Chapter 10

Tuesday, June 28, 2011

Eliza Roberts hated everything about her cramped office at Our Lady of Perpetual Help parish, from the fluorescent lights on the ceiling to the lumpy brown linoleum on the floor; from the dull institutional yellow-green on the walls to the ratty second-hand furniture. Then there was the safe. It was the largest item in the room, with stenciling on it that made it look like a refugee from a wild west assay office. She tried not to pay any attention to any of it; otherwise, it made her feel like she was parish secretary in a third-world mission outpost.

She was typing up some announcements for next week's church bulletin on a decades-old electric typewriter. Every few minutes, she stopped and checked the dainty jeweled wristwatch she wore and shook her head. The new associate pastor was due to arrive. The day was wearing on, and she was anxious for him to get there before she had to leave. Her curiosity was eroding her professional demeanor. She reached into one of her desk drawers and pulled out another butterscotch candy, unwrapping the cellophane and popping it into her mouth before better judgment could intervene. Although they threatened her trim figure, the sweets did blunt her nervousness—at least a bit.

The door behind her crashed open, and Yolanda rushed in. She was a squat, middle-aged woman with a warm, welcoming face, but her brown eyes looked especially intense. "I think he's here." She flailed her arms. "A fancy car pulled into the carport." She adjusted her hair net and tightened the white apron she wore over her flowered dress.

"Oh my." Eliza flicked off the power to the typewriter before standing up to straighten her skirt and vest. "It's getting so late, I thought we might not see him today."

Yolanda took a quick look around and moved the chairs a few inches one way and then another as if it might make the room look more inviting—but, in vain.

The door opened, and a young man stepped in—so handsome, Eliza was at first unsure if this was the priest. He had piercing gray eyes and a lock of black hair that fell over the center of his forehead. While he wore clerical black, his shirt was open at the collar and lacked the little white tab at his neck. But no, his bearing marked him as a priest. He pulled a large fiberglass suitcase on rollers behind him.

"Good afternoon," said Eliza in her most official administrative voice. "Welcome to Our Lady of Perpetual Help. You must be Father Röhrbach."

"That's me." The young priest held out his hand. "Please call me Father Jared."

"We're so glad you've come, Father." Eliza smiled as she shook his hand. "I'm Eliza Roberts, the church secretary and bookkeeper, and this is Yolanda Suarez, our housekeeper and cook."

"How do you do, Father?" Yolanda stepped up to shake his hand.

"Yolanda is getting ready to make your dinner," said Eliza. "I'm sure you'll be hungry after your long drive."

"I'm very much looking forward to a home-cooked meal," said Jared, "but the drive wasn't bad at all. I have to admit I bought myself a new car as an ordination present and this was a good chance to take it out on a nice, long drive."

"Yolanda said you parked in the carport," Eliza said. "You're fine there for now while the monsignor is away, but I'm afraid he's very possessive about his parking space."

"We wouldn't want to get off on the wrong foot with him now, would we?" His tone betrayed a surprising hint of sarcasm. "I'll move it tomorrow. When will the monsignor be back?"

"He left this morning after Mass, and we don't expect him back before noon on Saturday. He said he was sure you could take care of the daily Mass while he was away." Eliza caught the knowing glance Yolanda gave her as she spoke.

"Tell me, then," said Father Jared, "what's the story with the pile of stuff in the other parking space?"

Yolanda looked alarmed. "Under the carport?"

"Just building materials," Eliza said. "I don't know much about it, except it's been there for a long time—several months, I'd say. You'll have to ask our maintenance man, Frank Worth. You'll meet him tomorrow, I'm sure. However, I should warn you, the monsignor doesn't want his things touched."

"I'll have a talk with Frank first thing tomorrow morning. I'm sure we can get it all worked out." Father Jared turned to Yolanda. "I hope I'm not putting you out if I eat dinner here with you tonight."

Yolanda shook her head. "Of course not."

"Were you cooking anything special?"

"The monsignor is a meat-and-potatoes man, Father. I was going to cook a pork chop and some boiled potatoes. Would that be all right?"

"The pork chop would be fine. You could even make it two if it's no trouble. But how about something green instead of the potatoes? Could I have green beans or something?"

"Sure. I'll take a quick trip down to the market to get the extra chop and some fresh green beans." She shot a worried glance at Eliza. "That's all right with you, Eliza, isn't it?"

"Of course, dear." She took out a little key and opened one of her desk drawers. "Here's forty dollars. That should be more than enough for what you need. Don't forget to bring back the receipt."

"Yes, ma'am," said Yolanda.

"And the change," she added, before it occurred to her she shouldn't have.

70

It made Yolanda sound like a thief.

The new priest knit his brows but said nothing.

"Yes, ma'am. I'll be right back." Yolanda turned to Father Jared. "When you're ready for your dinner, just let me know. It'll take just a few minutes to get it to the table. Then you can tell me what you do and don't like to eat. We want to keep you around." She gave him a broad smile and left through the door marked Private.

"Yolanda will make your lunch and supper," Eliza said, "but for breakfast and on Sundays, you'll be on your own." She stopped herself. Was she being too curt? "She does the laundry on Fridays, because that's the monsignor's day off. She'll clean your room once a week, but we'll work out that schedule later." She turned the deadbolt on the front door. "I suppose I'd better show you around."

"Yes, thanks," said Father Jared. "This is the parish office, then?"

"Yes," she said, "such as it is. The closed door over there is the monsignor's office. He doesn't want anyone in there unless he invites you. The other door will be your office."

She crossed the room and stood beside the open door, trying to see the brown linoleum and yellow-green walls through charitable eyes. But how? There was an industrial fluorescent fixture on the ceiling, a single, naked window...and nothing else. Not a picture nor a piece of furniture—with one exception: on the floor in the far corner was a multi-line push-button phone, identical to the one on Eliza's desk.

She watched as surprise, then confusion, then concern, then resolve passed in sequence across the young priest's handsome face. It was hard not to feel compassion for the poor fellow. "I'm certain you'll make the place your own in no time," she said, trying to sound as if leaving him to fend for himself was standard procedure.

"I see," said Jared.

"If you'll take your suitcase and follow me," Eliza said, "I'll show you the

71

rest of the house." She opened the door marked Private and led him into a room painted the same color and with the same linoleum and fluorescent fixtures. There was a single unadorned window to their right and doorways straight ahead and to their left. A plastic laminate-covered dinette table sat in the middle of the room surrounded by eight mismatched chairs.

"This is our conference room." She kept her voice even, even though it was hideous, and she knew it. She could tell he was trying hard not to react. "The kitchen, over here, is Yolanda's realm, and as you can see, she does everything she can to make it livable."

Everything was arranged in neat rows on shelves or in glass-fronted cabinets. The brown linoleum floor was so clean it almost shone. Even the vintage appliances looked presentable Despite the occasional spots where the white finish had been chipped off. The sink, too, was spotless, though its white ceramic glaze had been scrubbed down past the shine decades ago. There were even a few cardboard-mounted pictures on the wall: one of the pope, another of the Virgin of Guadalupe, and a third (yellowed and faded with age) of John Kennedy.

Father Jared looked around with a satisfied smile. "This is more like it."

For a man who'd just bought himself a new car, she doubted it, but she didn't respond. She led him through another door and into the dining room. It was pitiful in its pretense to elegance. The wooden table and six matching chairs were second-hand acquisitions and looked it. The sole table decoration was a multi-line phone just like the ones in the parish office. The table sat on a threadbare imitation oriental carpet. Several hooks were missing for the red velvet drapes, so they hung at odd angles. An Eastlake-style buffet didn't match anything else in the room. There was nothing to break the monotony of the yellow-green walls but the flecks of white where the plaster had been chipped off.

In the living room in front of the fireplace sat a 1990s-vintage console television, giving eloquent testimony to the uselessness of the fireplace. The room smelled of dirty socks. Eliza pressed on, past an exterior door crudely nailed shut that she hoped he wouldn't notice. But by the look on his face, he had.

He followed her up the stairs, his suitcase thumping up behind him. Eliza opened the nearest door and went in.

Father Jared looked around and sighed. "The Bates Motel."

"Pardon?" said Eliza, pretending she hadn't heard.

"Oh, nothing." His smile now looked forced.

At least this room was furnished. A small desk held another multi-line push-button phone. There was a black spool bed—the kind Abraham Lincoln had died in—covered in tattered bedclothes that didn't hide the sag in the middle. Next to the bed was a dresser made of particle board, and in the center of the room sat a stained orange rug that looked as though it had been cut from a 1960s shag carpet.

She didn't blame the young priest for wrinkling his nose. A tiny empty closet stank of mothballs. The bathroom was a mess of rust stains and mildew, with a rusted metal shower enclosure missing its curtain. Threadbare towels hung from the single towel bar.

Eliza looked into his eyes and saw how tired he looked now. The light she had seen in them when he'd first walked through the door was dimming. The sad condition of the rectory was already working its soul-numbing dark magic.

She touched his sleeve. "Don't let it get to you, Father. You'll have a lot of support here. Trust me." She looked up at him and smiled. "Frank, Yolanda and I will make sure you're okay. We need you here." Perhaps she'd said too much, but there was something in his gray eyes that inspired her confidence.

"Thank you for that," he said. The shadow passed, and he smiled at her. "I'm afraid we'll have to make some changes around here."

Eliza nodded.

"I'll unpack a few things and then have an early supper, if that's all right with Yolanda. Would you mind telling her I'll be down in about half an hour?"

"Certainly, Father. I'll be leaving for the day. Weekday Masses are at eight. I'd better give you the key to the church." She reached into a little pocket on her vest and produced a single key on a metal ring. "You'll have to open up by 7:30. The key also opens the sacristy door. I'm sure you don't need me to find your way around the church," she added with a little wink.

"And the rectory key?" Father Jared asked.

"The monsignor keeps that himself. You'll have to lock up at night and open the doors in the morning from the inside."

"Are you serious?" His mouth hung open. "What if there's a sick call during the night?"

"Don't worry, Father," she said. "That almost never happens."

"And if it does?"

"You'll have to leave the back door in the kitchen unlocked while you're out."

"Damn!" He looked both embarrassed and annoyed. "Sorry," he added.

"I'll leave you to it. We can talk more tomorrow. I'll be in before noon." Eliza went down the stairs and into the kitchen.

Yolanda was already back, cutting some fresh green beans. "Well? What's he like?"

"The bishop knew what he was doing when he sent him here," said Eliza. "The monsignor will have a hard time intimidating this one. He may be young, but something tells me we may see some changes around here at last."

"It's about time," said Yolanda. "By the way, I'm sorry I had to ask for more money for the extra food. Here's the change." She picked up the money from the counter and handed it to Eliza. "I hope this doesn't leave you short."

"We'll do whatever we need to," she replied. "The monsignor made no provision for an extra mouth. That'll have to be between Father Röhrbach and him. All we have to do in the meantime is lay low and do what we're told."

As Eliza went back through the Private door to the office, she heard the thud above her of Father Jared's suitcase hitting the floor.

Chapter 11

Jared awoke in his new surroundings at Our Lady of Perpetual Help. It was Day Two. His back felt stiff and sore from sleeping on the saggy old mattress. His throat felt raw and congested, probably from the mildew. At least Yolanda had fed him well last night. She and Eliza were the only bright spots so far in this dismal assignment. He sat up, hoping the room might look a little better in the daylight. It didn't. His suitcase sat open on the desk chair, his clothes in a heap on top because he refused to put them in the grimy chest of drawers in the corner. *All of this junk has to go,* he decided. *A parish can be poor, but it doesn't have to be filthy.*

He climbed out of bed, took care of his morning duties, and threw on a pair of pants and a clerical shirt. It was 6:30, and he figured it would be best to go open the church before doing anything else. He hesitated and almost changed his mind. *What if the church is in as bad a condition as this place?* Well, there was no sense delaying the inevitable.

He hurried down the stairs and out the back door. There was no sign of anyone out and about yet. He unlocked the church door. When he went inside, it felt like he'd stepped back fifty years in time. The church was small, seating about a hundred worshippers. The pews were oak with beat-up old kneelers attached, each one upholstered in faded fake red leather and patched in various places with duct tape. The interior of the church was painted Virgin Mary blue, with white woodwork yellowed with age. The ceiling over the sanctuary was a half-dome, painted light blue like the rest of the church but with gold stars stenciled in. The plaster was cracked in several places, and on one side there had must have been a water leak because the back wall behind the altar piece was stained.

There were saints' statues everywhere. The whole ensemble looked like a spiritual junk pile that made no discernable sense. Jared's heart sank. He would find no spiritual solace here. He stepped up into the sanctuary and unlocked the door to the sacristy to the side of the main altar. He was beyond disappointment. He sighed at the shabby little sacristy room, shut the door again and headed back to the rectory.

Yolanda had set up his coffee maker for him the day before, and he got it started. By the time he had showered and put on some fresh clothes, his coffee was done, and his spirits started to lift. As he drank his coffee, he opened his laptop to check his email. There was one from Paul, hoping that the parish wouldn't be as difficult an assignment as he had feared. He laughed; if anything, it was worse.

There were a bunch of emails from Tony. He looked at one after another, laughing at Tony's sexual adventures since Jared had left him. It was funny how it lifted his mood. He decided he would need a trip back to LA very soon.

Checking the time, Jared finished his coffee, put on his clerical collar, and headed back out to the church. Five parishioners were waiting for him: four mature women, including Eliza and a woman whose red hair color did not occur in nature on man or beast, and one older man, slender, graying, and in work clothes. Jared smiled at them all and nodded hello. They greeted him with warm acknowledgement—all except the woman with the flame-red hair who seemed to ignore him.

When he entered the sacristy, a short, stocky man was waiting for him. His shoulders were rounded, and the bad posture made him look stooped with age before his time. His eyes met Jared as soon as he stepped into the room and followed him wherever he went, as though he were a chamberlain in a mediaeval palace in the service of his prince.

"Chuck Johnston. Sacristan. At your service." He thrust his hand at Jared, though Jared was so distracted by his bushy gray eyebrows, he avoided looking him in the eye.

Chuck had lit the candles on the altar and laid out everything necessary for morning Mass. Nothing was done the way Jared liked it, but whenever he questioned him, Chuck had the same answer: "That's the way the monsignor does it."

Jared checked the liturgical calendar for Wednesday, the twenty-ninth of June: the feast of Saints Peter and Paul. He retrieved a set of red vestments appropriate for the feast day, only to find the clasp at the neck was broken off and part of the embroidered applique was detached and hanging loose. He tried to make it as presentable as possible but without much success. He stood by one of the grimy windows gathering his thoughts. He always liked to say something that connected the day's liturgy with the people sitting in front of him, but today he struggled. His concern about his future here took center stage in his mind.

At last, led by Chuck, the sixty-year-old altar boy, Jared went out into the sanctuary to begin Mass. He took a few minutes during the Liturgy to share some reflections on how Saints Peter and Paul were the foundation of their Christian faith and formed an unbroken link back to the person of Jesus. Then he continued with the Eucharist, gave all present Communion, and finished up quite nicely, in his estimation, considering what he had to work with.

After helping Chuck put everything away, Jared stepped back out into the church. Eliza was waiting for him, surrounded by the little congregation (except Ms. Red Hair who sat glaring at him from her pew).

"Father, it's so nice to have you saying Mass for us," she said. "Everyone couldn't wait to meet you. Of course, you've already met Chuck. This is Paula Samuels." She indicated an elegantly dressed middle-aged woman who would have served admirably as president of any upscale PTA. "Paula is our parish council president."

Paula grinned and extended her hand. "You have no idea how happy we are to have you here. We desperately need your help."

Jared was caught off guard by her candor. There was something going on here that had escaped him.

"And this is Lupe Vargas," continued Eliza. "She's our women's guild president and serves on our parish council."

Lupe was the shortest and thinnest of the three women and looked like someone who had worked hard all her life. Her blouse and slacks were immaculate and impeccably pressed but of an outmoded style with signs of fraying around the edges. Her eyes sparkled with a quick intelligence that told Jared she might be someone he could count on.

Jared shook her hand. "I look forward to working with you."

"Welcome, Father," she replied.

"And this," said Eliza with a broad smile, "is Frank Worth. He's in charge of maintenance around here. To be honest, he's the only thing keeping the parish from falling down around our ears. I'm sure you'll want his help getting yourself settled."

Jared shook Frank's hand enthusiastically. "You're just the man I want to see. Will you be around this morning?"

"You bet, Father. I'm here for you whatever you need." Frank was a good-looking man, graying, slender, with a ready smile under a bushy mustache and sporting a day or two's growth of white stubble. He was wearing khaki pants and a khaki shirt with a heavy brown leather belt. There was a faded monogram on the breast pocket of his work uniform, but Jared couldn't make it out. He spoke with a hoarseness that suggested he was a heavy smoker. Jared caught the scent of pipe tobacco when he got close.

"Can we talk for a couple of minutes before you get to work?" Jared asked.

"Of course, Father."

"We'll be taking off for now," said Paula. "Will we see you at the parish council meeting next week? It's the first Wednesday of the month."

"I wouldn't miss it," said Jared. "Have a good morning, ladies." The women headed out the door.

"There's no need to add your comments to the Mass," said a raspy voice from behind him. Jared spun around to see the woman with the peculiar red hair staring at him with haughty, angry eyes. Her thin jaw was set tight, giving her pale cheeks an emaciated look. She held a worn leather purse close against her waist with her skeletal fingers gripping the handle. "The monsignor won't like it," she said, "and neither do I." Without another word, she walked out.

"Wow," said Jared. "Who was that?"

Frank shrugged. "That's Harriet Blake. Don't pay her any mind. Every parish has one like her, I guess. She's not happy unless she's griping about something."

Jared and Frank exited the church, leaving Chuck to turn off the lights and close the doors.

"What's going on with that pile of stuff under the tarp in the carport?" he asked once they were outside. "I have a nice new car, and I'd rather not leave it out in the weather. Is it something we could get moved?"

"That's odds and ends of building materials. It's stuff the monsignor had me put there two or three years ago. I don't have a clue what it's for. He's never used any of it, as far as I can tell."

"Is there anywhere else we could put it?"

"There's a shed behind the church we might use if I cleared it out some. Come see." Jared followed Frank around the back of the church, and Frank unlocked the door to the shed. Inside was old gardening tools, a hand lawnmower, and assorted junk—mainly broken appliances. "If I get rid of some of this old crap," said Frank, "I'm pretty sure the monsignor's stuff would fit in here."

"Would you take care of that for me?" asked Jared.

"Sure thing. It's about time we got rid of some of the junk cluttering this place up." They stepped into the bright sunlight. "But I don't dare touch anything without the monsignor's say-so. He's awfully particular." Frank made a point of emphasizing that word, *par-tic-u-lar*. As Jared turned to smile at him, he caught sight of red-haired Harriet standing near the carport, watching them.

"Anything else?" said Frank.

"Yes. Can we get hold of a pickup truck?"

"Mine's right over there." He pointed to a blue F100 sitting in the parking lot.

"Fantastic," said Jared. "There's a bunch of furniture I'd like to get rid of. I'm headed off to Monterey after I have breakfast. I need to get some bedroom furniture and a few things for my office. Maybe there's a poor family or a thrift shop that could use that old stuff. I'm afraid it's not good for much."

"Nobody's going to want that," Frank said. "I've seen it. I'll take it all to the dump."

"All right. I'll have to use it for another day or two, but I'll let you know when the new furniture is arriving, and I'll help you load up your truck." As he spoke, he kept glancing at Harriet. He had the uncomfortable feeling she was eavesdropping on their conversation. She gave him the creeps.

"What's next?" asked Frank.

The more they talked, the more energetic and enthusiastic Frank became. Jared thought he'd very likely been hoping for years that things might change someday.

"How would I go about getting a couple of rooms painted?" Jared asked.

Frank hooked his thumbs in his pockets. "Oh, the monsignor won't go for that. He'll say we can't afford it."

"*We* may not be able to afford it, but *I* can." He stared at Frank. "I want to paint my bedroom and my office before the new furniture gets here. Will you help me get the paint?"

"Will I?" Frank laughed. "I'll not only help you get the paint, I'll help you paint it."

"All right," said Jared. "I think it's time Our Lady got some perpetual help, don't you?"

Frank laughed again and slapped the young priest on the back. "Absolutely."

When Jared looked back toward the house, red-haired Harriet was gone.

Chapter 12

Saturday, July 2, 2011

Jared sat at the big dining table browsing through his brand-new iPhone 4S. A sandwich and a glass of beer sat in front of him—untouched. He was nervously awaiting the arrival of his new boss: Monsignor Terrence Sullivan. He'd been praying and thinking all morning. If the monsignor welcomed him, he'd be fine. If he wanted a fight, well, he was prepared for that, too.

The back door opened and slammed shut. "What the hell is going on here?" shouted a gravelly voice. "Who moved my things out of the carport?" There was a long pause. "And who's been painting? I can smell it."

Jared could hear the tremor in Yolanda's voice. "Father Jared and Frank cleaned out the carport and did some painting while you were away. We were hoping you'd be pleased."

"Pleased? Why in God's green earth would I be pleased? Would *you* be pleased if some stranger moved into your house and changed it without your permission? Hey?" There was silence. "Where is he?"

"In the dining room. We were waiting lunch for you," she said.

"Oh, were you?" he said. "We'll see about that."

Monsignor Sullivan stormed into the dining room. He was a lanky man with hard, angular features and mangy, yellowing hair. His complexion was so gray that his blue eyes looked out of place. In his clerical clothes, he looked like a black-and-white photo from the 1950s.

He set both palms on the dining table and leaned in over Jared. "Just who the hell do you think you are, coming in here and moving things around?"

Jared opened his mouth to answer, but the monsignor didn't give him a chance.

"I know your kind: punk kids who've had it all and think you know everything. You're all alike. You're spineless and spoiled, you and your fancy car. What kind of priest drives a sportscar?" he almost spat at Jared. "The people are going to see right through you just the way I do, you sissy fraud! I was here long before you showed up, and I'll be around long after you beat it out of here with your tail between your legs. In the meantime, you're going to leave my house the way you found it. Is that clear?" By the end, the monsignor was shouting.

Jared looked him in the eyes and didn't flinch. "There's something you've got very wrong, Monsignor," he said.

He folded his long arms at his chest. "And what's that, punk?"

"You may be pastor of this parish, but this isn't your house. It belongs to the diocese and the parishioners. I may be in residence here but let me remind you so are you. You have no more right to tell me how I can live in my own space than I have to tell you. So, let me be clear: you're going to leave me alone."

"Is that so, wise ass?" snapped the monsignor. "We'll see what the bishop has to say when I tell him you haven't been here a week and you're already stealing parish property."

"Stealing? What are you talking about?"

"The parish furniture. You stole it."

Jared burst out laughing. "I didn't steal anything. I gave it away. Tell you what, Monsignor. You want your junk back? Some of it's at the thrift store, but most of it they wouldn't even take. It's at the dump. You're welcome to it."

"I was right," said the monsignor. "You're no priest. I'll have you out of my parish so fast you won't know what happened. But while you're here, you'll do as I say. You're going to hear confessions from three to four every Saturday in the church. You'll say morning Mass every day and on Sunday. Other than that, you'll stay the hell out of my sight."

Jared shook his head, picked up his sandwich and glass of beer, and headed upstairs to his room. *Well, that went well.*

It was mid-afternoon when he got back from hearing confessions (there weren't any). He brewed himself a fresh cup of coffee from his little espresso machine and took it over to his new queen-sized bed. He fluffed up his pillow, sat back on it, and stretched out his legs. At least his feet didn't hang off the end of this bed. He picked up his phone and called Paul.

"Hey, hunk!" Paul said.

At the sound of his voice, Jared's whole body relaxed. "Hey, yourself. How's the bishop's secretary?"

"Right." Paul laughed. "Like after two days on the job, I'm an expert."

"Well, aren't you?"

"I wish. But it looks like I'm going to like it. The bishop's been taking it easy on me, and I can't get too lost with Monsignor Yates just around the corner from my office. At least I'm finding my way around, and I haven't screwed anything up yet—that I know of."

"O ye of little faith," Jared said with a laugh. "You'll do great. You take to that administrative stuff like it's second nature. Look at you: already working in the chancery office. I'd be willing to bet that you'll make bishop before me." He felt a surge of jealousy and had to wrestle it down. "You should see the mess I'm in."

"Did you meet the pastor yet? He's a monsignor, right?"

"Monsignor Terrence Sullivan. I met him over lunch."

"Is he as bad as the bishop says?"

Jared let out a long breath. "If anything, he's a bigger bastard than even the bishop knows. No lie. He looks like Ebenezer Scrooge."

"Ohhhh."

"Of course, he gave me shit for all the things I thought he would: the paint, the furniture. Called the bishop straight away, but Mickleson backed me up one hundred percent like he said he would."

"Nice of him. He told you he'd be on your side."

"I figured Sullivan won't be someone who'll respect my privacy, so I called Frank—the maintenance guy—and asked him to get me a deadbolt for my door. He'll have it installed tomorrow after Mass. He's a prince. Scrooge won't find out about it until he gets back next Tuesday."

"What about the parish? What's it like?"

"I said my first Sunday Mass this morning. I've got to say, for the first time in a long time, I felt something. The people in this shabby little slum of a church were so happy to see me. When I gave my homily this morning, it was like they were hungry for what I had to say. Even the babies were quiet. All the people in the church crowded around me after, telling me how wonderful I was. The kids were all hanging off me. Bro, I never realized how literally the Gospel meant 'feed my lambs, feed my sheep' until I was surrounded by a herd of hungry parishioners."

"So, there's potential there?"

"Scrooge has the people scared, but most of them want their parish to do better than he's willing to let them. I'll have to watch my step with him and not do anything that plays into his hands, but it won't take much to make them happy. All I have to do to show the man up is smile."

"Just turn on that old Jared charm and they'll be falling all over themselves to please you. The monsignor won't know what hit him." Paul paused. "I'm so glad you called. I was worried about you. You are a hundred miles from nowhere."

"You're right. With everything going on, I haven't been able to get away since I got here. I want to see you. Since Scrooge takes Mondays off, I'm going to take Fridays. That really means Thursday night to Saturday morning. I'll drive down to see you as soon as I can. The problem is there's still too much going on here, and I'm too new to get away just yet. Can you hold out for one more week?"

"I guess so."

"I'll make it worth your while."

"Promises, promises..."

"Tell you what," Jared said. "See if you can convince the bishop to let you have Fridays off. It would be awesome if we could spend our days off there together."

Just then, the phone vibrated in Jared's hand. He glanced at the screen: Tony K. "Sorry, Paul, there's a call I have to take. You call me next time, and don't wait too long." He made a kissing sound and whispered, "Love you."

At once, Jared tapped the phone to answer it before he lost the call. "Well, hello, Tony, you sexy thing. I was just thinking about you."

Tony laughed. "That's what they all say."

"Hey, thanks for the pics from last night's business meeting. You're one hell of a lucky man."

"Yeah, you're welcome. The dude was into photography. He wanted to have a record of our session. I told him, 'Sure, as long as I get copies.'" He paused. "You coming back to town anytime soon? You know this slick new condo is part yours. I could use a little help fixing it up."

It was Jared's turn to laugh. He was sensing from his tone that Tony was missing him more than he was willing to let on. "What would you say if I flew down Thursday night? Could you take a couple of nights off? I hope you can stand two nights in a row with me."

"Oh, I think I could. In fact, I'll clear my calendar for you."

"Awesome. You know I can't wait to get my hands all over that hot little body of yours."

"Okay, my man. C'mon down. It's here waiting for you."

A floorboard creaked outside his door. Jared's heart skipped a beat. "Hang on," he said as he dropped the phone and jumped off the bed. In two long strides he reached the bedroom door and opened it. The door to the monsignor's bedroom was just clicking shut. *The bastard was listing to my calls.* He shut the door and picked up his phone. "Sorry, Tony. See you Thursday night, okay? I'll call you back with the details."

Jared hung up, wondering how much the sound carried in this old house. Given the state of it, he suspected the monsignor had heard everything.

Chapter 13

Sunday, July 3, 2011

It was early afternoon and Jared was in his room, locked behind a shiny new deadbolt. He had the rest of the day to test his plan to break free of his isolation in Tres Robles. He had already contacted Sam Wright, the flight instructor at Hollister Aviation, about getting an appointment to renew his private pilot's license. He collected his flight log and paperwork and headed to the car.

It was a beautiful, warm, and sunny Sunday afternoon, soon enough into July not to be too hot. He rode the short trip to Hollister with his top down and, at the municipal airport, turned in at the large hanger standing near the road with "Hollister Aviation" painted in three-foot-high letters across the back.

The FBO office was quiet for such a perfect flying day. Jared had expected to make himself comfortable on one of the leather chairs, but the waiting room was empty. He approached a long, glass display case that served as a counter and felt a pang of self-doubt about having chosen the priesthood. The case was full of charts and manuals, navigation tools and new avionic devices—upgrades for the discerning pilot.

A teenage girl sat on a stool behind the counter.

"Slow day?" Jared asked.

The girl laughed and brushed her blonde hair out of her eyes. She pulled her bare knees up to her chest, set her heels on the edge of the stool, and wrapped her thin arms around her legs. "It wasn't this morning. You should have seen this place. They were all here." She looked up at him. "What can I do for you?"

"I'm here to see Sam Wright."

She dropped her feet to the floor and bounced off the stool. "Are you

Jared?"

"That's me."

She picked up a small PA mike and said, "Sam. Counter, please." Her voice in giant economy size echoed through the hangar and across the tarmac.

"Hollister traffic," came a voice on the Unicom radio. "Piper 2-1-4-1-Bravo, for downwind, runway 1-3." Somebody was getting ready to land. A door behind the counter opened, and a tall man in his early fifties with thinning brown hair and a weather-beaten face walked into the room with an easy authority. He wore a blue shirt with "Hollister Aviation" emblazoned in white on the pocket. The visor of his white baseball cap sat so low on his forehead Jared could barely see his eyes.

"Mr. Röhrbach?" He looked at Jared.

"Please," he said. "Call me Jared."

"I'm Sam Wright—no relation."

Jared rolled his eyes. "I'll bet you get that all the time."

"Yes, sir. I had to get into the business just to keep my sanity." He grinned. "That your flight log?"

"Yup." Jared held it out to him.

Sam gave it a cursory review. "Been at this a while for a young guy."

"Ever since I was eighteen," Jared said. His father had started him flying. It was a fond memory he had of the two of them.

"How come you never went commercial?"

"I had other interests," Jared replied. "Besides, I loved flying too much to ever make it into a job."

"I know what you mean. C'mon, let's take you up and get you checked out. This'll be a piece of cake." He handed him his log back. "Your medical current?"

"Six months." He held out a piece of paper, but Sam didn't even bother to glance at it. Jared followed him out one of the side doors and across the ramp to where a little blue Cessna 172 Skyhawk was tied down. Sam unlocked the pilot-side door and handed Jared the key. Jared unfastened the ropes holding the plane to the tie-downs. Then he climbed up and in and lifted the locking lever on the passenger side to open it for Sam.

He studied the flight instruments. Every plane is configured a little differently, and Jared was more used to flying with a glass cockpit of more advanced and sophisticated electronic avionics than the array of 1970s instrumentation that greeted him in this one. At least it had an updated Garmin GNS430 GPS for navigation. That would have to do.

Sam climbed into the second seat and handed Jared the checklist from the side pouch. "Let's get her checked out, then we'll check you out."

Jared read aloud. "Brake: set. Wheel lock: off. Ignition power: off. Master: on. Fuel: full both tanks. Pitot heat: on. Avionics: on. Fan: audible. Alt pressure: off. Flaps: full." After the preliminaries, Jared got out of the plane for his walk-around, checking the fuselage, wheels, tail, wings, struts, and fuel sumps.

Then he climbed back into the pilot's seat. Time to get her started. "Throttle: half-inch. Mixture: rich. Carb heat: on. Prime: pumped and locked. Fuel pump: on. Prop area..." Jared opened the window beside him and shouted, "Clear!"

"Master switch: on. Beacon: on. Ignition..." He turned the key. The engine turned over twice and sputtered to life. He adjusted the throttle to a comfortable purr. Once he'd checked the rest of his instruments and engine readings, he adjusted his gyrocompass, tuned his navcom radio to 123.0, Unicom, and turned to Sam. "Where to, chief?"

"We're using runway 1-3 today."

Jared revved the engine, released the brakes, and the little plane bounced along the taxiway. When he got to the end, he turned the plane into the wind and parked for his runup. "Throttle: up to 1800. "Magnetos—right: check. Left: check. Suction: check. Engine instruments: check. Ammeter:

check. Throttle: back."

"Let's go," said Sam.

Jared picked up the mike from between the seats and squeezed the button. "Cessna 3-0-7-Golf departing runway 3-1, Hollister." He revved the engine again, stepped hard on the right brake pedal and the plane swung around into position. He pushed the throttle all the way in and, in just a couple of hundred feet, the noise of the wheels on the concrete went silent except for the tiny vibration that remained for a short time while the wheels spun aimlessly in mid-air.

"Climb to two thousand feet, but stay in the area," said Sam.

When he had reached two thousand feet, he leveled off, rotated the trim tabs so the plane could fly by itself, pulled the throttle out to partial power, and pulled the mixture valve out a little to lean the engine. Antique though it was, the plane purred.

Sam put Jared through his paces: turns, steep turns, standard turns, slow flight, stall recovery, all the while questioning him on operating and emergency procedures.

As expected, Sam turned the ignition key off in mid-maneuver. "Now what?"

Jared gave him the standard responses: "Fly the plane. Look for a landing site. Fly to the landing site. Deploy flaps if necessary. Attempt to restart the engine."

As they glided downward, Sam said, "Okay, it's night. You've done all that. What do you do now?"

That question took Jared by surprise. "Turn on the landing light?"

"Good. Now, you turn on the landing light and there's a tree right in front of you. What do you do?"

"I don't know," said Jared. "I've never been asked that before. What do you do?"

"Turn off the light."

Both men laughed.

"Let's go home," said Sam.

Once they were back on the ground and parked at the ramp, Jared and Sam headed back to the office. Sam took Jared's logbook, entered the engine time and his flight check information, signed it, and handed it back.

"I understand this plane doesn't get a lot of use," Jared said.

"Nope," said Sam. "Most folks want the fancier planes with the newer avionics. This one just sits here gathering rust."

"How about I rent it from you every week, Thursday noon to Saturday noon, starting this Thursday?"

Sam narrowed his eyes. "That'll leave me one plane short now and again," he said. "And I'd have to have it sometimes for regular maintenance."

Jared nodded. "Of course."

Sam looked at him square in the face. "But to be honest, I'd rather it be with you making me money than sitting here on the pavement costing me." He stuck out his hand. "Deal."

"Deal," said Jared, and they shook on it.

He felt like down the pavement back to his car. Just like that, he had a ticket out of Purgatory.

Chapter 14

Eliza slipped through the back door and into the rectory. She never arrived at nine o'clock in the morning, but something had been on her mind for a long time, and she had to talk to Father Jared alone. The monsignor's parking place was empty, so she knew he was gone, and they wouldn't be disturbed. The kitchen was quiet, empty, and dark except for the morning sunlight streaming through the one window. There was nearly a full pot in the Mr. Coffee, and she was surprised to find that it was still hot. She filled two mugs. As Father Jared entered the kitchen, Eliza noticed an odd expression on his face. "Is something wrong?"

"I'm not sure," he said. "It's probably nothing, but as I was coming downstairs, I couldn't help thinking back to something peculiar that happened yesterday when the monsignor came back from his day off. You've been around him quite a while; maybe you can tell me what you think."

"Okay." She poured some half-and-half into her coffee. "Cream and sugar?"

"No, thanks," he said. "You know I had Frank install a deadbolt on my door over the weekend."

"Yes, of course."

"Yesterday, when I was leaving my room, the monsignor was standing in the hall staring at the deadbolt. He looked straight at me. I expected another shouting match, but he just stood there and didn't say a single word. But I could have sworn the corners of his lips twitched. I think he almost smiled. It was the most peculiar expression you could imagine. I don't know what to make of it. Do you?"

"I don't know, but seeing the way he is with you, I'd bet it wasn't a happy face. You know, Father, I don't think I've met an unhappier man."

"I might have imagined it."

"Courage, Father," said Eliza with mock gravity. "I'm sure you can hold on until your day off." She picked up both mugs and handed the black coffee to Father Jared. "Would you mind if we talked in your office? It's so much brighter and more cheerful than where I sit."

"Of course."

She followed him through the Private door into the office. As she passed by her desk, she picked up one of the binders she had left there.

Father Jared turned on the light. When Eliza closed the door behind them, he raised his eyebrows in surprise.

"Father," she said in almost a plaintive tone.

"What is it?" he asked. "Is something wrong?"

She sat down and leaned forward in her chair. "You've got to understand. I've never said anything like this to another living soul ever in my life." She paused to collect her thoughts.

"Go on," he said.

She sat back and adjusted her skirt. "I just don't trust him."

"Trust whom? The monsignor?"

"Yes."

The new priest's office smelled of fresh paint and with new carpet on the floor and new furniture, it looked like a different place. It made Eliza feel like she could take a deep breath for the first time in a while. "He *listens.*" She was almost whispering. "I wouldn't be talking to you now if he was here. I don't trust him at all."

Father Jared sat back in his chair with a broad smile. "What makes you think you can trust me?"

"Please." She hugged the binder to her chest. "You saw everything the moment you got here. I know you did. I watched you. And it hurt you as much as it's hurting us."

"You're right."

"Besides, there have been other associates here before you—three or four. And not one of them ever stood up to him the way you have. I saw some of them—grown men, experienced priests—leave here in tears. He has a way of beating people down to get his way. Let me tell you, if we in this parish have any hope of turning this around, you're it."

"I'll do what I can. And, maybe I can help more than some of the others. There are certain things you don't know—that the monsignor doesn't know—that might help you." He leaned forward and rested his forearms on the desk. "You've trusted me with your job. Can I trust you with mine?"

"Father," she murmured, "if we don't trust each other, then he's already won."

"All right," said Father Jared. "But what we say to each other can never be repeated. Do you understand?"

"Yes. You have your seal of the confessional, and I have mine."

"The bishop himself sent me here to help. He knows what the monsignor is like. There's nothing the monsignor can say that will turn the bishop against me. He's already tried that once—with the paint and furniture— and failed."

"Oh, thank God." Eliza grasped her hands to her chest. "Then you've got to tell the bishop that there's something not right in this parish."

Father Jared's brow furrowed. "Not right? You mean besides the way he treats the people?"

She opened the binder she'd been clutching and said, "Look at this." She set it on his desk. "See this family? And this one? And this one?" She pointed to the names.

"Yes?"

"They're all big vegetable growers. Commercial farmers. They've been in

96

the parish for decades. Generations, even. They don't all come to church every Sunday—sorry, Father—but they do come."

Father Jared shook his head. "Why would anyone want to come to Mass here? It's depressing. Why hasn't anything been done to fix up the church?"

"The monsignor says we can't afford it, that we're too poor."

"Well, are we? You're the bookkeeper."

"That's just it. The families I'm showing you are all wealthy people, and they're not the only ones."

"Do you think I should start visiting these people to see if they'll support the parish? I'll beg if I have to."

"No, Father. We have no idea who's supporting the parish, and who isn't."

"But don't you record all the donations?"

"We do," Eliza said.

"Well...can I see the records?"
"I don't have them. He won't allow it."

Now the new priest looked bewildered. "What do you mean? How can he keep the donation records away from the bookkeeper?"

"He says that what people give is nobody's business but theirs and God's. He doesn't want people's finances blabbed all over the parish. So, he's made it so that nobody but he and a couple of his trusted friends ever see details."

Father Jared frowned. "That doesn't sound right."

Eliza's pulse was racing. She'd been wanting to talk to someone about this for years. She had to force her voice to stay calm. "I'm sure you've noticed that Harriet Blake and Chuck Johnson lock themselves in the conference room after every Mass on weekends. They count each collection and put it in a bag. When they're done, they drop the bag into the strongbox in the

97

monsignor's office."

"What about you? Don't you get a look at what's going on?"

"No. Nobody else but those two. When I asked the monsignor why, all he said was that everyone had their job and that was theirs and I needed to do mine." She took a deep breath. "On Tuesdays, when the monsignor comes back from his day away, he takes the collections, makes out a deposit slip, and takes it down to the bank himself. All I get is the bank deposit receipt when he gets back. That's what I use for my accounting."

"But the checks appear on the bank statement."

"No. He won't let me see the statement. He says it's too private."

Father Jared crossed his arms at his chest. "So, even if we wanted to go door to door, we have no idea who's contributing and how much."

"Right." She closed the binder and held it against her chest again. "We've always been a poor parish, but it wasn't this bad before he came here. And it's getting worse. Every month, there seems to be less money to pay our bills, and we have to keep asking for more from the diocese. And now he's making us take your salary and the cost of your food from the little we have left." She looked down at the carpet. "Do you think he wants the parish to close?"

"It sounds like it, from everything you've said, but what would he get out of it? It doesn't make any sense." He scribbled a note on a pad of paper and said, "I'll talk it over with the bishop, but I don't know what else we can do right now without raising a fuss. We'll both have to watch everything that goes on here from now on." He sipped his coffee. "Is there anyone else we can trust?"

"Some. I introduced you to them the first morning you said Mass here. I know that Paula, the parish council president, thinks the way we do. I've had many long talks with her—out of the office, of course. And Lupe Vargas, the Director of Religious Education. She's very quiet, but she misses nothing and she's loyal to the parish."

"Maybe I should talk to them before the parish council meeting tonight. The monsignor won't be here, so it'll be safe."

Eliza shook her head. "Not as long as Harriet Blake is around. She thinks she's the monsignor's eyes and ears in the parish."

"I got that one's number right away."

Eliza laughed, even though a part of her thought it was uncharitable.

"Call your friends," Father Jared said, "and ask them to come early, before she gets here."

Panic made Eliza grip the binder. "You won't tell them anything I've said, will you?"

"Not a word. I'll just say I suspect there's something odd going on, and that I'd appreciate their help keeping an eye on things and letting me know if they see anything out of the ordinary."

"That's wonderful. I just hope we find out what's happening before it's too late. We can't go on forever like this." Her eyes filled.

Father Jared stood and gave her a hug. Eliza opened the door, stepped out and let out a small cry. Harriet Blake sat in one of the chairs in front of her desk. She could feel her face redden. "Goodness, you startled me," she stammered.

"It's about time you two were done in there," Harriet said with a sniff. "I need a Mass card. My great aunt died."

"I'm so sorry to hear that," said Eliza in her most professional voice. The cloying scent of Harriet's perfume made her want to open a window.

Jared made noises of sympathy and escaped through the Private door.

"Were you close?" Eliza asked.

"No. I never met the lady. Just get me a Mass card, will you, please?"

Eliza knew that Harriet's grating voice would carry through the house. She had no doubt the new priest was listening.

"Where's the monsignor?" Harriet squawked.

"Why, you know he's away every first Wednesday of the month." She placed the Mass card on her desk and filled in the next available date.

"Right. The parish council. I presume you'll be there?"

"Yes, Harriet." Eliza sweetened her tone just to add to Harriet's aggravation. "I wouldn't miss it for the world."

Harriet snatched the card off the desk and left, slamming the door behind her.

Eliza could hear Father Jared giggling from the kitchen.

Chapter 15

Jared was dreaming again. He could tell because, once again, his mother and father were there at the front of some sort of line, only this time when they stepped aside, his twin brother Justin and Tony stood between them. He reached out to touch Justin, but the group faded into the night. Jared shivered and forced himself awake. The experience left him with a knot in his stomach. He hadn't thought about Justin in a long time. *God knows where he is.* He felt a twinge of guilt that he hadn't invited him to the ordination, but how could he have? He hadn't heard from Justin in years. Why was his subconscious dredging him up now?

He dragged himself out of bed, careful not to wake Paul, and took a moment to reorient himself. It was his first morning in the apartment in San Luis Obispo. The space was nice—wide open, bright—and Paul had done a great job furnishing it. Paul's taste was very much like his own.

He didn't bother to get dressed but tiptoed into the kitchen to grab some strong coffee and maybe something to eat. His stomach was unsettled as much from the dream as from what he'd had to drink last night. The coffee maker had gone off right on schedule, and the kitchen was filled with the aroma of fresh-brewed coffee.

Jared grabbed the largest mug he could find and poured himself a cup. He took a tiny sip, letting the bitter liquid wake his pallet. He couldn't stop thinking about that dream. Why Justin, and why Tony? He thought about his relationship with Tony. He'd let his anger and resentment get the best of him when he'd taken off from Rome to LA. He'd had a bad case of the fuck-its and he'd wanted a hook-up...for what? To hurt Paul? To sabotage his priesthood that was only hours old? Hadn't he just been looking for a one-night stand? He'd gotten that, all right, and a lot more. He hadn't intended to fall for anybody, but he had, and now he felt fragmented. A big piece of him was back in his parish in Tres Robles, another piece was here with Paul, and still another was down in LA. He couldn't blame Tony. It was his own fault. He'd known what he was doing, and he'd chosen to ignore the consequences. *If you play with hot men, you're gonna get burned.*

He opened the fridge more from habit than hunger. There were two large, unmarked cardboard food cartons there with the remains from last night's welcome home dinner. He opened them to remind himself of what they'd eaten. There was something Parmesan in one and something Marsala in the other.

"Hungry again?" Paul stood in the doorway in all his naked glory.

"Unh," said Jared. "Coffee." He held up his mug as if providing evidence of his honorable intentions.

"Where's mine?" asked Paul.

"In the pot. You're not helpless."

Paul flinched.

That was a little harsh. Jared moved over to the island, pulled out a stool, and sat.

Paul filled his mug, then came over and topped off Jared's and took the seat next to him.

"How do you like the apartment now that you've had the chance to try it out for yourself?"

"It suits us." The kitchen was crisp and modern, a study in black and white and stainless steel with a backsplash of electric blue above the counter all the way around. "This could work for us."

"I should hope so. You're paying enough for it."

"Nothing but the best for you." He kissed Paul on the cheek. "Though I didn't sleep well last night."

Paul gave him a *go on* look.

"I dreamed about Justin. I haven't thought about him in forever."

Paul frowned. "Have you been in contact with him?"

"Not since the accident. I figured he left the country. I always hoped he'd find a way to contact me that wouldn't lead the authorities to him, but he never has." He took a thoughtful sip of his coffee. "You haven't heard from him, have you?"

Paul shook his head, but an odd look flashed across his face.

"You haven't, *have you?*"

"Uh, no. Nothing."

There was something Paul wasn't saying, and it annoyed the hell out of him, but he decided to let it go for now. "So, what's it like working for the bishop? All I remember us talking about last night was me and Our Lady of Perpetual Hell."

Paul went to get a bathrobe from the back of the bathroom door and put it on. "Stop calling it that, will you? It's disrespectful."

"It's the truth." Even first thing in the morning, Jared could feel the resentment in the pit of his stomach. "Enough about my crap. How's your job?"

"It's pretty cool. Of course, I work with Sister Margaret and Monsignor Yates a lot more than I do with the bishop. I'm a kind of an information gatekeeper for him. I let in what he wants to see and keep out what he wants to avoid. I also keep the master calendar. I'm still new at that, but I'm catching on, thanks to my two mentors." Paul took out a frying pan and heated it up. "Eggs?"

"Of course. Over easy, please. No scandals?" Jared asked with a wink.

"I haven't been there long enough for anything interesting to happen," Paul said as he cracked the eggs.

Jared searched around for a toaster. "Are you doing any *priest*-ing over there?"

"Not yet."

So, he was a glorified secretary. All that jealousy Jared had felt at the idea that Paul was getting to work elbow-to-elbow with the bishop, that he was getting ahead while Jared was stuck in backwater Tres Robles with Scrooge—it had all been for nothing. They'd both ended up with shit jobs, if the truth was being told.

Once breakfast was ready, they settled themselves at the table and Jared poured fresh coffee. "So, what's the story with Saint Theresa's?"

"Their pastor is new there since we left for school," Paul said. "His name is Richard Loring. He wants me to help out on weekends. How do you like that? Of all the places I could be doing weekend ministry, they chose your old parish. It'll be like coming home."

"Really?" Jared didn't even try to hide his lack of enthusiasm. "You must be excited."

"I am. And Father Richard is super nice."

He curled one hand into a fist under the table. "Just like my pastor, hey?"

Paul's smile disappeared. "Oh, Jared, no. I didn't mean…"

"It's okay. Life's not fair. But that doesn't mean we can't enjoy it when something good happens to someone else." Jared sipped his coffee. "So, tell me more."

But Paul's excitement seemed tempered now. "I'm going up there tomorrow afternoon for dinner to see the set-up. He'll have me stay overnight at the rectory, and I'll take one of his Sunday Masses."

"Sounds ideal." He struggled to feel his partner's joy; all he could find inside was bitter envy.

"There's something else I need to tell you." Paul went to fetch refills for their orange juice.

Great.

He sat back down. "I got a call from your father yesterday."

"And?"

Paul looked at his plate. "He asked me to come by and see him."

"So, go. I don't care."

"He said he had something important to talk to me about."

"No doubt." Jared ripped off a piece of toast with more force than necessary.

"I just thought you'd want to know. If you want, I'll let you know what it's about after I talk with him."

"Don't bother."

"Don't be like that," Paul said. "He's your father."

Jared scowled at Paul and went back to finishing his eggs.

After a few minutes of silence, Paul finished up his own breakfast and carried his dishes to the sink. "I'm going to shower. Want to join me?" he said.

"Sorry, studmuffin, but the tanks are empty after last night. Catch me later."

Paul took off toward the bedroom, and Jared welcomed the break in the tension. He wanted his relationship with Paul to be fun, not the hard work it was becoming. The last thing he needed was more pressure in his life.

As soon as he could hear the water running, Jared took his dirty dishes to the sink and washed them. No use loading the dishwasher with the breakfast dishes.

"You gonna shower?" Paul called. "I'm done."

Jared dropped the last dish into the drying rack. "Be right there."

The kitchen led out to a good-sized living area with a large window across one wall. The sectional couch, positioned under the window, was a perfect spot for napping. On either side of the living room was a bedroom, each with ensuite bath. In effect, the apartment had two master suites: one for Paul and him, and one so that no one in the chancery would talk.

Jared sauntered into the bathroom where Paul was brushing his teeth. He turned on the water in the shower and stepped right in, since Paul had already gotten it nice and warm. He soaped up and shampooed and, by the time he opened his eyes again, Paul had left the room. He took his time luxuriating in the soapy warm water, making his skin slick and slippery. He enjoyed sliding his wet soapy hands over the more sensitive and responsive areas of his body, and respond they did. A squeeze here and a flick there, and he was playing his rigid body like a well-tuned instrument. His mind drifted to Paul. Over time, he had lost some of his virtuosity at playing this instrument—lost melodies that Tony had been able to rediscover in him, and even to coax out a few new harmonies he hadn't realized himself capable of. But he couldn't abandon Paul. There was too much of each of them woven into the fabric of the other. He leaned back against the shower wall thinking that he could go on feeling like this all day, but he dared not. So, he rinsed, turned off the water, and stepped out of the shower.

As he was drying off, he couldn't help himself. He locked the bathroom door and texted Tony: *In SLO for the weekend. Missing ur hot bod. Hows biz? Miss U CU Thurs.*

A couple of seconds later, his phone dinged with a return text: Done with biz. Not a 10. U spoil me. Biz is slow. Miss U 2. T.

It felt good to have someone in his life who thought the sun rose and set on him. He clicked off his phone, unlocked the door, and wandered into the living room, saying, "What did you want to do for the rest of the day?" When he pulled the towel away from his head, all he could do was stare. Jeff Hensen stood there.

"Woah, dude!" Jeff said with a grin. "Nice package."

Jared shot a look at Paul. "Thanks for the warning that we were having company."

Paul looked like he wanted to jump off the balcony, but Jeff didn't seem at all uncomfortable. He grabbed Jared by the shoulders. "Good to see you, man. I've missed you."

"Good to see you, too." Jared wrapped his towel around his waist.

Jeff sat down—uninvited. At least, not by him.

"I don't want to be rude," Jared said, "but what are you doing here?" He glanced at Paul, but Paul wouldn't look up. Jared couldn't help but think of the letter he'd slipped from the pack back in Rome. Jeff hadn't noticed—had he? Could he be here for that?

"You wouldn't believe the coincidence," said Jeff.

Jared crossed his arms. "Is that what you'd call it?" Those erotic letters—as if Jeff hadn't planned this.

"Of course," Jeff said with a nervous laugh. "What else would it be? I'm applying to law school in the fall, so my uncle Roger has decided to take me under his wing as a summer paralegal—not just this summer, but for as many summers as I want until I graduate. The last thing I expected was to run into Paul here—or you."

Right. "So, you're going to be here in San Luis every summer?" asked Jared.

"It looks that way."

"Where are you staying?" Paul asked, looking at Jared out of the corner of his eye.

"I'm in Uncle Roger's guest room for now, but it's not the best. I feel like I'm always under foot and, to be honest, it's putting a big damper on my social life. He's good with my being gay, but both of us would feel weird if I ever brought anybody home."

"I'll bet," said Jared. Don't look at Paul. Don't.

Both Jeff and Paul were staring at the closed door of the second bedroom as if it might miraculously pop open.

"You guys don't have any extra room, do you? I'd be happy to share the rent," Jeff said.

"Well," Paul said. *Of course.* Trust Paul to open his mouth. He couldn't lie if his life was on the line. "Jared and I share one bedroom and the spare one isn't being used." He glanced at Jared. "Would you mind?"

Jared shrugged. "Why would I?" *If they're gonna mess around, who am I to complain?* It would make his trips to LA guilt-free.

"I thought you might have...reservations," Paul said.

"Nope," said Jared. "If that works for you guys, I'm okay with it."

When Jeff and Paul looked at each other, Jared knew all too well the conflicting thoughts and feelings that were passing between them.

"This will be fun," said Jeff.

"I'm counting on it," said Jared. He could hear his phone buzzing in the other room.

Chapter 16

Sunday, July 31, 2011

When Sunday morning Masses were over, Paul turned out of the parking lot at Saint Theresa's parish and onto Main Street. He headed along the familiar route to Exeter Lane and Jared's family home, where he and Jared had spent so many great hours together as teens and young adults. Although he had spoken with Kurt and Hannah countless times over the years and shared meals with them, most of what he knew about them came from Jared.

He pulled into the circular driveway and parked in front of the door. For a man with almost unbelievable wealth, Kurt did not have an extravagant home. It was a modestly impressive two-story house with a large turret to one side of the entrance, more suitable for an upper-middle-class family than a billionaire.

Paul rang the doorbell. He was a bit startled when a woman he didn't recognize opened the door. It was not like Kurt to have staff. He had always run his own household.

"You must be Father Paul," said the woman.

"Uh, yes," he stuttered. "I'm here to see Mr. Röhrbach." Paul decided he'd best proceed formally until he found out more about this new state of affairs.

"Of course. Please come in." She opened the door wide enough for Paul to see Kurt hurrying down the hallway toward him.

"Come in, son. Come in." Kurt seized Paul's hand and shook it. "Thank you so much for coming to see me. I've wanted to talk to you for a long time." The older man almost dragged Paul into his study—a comfortable room that took up the entire first floor of the turret and was lined with overcrowded bookshelves. "Sit down, my boy. Please." He indicated a well-stuffed club chair. "Vodka and tonic? Rocks?"

"Yes, thanks," said Paul. "Tonic, please, but just one. I have to drive back to San Luis Obispo tonight."

Kurt went to a small wet bar nestled among the books at one side of the room and poured drinks for both. "Paul," he said, "I have known you for many years." He carried Paul's drink to him and set it down on the little table beside him on a white paper napkin. "How long has it been? Fifteen or twenty years, I think?"

"Yes, at least that," said Paul.

"I have many serious things to say to you, but I've been waiting until you were out of school and on your own to say them. You know about the accident."

Paul felt the color drain from his face. *Please don't ask me about that night.*

"I think perhaps you know even more about it than I do," Kurt said, "but no matter." He took a sip from his drink. "I lost one son that day. Jared is all I have left."

His stomach tightened. Kurt had no idea that he knew all about the fatal auto accident eight years ago that had sent Justin running from the law. He intended to take that secret with him to the grave. Strange. He hadn't thought about it in years, and now first Jared, then his father, had brought it up.

"I watched you grow up," Kurt said. "I know you're a good man, so I trust you. I trust you more than I trust my own children. I love my family, but life has not been easy for them, despite my wealth. At this stage of my life, I might as well have been childless."

"Sir, I know Jared loves you very much in his own way. He just feels so hurt."

"I only wish he could learn to forgive the way he believes God forgives. Still, wishing will not make it so. That is why I asked you to come see me."

"Yes?"

"I want to explain something to you so that maybe, when Jared is ready, you can tell him about his stepmother, Hannah."

"And..." Paul could see Kurt wanted to say more.

"And to make sure Hannah is taken care of should anything happen to me. You see, I have cared for her for twenty-five years." He heaved a sigh. "I need my boy to know the truth. Besides Hannah, only my Lilly, her brother, Father Hans Pflüger in Austria, and I know the whole story. I am trusting you with it so that one day he will understand."

Paul nodded.

"Hannah was born in Salzburg during the war. Her mother Ada and my late wife Lilly's father, Johann Pflüger, were brother and sister, but the two had very different ideas about life." Kurt crossed the room and fetched a wooden box off one of the shelves. "Hannah kept a souvenir of her parents." He patted the top of the box. "It's the only possession she had for much of her young life. She kept it so she would never forget what those days were like."

He opened the lid and took out a silver locket on a fine silver chain. He popped open the locket and handed it to Paul. Inside were two pictures, head and shoulders, one of an attractive woman with blond hair tightly braided in the German style, the other of an officer. A Nazi officer.

"Who is this?" Paul asked.

"That, son, is Ada and her husband, *Reichsstatthalter* Friedrich Rainer, Reich Governor of Salzburg. He was one of the Nazi officers involved in the Theresienstadt concentration camp. He was also Hannah's father. You see, they were both committed Nazis. Hannah was the youngest of six. At the end of the war, Rainer was arrested, taken away and Hannah never saw him again. He was executed."

Paul stared at the portraits in his hand.

"Hannah's mother fled Salzburg with her children. Nowhere was safe for the wife and children of a high-ranking and infamous Nazi officer. They travelled Austria and hid for months, until Ada couldn't take it anymore. Taking care of a toddler on the run was impossible."

"What did she do?"

"She took Hannah to an orphanage near Salzburg and left her with the nuns."

"So, she grew up in an orphanage?"

"If that's what you want to call it. The nuns were aware of who her father was, and they punished her cruelly for something she had no nothing to do with. She was given the worst tasks and beaten severely for the least transgressions. You can only imagine how she felt about the Church after that experience."

He looked up at Kurt. "No wonder. Does Jared know about this?"

"No, son. He has no idea. He only knew her as Hannah Schümer growing up. He was young when his mother died. After that, he came to hate Hannah, so he refused to talk to me about anything concerning her. He is such a stubborn boy...and he was so angry."

Paul couldn't argue with that.

"The one good thing the nuns did for her was to teach her to cook, do housework, and sew. They taught her to care for babies and, even as a young child, the nuns made her care for the babies in the orphanage. When she was a teenager, they hired her out to wealthy families. Of course, the orphanage kept her wages. You see, that's why she couldn't be adopted. The nuns wanted her to work for them. They told prospective parents who she was so that they would lose interest. So, for her entire young adult life, she survived as a domestic for one family after another." His sadness was palpable.

"After many years, her cousin, Hans, found her by scouring the war records and writing every orphanage in Austria. He told her she had another cousin, Lilly Röhrbach, in the US, but he had no idea what had happened to the rest of her family."

Paul sipped his drink, grateful for the little buzz.

"After she left the orphanage, she found a steady job with a wealthy Austrian family. She had her own quarters and they paid her enough to get by. The family also employed a gardener and handyman named Max Schümer. He courted her, and she agreed to marry him. She was both naive and very anxious to be someone other than Hannah Rainer. So, they married." Kurt looked over at Paul's empty glass. "Another drink?"

"Yes," he said, "I'd like that."

A few moments later, Kurt returned with a fresh drink. "Where was I? Yes. So, Hannah married Max. As it turned out, Max was a drunk and a gambler. He would stay out for days and beat her when he was home. He was also a thief. He was caught stealing from the family to pay for his gambling, and they were both fired and kicked out. Hannah took part-time housework wherever she could find it, but Max drank and gambled up everything. They were nearly homeless. When he was out gambling one night, she ran away from him. That's when she took a chance and wrote to Lilly out of desperation."

"Ah." Paul nodded. "That's how she came to be with you."

"Yes. Lilly and I were returning to Salzburg so I could expand my company into Eastern Europe, and we brought her to live with us. She worked for us for about six months while we were in Austria. Not long after, we heard that Max got drunk and was hit by a train. We have no way of knowing whether it was suicide or not." He took off his glasses and wiped them with a handkerchief from his breast pocket.

"Wow," said Paul. "One tragedy after another." He realized he was clutching the locket.

Kurt shook his head. "It was while we were in Salzburg that the twins were born. Of course, Hannah wanted to care for them. We were happy to have her with us." He sipped his drink. "But we couldn't stay in Europe forever, so we arranged to bring her back here with us as our housekeeper. She has been here ever since." He looked down at the floor. "And when my Lilly died, Hannah took over. In hindsight, I gave her too much leeway with the boys, because she was too hard on them, and they resented her taking their mother's place."

A clock in the room struck the hour, accentuating the sudden silence. "But you married her," Paul said.

"That's right. The boys left, and I was alone. I knew Hannah had no one to look after her, and if I died, she would have nowhere to go. I married her because I care about her, and she takes good care of me. She is strong, but not on her own. She can't survive in this world on her own. Jared doesn't understand that."

"Are you coming to the kitchen soon?" Hannah's loud voice carried down the hall and into the study. "Everything is almost ready."

"In a moment, *meine shatz*," Kurt called back. He took the locket back from Paul and placed it in the box. "Someday you'll explain all this to Jared. When that time comes, you need to give him this. It is important." He closed the wooden box and handed it to Paul.

"But, sir," he said. "I can't take this from you."

"It's not for you," Kurt said. "It's for my boy—when you think he is ready."

Whenever that will be. "I'll see that he gets it when the time comes." When Paul looked at Kurt, it occurred to him he was looking very old. *What isn't he telling me?*

"Good." The ice cubes rattled in Kurt's drink as he took a long sip. "Now, we have one more detail to go through before I get to fatten you up with Hannah's strudel." Kurt's mood seemed to have lifted now that he was assured his message to his son would someday be delivered.

"Yes, sir," said Paul. "What else can I do for you?"

"Do you know anything about Alzheimer's?"

114

"A little."

"It starts out with forgetting little things, occasional confusion, getting lost once in a while." He pushed his wire-rimmed glasses back up on the bridge of his nose. "I'm starting to see these things in Hannah, and it worries me. If anything was to happen to me, Hannah would be unable to care for herself. That's why I hired a companion for her. You met her. Rosario Alvarez. She answered the door."

"I was wondering."

"I've had Hannah to the doctors, but the tests have been inconclusive."

"Oh, dear," said Paul.

"Yes, and I can't count on my children to care for her. That's why..." Kurt rose, went to the desk across the room and fetched some papers that he handed to Paul.

Medical Power of Attorney. Paul's name was on it. "What's this?"

"It gives you full authority over Hannah's care should I become...incapacitated." He looked at Paul over the top of his glasses. "I'm not going to live forever."

"I wish this weren't necessary." *What will Jared think when I tell him? If I tell him.*

Kurt shrugged. "The alternative is Jared, and I'm afraid Hannah wouldn't survive in his care."

"What do you need me to do?"

"I've taken care of everything. There are two copies there. Hannah and my signatures have already been notarized. You only need to sign the copies, have them notarized, and return one to me."

"No problem. Sister Margaret at the chancery office is a notary. I'll take them back to San Luis with me tonight and drop your copy off when I'm up here again next weekend."

115

Kurt's shoulders softened, as though a burden had been lifted. "Do you need somewhere to stay while you're here? Jared's old bedroom is just as he left it."

"No, thanks. I'm staying at the rectory over at the church. I'll be helping out there every weekend."

"Perfect." Kurt clapped his hands. "We will fatten you up. You come see us every Sunday; we'll take care of the rest."

"Thanks, sir, but I can't promise that. I *will* promise I'll visit as often as I can, though."

"That will have to be good enough for Hannah and me. In the meantime, let's go to the kitchen now and have some strudel, yes?"

Paul held up his hands in mock surrender. "If you insist."

Kurt led them out of the study and into the well-provisioned kitchen where Hannah was pulling a bubbling pan of strudel from the oven.

"See who is here, Hannah? Paul is working down at the church now and will be coming by to visit us."

"Oh, that will be nice," she said, smiling. "Sit down. You can't eat standing up. Bad for digestion." The fragrance of the baking pastry filled the kitchen.

"Would you like some coffee with your strudel, Paul?" Kurt asked.

"I'd love some."

Kurt filled three mugs. "You take a little cream, no?"

"Right. What a memory." It dawned on Paul that his relationship with these two people had forever shifted. Kurt was no longer just his best friend's father. He had taken Paul in as a trusted friend and given him a heavy responsibility. He felt now almost like a member of the extended family. He wanted to tell Kurt how much that meant to him, but the words failed him. Kurt set the coffee mugs down on the table and Paul looked up at him, hoping his smile would convey what his words could not. The look in Kurt's eyes told him he had been at least partially successful.

Moments later, Hannah carried over the plates heaped with steaming hot strudel. Paul and Kurt put their napkins in their laps and waited for the chef to join them. She stood in front of Paul with the carafe, smiling at him.

"More coffee, Justin?" She patted his hand.

Kurt went pale.

"No," Paul managed to say. "No, thank you, Hannah."

Chapter 17

Jared listened as Guadalupe Vargas, Secretary of the Our Lady of Perpetual Help parish council, read the minutes of last month's meeting. The same familiar faces sat in the rectory meeting room around the dinette table that served as a conference table. Besides Lupe, there was Paula Samuels, council chair; Chuck Johnson, vice chair; Eliza, the treasurer; Frank Worth, buildings and grounds; and Harriet Blake, ways and means. Monsignor Sullivan never came to these meetings.

It was Harriet's behavior that piqued Jared's curiosity the most. Although Eliza reported a deficit from the month before of over two thousand dollars, Harriet, as head of ways and means, had nothing to report. On top of that, she was the one council member who opposed his proposal to add an extra Mass on Sundays in Spanish, as well the suggestion from Frank to paint the church offices.

"Do I hear a motion to accept the minutes as read?" Paula Samuels said, breaking his train of thought.

"So moved," said Frank Worth.

"Second," said Jared.

"All in favor?" Every hand went up. "Carried unanimously. Now, for our reports. Administration committee. Eliza?"

"I was hoping we had done a little better last month, considering church attendance goes up for Christmas, but we still haven't been able to collect much over two thousand dollars on any given weekend. We ended the year owing the diocese over forty-nine thousand dollars. We'll have to come up with something to turn our finances around, or I'm afraid the bishop will have no choice but to close the parish. The committee is open to suggestions. That's all I have."

"Thank you, Eliza," Paula said. "Now, for buildings and grounds. Frank?"

"After Eliza's report, I hesitate to say anything, but here goes. The leak in the sanctuary ceiling is back, and it's getting worse. As you know, there have been issues with the church roof for some time. I can try to patch it again, but there's a limit to how long these temporary fixes will last. I know there's no money, so I won't ask for any, but I want to go on record to warn the parish this can't go on forever."

Jared stifled a sigh, thinking of the bucket in the middle of the sanctuary that was collecting drips as they spoke.

"All in favor of accepting his report?" All hands went up. "Would Lupe please give the education committee report?"

"Thank you, Paula. We had a very nice Christmas pageant. The children worked hard and did a wonderful job considering Jimmy Knox got the stomach flu and Peter Nichols had to step in and play Joseph at the last minute. Some of the parents chipped in, and we bought all the children nice rosaries as Christmas mementos. That's about it."

Everyone accepted her report.

"I'm sorry to say we won't be having a report from the Knights of Columbus tonight," Paula said. "I heard from Mabel Johnston that Chuck fell earlier today and broke his hip. He's in the hospital in Monterey, and we're waiting to hear what they're going to do for him. The one thing that's certain is he won't be able to do work with the council for some time. We'll find out more as soon as Mabel is back from Monterey."

Jared looked from Paula to Lupe. *Poor Chuck.* But he was getting an idea and could hardly wait for the meeting to end so he could take the two ladies and Eliza aside for a serious talk. He felt like a mother hen, hatching a conspiracy.

"Harriet, do you have a report from the ways and means committee?" Paula asked.

"No report," was all she said.

As usual. Jared held in a sigh. It should have been called the no ways and no means committee.

Paula gave the report from the women's guild, and then it was Jared's turn.

"I have some news from the worship committee today," he told them. "Monsignor Sullivan did not approve our request for the addition of a Mass in Spanish on Sundays." The council members looked at one other in disappointment, all but Harriet Blake who sat there with a satisfied smirk on her face.

"However," Jared went on, "I spoke to Bishop Mickleson this morning. He is strongly in favor of our request and gave us the go-ahead. He told me to let you all know that if we wanted an additional Mass in Spanish, he would grant it as well."

"How wonderful," Paula said.

Harriet's face turned red with fury.

"All in favor of accepting Father's report?" Paula asked. Every hand but Harriet's went up. "Harriet? Do you have an objection?" Reluctantly, Harriet raised her hand, never taking her glaring eyes off Jared. "Thank you," said Paula. "Now, is there any new business?"

Jared raised his hand. "Since Chuck is temporarily unable to carry out his duties, his absence will leave the parish shorthanded. Everyone knows Chuck and Harriet have dedicated every Sunday morning to sorting and counting the collections for as long as anyone can remember. I think both deserve a thank you for their service to the parish." Jared started the applause, and the rest of the council members joined in enthusiastically. Harriet looked confused.

"But now, with Chuck recovering, I think the council should give serious thought to appointing someone in his place to give Harriet the help she needs."

Harriet had a panicked look on her face that she tried to cover with a sort of smile. It was exactly what Jared had hoped for.

"May I suggest Lupe Vargas?" Jared said.

Paula's face brightened. "Lupe, would you be willing to do this?" She gave Lupe an almost imperceptible nod of her head.

Lupe looked first at Paula, then at Jared, and a look of comprehension crossed her face. She smiled. "I would be pleased to take this on for my parish."

Paula wasted no time. "Do I hear a motion to appoint Lupe Vargas to assist with our weekend collections?"

Jared jumped in. "So moved."

"Second!" Frank shouted.

"All in favor?" said Paula. All hands but Harriet's went up. "Opposed?" Harriet sat there looking stunned. "The motion is carried."

As soon as the meeting was adjourned, Harriet stormed out, slamming the office door behind her. A few minutes later, Frank left, and Jared asked the three women to join him in his office. He sat behind his desk feeling energized.

"I couldn't let this opportunity pass us by," Jared said. "I hate to say this, but Chuck's accident may be a godsend to us."

        "How does the collection-counting work?" asked Lupe. "What do I need to do?"

"What happens, as I understand it," answered Eliza, "is that they separate out the checks from the cash, sort the cash into denominations, and write down a tally of the receipts on a slip of paper. They put the tally slip into a bag with the money and drop it into the lockbox in the monsignor's office. On Tuesdays, when he comes back from his day off, he goes through the money and checks it against their tally. Then he takes it to the bank and drops the bank receipt on my desk. I never see the tally slip."

"What we'd like you to do, Lupe," said Jared, "is get those figures from the tally sheet and pass them on to Eliza. If there's anything suspicious at all, we want Eliza to know about it."

"It sounds easy enough," said Lupe. "The monsignor is never here after Mass on Sundays or Mondays. All I need to do is not let Harriet catch on."

"What if the monsignor won't let Lupe count the money?" asked Paula.

"Let me level with you all. Bishop Mickleson is committed to turning this parish around, with or without the pastor's cooperation. The parish council unanimously selected Lupe to replace Chuck. Every time the monsignor tries to go against a reasonable decision by the parish council, the bishop himself will overrule him. I'm hoping the monsignor will get tired of having his wrist slapped and will stop picking fights he can't win. If he's wise, he'll let Lupe count the money. If not, I'll inform the bishop, and he'll be ordered to let her. Either way, we can count on Lupe being our eyes and ears with the Sunday collections."

"What a wonderful way for our parish to start a new year," said Paula. "Please thank the bishop for his support—and for sending you to us." She gave Jared a giant hug, followed by Eliza and Lupe.

This assignment might not be so bad after all. It occurred to him that every time he had to contact the bishop about something the monsignor was doing, it put him one step closer to the position he wanted. Soon enough, the bishop would be in his back pocket and if (*no, when*) he was named archbishop and the position came free, Jared would be his first choice.

He closed his eyes and hugged the women back.

Chapter 18

Monday, April 2, 2012

Frank Worth felt almost warm in his light jacket as he stepped around the puddles of rainwater from last night's downpour. He crossed the church parking lot from where he always parked his pickup, scanning the asphalt to see if wear and tear had created any new issues. The water-slick surface seemed to bring to light any new irregularities. It was in remarkably good condition, considering how little maintenance it had received over the years.

It was a little after seven o'clock in the morning, but Frank knew Father Jared had already been out to unlock the church. This was his Monday morning routine: come in early, duck into the church first thing in the morning and give the interior a quick once-over before the eight o'clock Mass. Today was the Monday after Palm Sunday. There would be a lot of material for him to clean up. The things he found in the pews after weekend Masses sometimes surprised him. Once, he found a half-eaten burrito. Another time, a pair of boxer shorts. As far as he knew those were still unclaimed in the lost and found.

Sunday Mass attendance was picking up, not only because Easter was approaching, but also thanks to the new Mass in Spanish. Word had gotten out that Father Jared was offering the Sunday liturgies. People found his homilies inspirational and enjoyed listening to him. As far as Frank was concerned, the less said about the monsignor's homilies, the better.

The church was still dark. Father Jared knew Frank would be there first thing, so he often left it to Frank to turn on the lights and straighten up. As soon as Frank stepped inside, though, he knew something was wrong. A sour, musty smell hit him in the face. He flipped on the light switch and his heart sank.

The floor of the sanctuary was piled with rubble. He looked up. About a quarter of the ceiling had let go and come crashing down, spreading wet plaster and debris over the floor. All he could see was a gaping hole. He turned on more lights so that he could look up to where that portion of the half-dome had been. Now he could see all the way up into the rafters and to the underside of the roof. It was discolored and streaked with black. Water still fell drop by drop to the floor. Most of the debris had landed on the right side of the sanctuary, somehow missing the altar and statuary. Maybe once he cleaned up the mess, they could still have morning Mass.

Frank hurried out to the shed and came back with a shovel, a mop and a broom, and a pair of trash cans. He dug right in, gathering the plaster, and loading it in the trash cans. Before long, Paula, Lupe, and Harriet Blake arrived. Once they got over the shock of seeing the damage and the mess, Paula and Lupe pitched in with the mop and broom.

Harriet, on the other hand, sat in the front pew. "Lupe, don't you dare get any of that on my clean altar linens."

By the time Father Jared came in to prepare for Mass, the sanctuary was at least serviceable.

"Frank, I'm so sorry," he said when he saw the damage. "I never even opened the church door this morning. I had no idea this happened. What do you think caused it? Last night's rain?"

"I've been worried about this for a long time," he said. "I keep patching the roof, but it's a losing battle. Water travels. God knows where the leaks that caused this might be. They could be anywhere on that roof. From the looks of those beams up there, I'd say they're pretty well soaked. We'll have to get a contractor in here. This could be serious."

"Do you think it's safe to have Mass with it in that condition?" Father Jared asked.

"Should be, for the time being," said Frank. "I figure what was loose already fell. I was on that roof a couple of weeks ago and it held me all right. But after seeing this, I won't get back up there anytime soon."

"I'll get ready for Mass, then. We can talk in the rectory afterward and figure out what needs to be done." Father Jared thanked Paula and Lupe for their help and then went into the sacristy. Aside from the occasional *plop* as water dripped from the gaping hole in the ceiling, the Mass proceeded without further mishap.

Frank waited for Father Jared to finish putting everything away. Then the two men locked up the church and headed for the kitchen. They sat down together at the dinette table in the conference room.

"What do we do now?" Father Jared asked him. "Holy Week starts Thursday, and Easter is just six days away."

Frank leaned over the table on his forearms. "Like I said, we need to get someone out here to look at the damage and let us know how bad the situation is."

"Do you know anyone?"

"The best man I know of is José Hernandez. He's reliable and honest. If he tells you something, you can take it to the bank."

Eliza appeared in the doorway. "Paula just called and told me what happened. What can I do?"

"Do you have José Hernandez's phone number?" Frank asked. "We need him to take a look at this right away."

"I'm sure I do." She disappeared into the office.

"This could get expensive," said Frank. "There's no telling how much water damage there is up there. Where are we going to get the money to pay for it?"

"I'm not sure," said Father Jared. "Maybe our insurance will cover it. I hope we won't have to get the bishop involved."

Eliza returned with a slip of paper and handed it to Frank. He called José and explained the situation, then set down the receiver. "He'll be right over."

"We'll have to pay him for this, of course." Father Jared turned to Eliza. "Do we have any petty cash?"

"I'm sorry, Father," she said, "but Yolanda just did the shopping. I'm afraid we're cleaned out."

"That's okay," said Jared. "This is an emergency. I'll cover it myself if I have to."

Eliza gave an ironic chuckle. "You know what the monsignor calls you, don't you?"

"No, what?"

"Father Moneybags. He's always saying, 'Don't worry about it; Father Moneybags will take care of it.'"

Father Jared shook his head. "I don't see old Scrooge stepping in to help."

Frank exchanged a look with Eliza. He'd never heard Father Jared disparage the pastor.

"Frank," said Eliza, "may I borrow Father Jared for a few minutes before José gets here?"

"Sure," said Frank. "Sounds like you've got some important matters to discuss. This little problem of ours won't get solved with petty cash."

Father Jared followed Eliza out into the office, leaving Frank alone to sip what was left of his coffee. He returned about five minutes later with a solemn look on his face.

"More trouble, Father?" Frank asked.

"I'm afraid so," he said. "It looks as though our financial situation may be worse than we thought. Eliza and Lupe have discovered an unexpected shortfall that's going to make it very difficult to meet our obligations. Our situation is no secret to you."

"I've dealt with it every day for years," he said with a slow nod.

"You have," said Father Jared. "But please don't say anything about this to anyone. We're not sure how bad it is. Just know that Eliza and I will try to get you everything you need to keep this parish running. This roof problem could not have happened at a worse time."

"Understood, Father," said Frank. "I know you're doing the best you can."

Eliza came to the doorway of the conference room. "Mr. Hernandez is here."

"Good," said Father Jared.

The two men rose and headed for the office door.

"José! Let's get over to the church," said Frank when he spotted the contractor at the door. "You'll need your ladder."

José's truck was parked in the driveway between the church and the rectory, and in a few steps, he was pulling a good-sized extension ladder off the rack over the cab. Balancing the ladder on his shoulder, he followed Jared and Frank into the church. When he looked up and saw the damage, he let out a low whistle.

"That doesn't sound good," said Father Jared.

José turned to Frank. "Help me get the ladder up there and I'll take a look around. Then I'll have a better idea."

The two men raised the ladder up through the hole in the ceiling and rested it against one of the joists. José climbed up into the ceiling until only his work boots were visible. "Holy crap!" was all Frank heard from on high. He watched José's flashlight scanning the roof beams. After about ten minutes, José backed slowly down the ladder.

"Guys, I'm afraid you've got a real mess on your hands."

"How bad is it?" asked Father Jared.

"Pretty bad," said José. "You have a bunch of leaks up there, and they've been going a long time. Some of the joists are almost rotted through, enough so that the roof is starting to sag in places. I saw some fresh patches up there." He looked at Frank.

"Yup, that was me." He knew he'd been taking a risk.

"For your own good, I wouldn't get up on that roof again in its present condition."

"What do you suggest we do?" asked Frank.

"Ordinarily, I'd say we could reinforce the beams—put some new ones up there and tie them into the old ones. But, in this case, I don't recommend it. There's not enough solid wood left in some of those old rafters to hold onto. Besides, it looks like there's mold starting up there. For the time being, we'll have to cover that hole in the ceiling with plastic to keep the moisture and mold from getting down into the church. At least then you'll still be able to use the church. And Father, pray it doesn't rain."

"But that's just a temporary measure," said Father Jared. "What's the permanent fix?"

"I recommend taking the roof off in this whole section and replacing the rotted beams from the joists up. If you don't, you'll be asking for a lot more trouble down the line."

Frank and Father Jared exchanged a long look.

"What would *that* cost?" asked Father Jared.

"I can't tell you with any certainty without doing a formal estimate, but a thumbnail guess would be between eighty and a hundred thousand to do the job right."

It was Father Jared's turn to give a low whistle.

"Can we afford that, Father?" asked Frank.

"We'll do whatever we have to do. Can you two put the plastic up for now?"

"Sure thing, Father," said José. "And I'll get you that estimate."

"Will the church be usable while you're doing the work?" asked Father Jared.

"We'll see," said José. "You should at least be okay for Easter."

Frank tipped his head toward the young priest. "Guess you'd better find out if the insurance premiums are paid up."

Chapter 19

Paul climbed the chancery steps alongside Bishop Mickleson. The bishop was a kindly-looking African American man with graying temples and wire-framed glasses. He was dressed in a tailored black suit with a Roman collar and a silver chain around his neck, a small silver cross tucked into his jacket pocket. The only sign of his status as bishop was a small purple tab just below the opening in his collar.

Paul had come to enjoy his luncheon excursions with the bishop. Though infrequent, the meals were always full of stories and laughter. He always came back to work refreshed and in a better mood.

It was Monday of Holy Week, and there were still last-minute details to handle to make sure the bishop's busy schedule went without a hitch. Wednesday afternoon would be the annual Chrism Mass in the Cathedral where all the priests of the diocese would celebrate their common bond of priesthood and renew their priestly commitment. It was the bishop's custom to provide an evening meal at a local hotel for all the participants. Arranging dinner invitations and logistics for over five hundred priests was like trying to organize a room full of hummingbirds. Paul felt out of his depth. It was at times like this that he appreciated his relationship with the bishop. He knew that, regardless of how the final product turned out, the bishop would appreciate his work.

As they entered the chancery, the bishop was finishing a story about last year's Chrism Mass and how the priests had lined up outside the cathedral waiting for the procession to begin.

"The organ cranked up," he said, "and the choir began singing very loudly as the procession started down the main aisle. Only a handful of priests made it inside the cathedral before the skies opened and the rest of us were caught outside in a deluge with nowhere to go. The people inside couldn't hear the rain, so they kept the procession moving nice and slowly. By the time I got inside, I looked—and smelled—like a wet dog." He laughed. "As we were going down the aisle, I heard one of our priests—it could have been your friend, Richard Loring—say, 'And the rains fell on the just and the unjust!' Those of us with a sense of humor had a good laugh at our own expense."

"We're lucky this year," said Paul. "No rain predicted all week."

"God is, indeed, merciful," said the bishop. As they got to his office door, the two men parted company.

Paul had just sat down at his desk when his phone rang. It was Jared.

"Hey, handsome," said Paul. "How're things at Our Lady of Perpetual Hell?"

"Don't be an ass." Jared's serious tone caught Paul off guard.

"Is something wrong?"

"You might say that. The ceiling in the church collapsed last night."

"Oh, my Lord!" Paul sat up straight in his chair. "Was anyone hurt?"

"No, thank God," said Jared. "But the bishop needs to know."

"I'll put you right through to him."

"No, wait." Jared said. "I want to talk to you first."

"Okay. What do you need?" Paul picked up a pen and a pad of paper in case he needed to take notes.

"You remember how I told you that Eliza—the church secretary—and I suspected there was something odd going on here?"

"Yes. You got someone to keep an eye on the collections, right?"

"Right. It's been a couple of months now, and Eliza's been getting the tally sheets from the money counters. She's been comparing them to the deposit receipts."

"And?"

"There's a discrepancy. We're missing almost five hundred dollars a week from the collection. That's about a fifth of what we receive."

"What are you going to do? Are you going to tell the bishop?"

"Not yet. I want to wait until things slow down after Easter. Then, Eliza and I will drive down and meet with him in person."

"I'll get you on his calendar. You want to see him sometime next week?"

"Preferably on a Friday, so the monsignor won't suspect anything. I'm always out of town on my day off anyway."

"I know," said Paul with a smile. "Okay, you're on for the morning and, just in case, I've blocked out some time in the afternoon, too." Paul thought for a moment. "You're sure you don't want to tell him now?"

"It's too sensitive. Besides, I want to show him the evidence firsthand. I'm glad I'm not the one who has to decide where to go from here. Anyway, I feel better that someone else knows about the mess."

"Speaking of messes, what are you going to do about your church?"

"It looks like our insurance will cover the damage, but we'll have to replace part of the roof. It will be an expensive job. I'd better break the bad news to the boss before ol' Scrooge gets back from his day off. Will you transfer me over?"

"Sure. Just a second."

"And Paul?" Jared said.

"Yes?"

"Not a word about the other matter to anyone. Okay?"

"Of course." He transferred the call and sat in silence for a couple of minutes. Although he had no fondness for Monsignor Sullivan, he hoped that what Jared had found was a mistake. The alternative made him sick to his stomach.

He was deep into paperwork when the phone on his desk rang again, startling him.

"Father Paul? It's Rosario Alvarez, Hannah's companion."

"Yes, of course, Rosario." He bit his lip. Rosario never called him. "Is everything okay with Hannah?" He didn't relish the thought of delivering more bad news to poor Jared.

"No, Father. It's not Ms. Hannah, it's Mr. Kurt. He's sick."

Paul's chest tightened. "What do you mean? What's wrong?"

"He's been feeling weak for the past several days. He doesn't want to get out of bed."

"Have you called a doctor?" Paul said.

"He wants to see you," Rosario said. "Can you come, please?"

Me, and not a doctor. That seemed odd. "I'll be there as soon as I can. Thanks for letting me know." He put down the receiver and ducked out of the office.

He rapped on the bishop's door and put his head in. The bishop was still on the phone with Jared, so he made *I'm going out* signs, and the bishop nodded. In a few minutes, he was on his way to Cambria. The trip took a little over a half hour, and then he was parking in the driveway. Rosario met him at the door and ushered him up the sweeping staircase to a gigantic master bedroom.

He was surprised to see how much Kurt had changed since their last visit a month earlier. He looked like a gaunt caricature of himself, nearly lost in the folds of the bedclothes. Hannah sat at a chair beside his bed, arms crossed at her chest. The room was dark, the curtains drawn despite the bright sunny day.

Paul sat on the side of the bed and took one of Kurt's cold, slim hand in both of his. "What's going on?" He looked from Kurt to Hannah and back again. A plate of toast sat on a tray beside Kurt. Paul was quite sure it had been sitting there for hours.

"The cancer is winning," Kurt said.

"What?" Paul felt like he'd walked into a movie halfway through. "What cancer?"

"It's his lungs," said Hannah. "He smoked all his life. Now, he pays for it."

"But...when was this diagnosed?" Could he have gotten this sick this fast?

"I've known for maybe a year," said Kurt.

What? "And you didn't tell me?" Paul swallowed the lump in his throat.

"Why? What could you do—other than feel sorry for me? No. I told nobody but Hannah."

"I could have done something to help you," Paul said.

"How? The cancer was already spreading when they found it. They wanted me to have radiation and chemo, but I said no."

"Why?"

"Because I asked my doctors, what are my chances if I take the treatment? Not one of them could give me even a fifty-fifty chance. So, I asked them if they were me, would they do it? They all hemmed and hawed. So, I said no. They gave me pills, and I've had a good year until now. Now, the cancer is doing better and I, not so much."

"Have you told Jared?"

"No. I've tried calling him several times, but he won't take my calls." Kurt gripped Paul's forearm. "You talk to him. You tell him. Tell him I'd like to see him. It would mean a great deal to me. If—if he's willing."

He shook his head. "I know Jared. He's stubborn, but he's a good man. He wouldn't refuse you this."

Hannah crossed the room and stood by the window, peering out through a crack in the curtains.

"Good," said Kurt. "I trust you like my own son." He drew Paul closer and said in a hoarse whisper, "You remember our agreement, yes? You'll make

134

sure my Hannah is looked after."

"Yes, I remember," Paul said. "I'll take care of everything."

"I know you will. Now, I need to rest a little. Thank you for coming all this way to see a sick old man. I'm so very glad you came. Come back and see me soon, okay?"

"I will," said Paul. "I promise."

"Good. Very good." Kurt closed his eyes in a way that made Paul think he must be in pain.

Paul turned to Hannah. "Is there anything you need? Anything I can get you?"

Hannah scowled. "Make my husband well. That's what I need. Nothing else." *And certainly not your prayers.* She didn't say that, but the way she frowned at the crucifix at his neck, he knew it was what she was thinking.

Paul ignored her bitterness. "If you think of anything, just have Rosario call me, okay?"

Hannah didn't answer.

"I'll see you soon, Hannah. Goodbye for now." As he turned to leave, Rosario followed him out.

When they reached the front door and Paul was certain he wouldn't be overheard, he said, "How bad is it?"

She shook her head and looked at the floor, grasping both her arms as if she were getting a chill. When she looked up, tears welled in her eyes. For a paid companion, she performed her duties with sensitivity and attentiveness. She took a deep breath as if to compose herself. "It's bad, Father. The doctor says it's stage four. He told me that means it's gone into other organs. I wish he would eat more to keep up his strength, but he's lost his appetite. They say it could be a couple of months, but maybe sooner. I think they're guessing."

"Is he in pain?"

135

"Sometimes, but they have me give him morphine when it gets too bad. He sleeps a lot."

"Why didn't he tell me?"

"Mr. Kurt and his sister are very stubborn people."

"Like his son, I'm afraid."

"Yes," said Rosario, "That's what I've heard about him." She took Paul's hand. "It would be good for him if his son came to see him. It's the one thing he's been asking for."

"I'll do my best," said Paul. "And Hannah—is she alright?"

"She has her good days and her not so good days. She knows her husband is dying, and she's already sick with grief. Sometimes I have to give her something to calm her down and make her sleep."

"Please keep me informed—about both. Thank you for all you're doing for them."

"They are good people, Father," Rosario said, "despite how it sometimes looks."

"Yes, I know," said Paul. "Let me know if you need anything."

"I will." Rosario turned and trudged back up the stairs to Kurt's room.

Paul got in his car and drove back to the chancery. He knew what he had to do, regardless of his doubts about how Jared would react. When he got back to the office, he dialed Jared's number.

"How're you doing?"

"It could be worse," said Jared.

Yes. And it's about to be.

"I just came back from the church," Jared said. "They've almost got the plastic up to cover the hole in the ceiling. It looks like hell, but at least we can get through our Holy Week services. I talked to the bishop, and he's been supportive."

Paul thought he sounded tired. He let out a long sigh. "I'm afraid I've got more bad news for you."

The line went silent for a moment. "What now?"

Paul stared at the wood grain of his desk. "It's your father."

"What's wrong? What happened?" Jared's voice was tight with anxiety.

"I just came back from Cambria." He hesitated. "It's cancer, Jared. Stage four. They say he has a few months, max."

"Oh, crap. Leave it to him to keep that a secret."

May as well jump right in. "He wants to see you when you can get away."

"You saw him?"

"Yes," Paul said.

"How did he look? Do you think I need to get over there now, or can it wait until after Holy Week?"

"I can't say. He's lost weight and spends most of his time in bed, but Hannah and the nurse he hired are looking after him. He seemed strong and was in good spirits, but it's impossible to guess. Even his doctors don't know."

There was a long pause on the other end of the line. Paul wished he could say something helpful, but nothing came to mind.

"I'm already coming down there next week to meet with the bishop. I'll come a day early. Tell Papa I'll see him first thing next week. No, never mind. I'll call him and tell him myself."

"Good," said Paul. "He'll be glad to hear from you."

"I know. Say a prayer that this will all work out, will you?"

"Sure, Jared. Whatever you need."

"And you'll go see him whenever you can, right?"

"I promised him I would," Paul said.

"Gotta run," said Jared. "I'll call him right now. Thanks for letting me know." He paused to catch his breath. "No. Thanks for everything. Catch you later."

Paul hung up and stared bat the paperwork spread out in front of him, not seeing any of it. He got up and made sure his office door was closed tight, took a deep breath, and picked up the receiver again. He dialed the thirteen digits from memory. There was a loud buzzing at the other end of the line.

"Justin Röhrbach, *guten Tag*," said Jared's brother in a sleepy but familiar voice.

"Justin, it's me, Paul."

"Dude. What's up? It's two o'clock in the morning."

"I'm sorry, man. It's not good news." He filled Justin in with the news about his father. "Can you come home? You know what it would mean to him."

Justin made a noise of deep anguish. "They'd never let me through immigration."

"Can you call him and let him know you're okay?" Paul said.

"You know what he thinks of me. He's never accepted any of my calls."

"Can you at least try?"

"All right, buddy, for you I'll do it. I appreciate what you're trying to do. Now, let me get back to sleep. I've got an early shift tomorrow."

The call went dead. Paul buried his face in his hands, wondering for the hundredth time how he'd allowed himself to end up in this position.

Chapter 20

Thursday, April 19, 2012

Eliza stood up and adjusted her skirt before grabbing a pen and notepad and entering the monsignor's office. These days, every time he called her in, she braced herself for a confrontation about the donations.

"Sit down, please," he said. She pulled up one of the chairs, pen poised over the paper as if it would somehow keep trouble at bay.

"I've been in contact with the diocese, and it seems our insurance will cover most of the repairs on the church roof. I have hired José Hernandez to do the work. Mr. Hernandez will submit his invoices to this office, and I will forward them to the chancery and make sure he is paid. If you receive any invoices from him, you must give them directly to me. This is nobody else's business, especially not Father Moneybags. Do I make myself clear?" He peered out at her from under his bushy gray eyebrows.

"Yes, Monsignor," she said. *Invoices to Monsignor*, she wrote on the pad.

"And, if anyone asks any nosy questions about the repairs, you can also refer them directly to me. I know how some people around here love to gossip about things that are none of their business. I will have none of that in my parish. You've always been good about keeping our parish business private. I expect that to continue."

"Of course, Monsignor," she said in her most professional tone of voice.

"Thank you. You may go." He dismissed her with a wave of his hand. As she stood to go back to her desk, he stopped her. "One more thing. I'm driving over to Monterey this afternoon to visit one of our parishioners in a nursing home there. Please let Yolanda know I won't be eating at home tonight."

"Yes, Monsignor," she said.

He went back to his paperwork and Eliza escaped through the door marked

Private.

In the kitchen, Yolanda was stirring up a batch of batter.

"Biscuits?" she asked.

Yolanda laughed. "You must have some kind of biscuit radar in that head of yours. You always seem to appear when I'm making them."

"You'll save me some, won't you?"

"Don't I always?"

"The monsignor won't be home for dinner tonight."

"That so?" Yolanda stopped stirring. "Where's he gallivanting off to?"

"Monterey. He's going to visit a parishioner in a nursing home this afternoon."

"That old crook," She whispered. "He's not going to Monterey to visit a parishioner. We don't have anybody in Monterey."

Eliza's eyebrows knit together. "Are you sure?"

"Course, I'm sure. I'd be the first to know about it. They tell me everything."

"Regardless, my dear, he won't be here for dinner."

"Just as well," she said. "Less work for me. I'll just make dinner for Father Jared then."

Right. Eliza shut the door, came back, and leaned across the counter. "I need you to keep a secret for me."

"Of course." Yolanda set down her spoon and pushed the bowl aside. "What is it?"

"You know Father Jared is a pilot and flies himself all over the place on his days off."

"That's not much of a secret," she said. "Everyone knows that. Our fancy gallivanting priest." She waggled her eyebrows.

"Stop it," said Eliza. "The secret is that he's taking me with him tonight. We're going down to San Luis Obispo for the day."

"Oh, my," said Yolanda. "He flies one of those puddle-jumpers, doesn't he? You'd never get me up in one of those things."

Eliza laughed, throwing her hands up. "I'm sixty-two years old. What have I got to lose?"

"Getting to sixty-three."

"I'm sure there's nothing to worry about," said Eliza. "Father Jared's been flying for years."

"Still and all, if I were you, I'd worry."

"Worry about what?" The monsignor bustled through the kitchen door.

"Oh, it's nothing, Monsignor," Yolanda answered, picking up her spoon and returning to the biscuits. "Eliza is just so much braver than I am. I worry about everything."

"I think you're right to worry," he said. "Things would go a whole lot smoother around here if some people worried a little more." He shot Eliza a weighted glare. "Good afternoon, ladies."

"Good afternoon, Monsignor," the two women said in unison, like schoolgirls in front of Mother Superior.

He went through the back kitchen door, letting it slam shut behind him. Eliza and Yolanda stood by the kitchen window watching until he got into his car and drove away.

"What was that about?" Yolanda said.

Eliza shook her head. "Life, I suppose. Can you make up some excuse for why I'm not here tomorrow?"

Yolanda gave a conspiratorial smile. "I'll think of something."

Eliza dialed Jared's room and said quietly, "He's gone for the rest of the day, Father."

Almost immediately, she heard footsteps on the stairs, and Father Jared appeared at the kitchen door. "Let's go to my office," he said. Then he turned to the housekeeper. "Yolanda, I'll be ready to eat whenever you have supper ready. You don't have to wait until six o'clock. That way you can get home at a decent hour."

"That's kind of you," Yolanda said. "It'll be about a half an hour, Father, if you don't mind eating that early."

"That'd be great."

Eliza followed him to his office. As he sat behind his desk, Father Jared whispered, "Close the door."

Eliza laughed as she pulled it shut behind her. "We've made you as paranoid as we are." She sat down opposite him.

Father Jared laughed. "That's right. He's gone, isn't he." He shuffled some papers on his desk. "About our trip. All you have to do is get yourself up to Hollister Aviation at the airport. It's a big hanger right off the highway. You can't miss it. And don't worry about the timing. I'll call you when I'm leaving here. Okay?"

"Easy enough, Father."

"When we land at San Luis, Father Paul Fortis will be picking us up. I've booked you into the Granada Hotel on Morro Street. It's a couple of blocks from the chancery. We can drop you off."

"Where will you stay?"

"Father Paul is a classmate of mine and I always stay with him when I'm in town. But first I have to drive home to Cambria. My father is sick."

"Father! You never told us that. I hope it's nothing serious."

"Unfortunately, it is," Father Jared said. "But I'll be back in time to meet with the bishop, don't worry.

Eliza clasped her hands in her lap. "Good. I have the books and tally sheets and bank receipts all ready to go."

Father Jared consulted his agenda. "Our appointment with the bishop is at ten o'clock, so Father Paul and I will meet you tomorrow morning at the Granada for breakfast. Then we can all walk over to the chancery. Is there anything else you need to know?"

"No, but there's something else I need to tell you, Father," she said. "The monsignor told me he was hiring Mr. Hernandez as the contractor for the church roof." She explained about the invoices and how he specifically wanted them kept away from Father Jared.

He sat for a long time staring at her in silence. "He doesn't seem concerned about raising suspicions. I don't know what his game is—and I hope we're wrong about all this—but I'm sure the bishop will want to get to the bottom of it. We'll just add it to our list of things to tell him tomorrow."

"Is there anything else we need to go over, Father?"

"I don't think so. Why don't you get your things together and head home? Grab yourself some supper with your husband. I'll call you when I'm done here."

When Eliza opened the door, the room filled with the heady aroma of fresh-baked biscuits. They left the office area together. In the kitchen, Yolanda was sliding a baking sheet full of hot biscuits into a plastic container.

"I've packed you a little something to take on your trip," she said. "I don't think your airline serves snacks." She handed the container to Eliza.

"What about the pilot?" Father Jared said. "Doesn't he get fed?"

"The pilot will get his before he goes." She pointed to a platter piled with more of the golden-brown pastries. "Now, if you'll go get washed up, I'll feed you."

"I'll see you at the airport, Father," said Eliza. Then, saying goodnight to Yolanda, she left for home.

Two hours later, she parked her white Ford Focus by the front door of the Hollister Aviation hangar. She pulled a plaid carry-on bag from the backseat and retrieved a shopping bag loaded with the box of biscuits and a thermos of hot decaf.

Father Jared sat alone in the waiting room. He rose as she approached. "All set?"

"As ready as I'm going to be, Father."

They walked together to the plane. The little luggage hatch in the tail was standing open and ready. Eliza's heart beat a little faster. The plane looked substantial enough...but it was so small. She reminded herself how she had been looking forward to this adventure. She was not going to let last-minute nerves deter her.

Once she was settled into her seat and saw how professionally Father Jared went through his list of tasks, her anxiety left her. Although when the wheels lifted off the ground, she did feel a nervous twitter in her stomach. But once they were leveled off and on their way, she settled into pure enjoyment. Coastal northern California was a beautiful sight from the air.

She had flown in commercial planes often enough to know what to expect during a landing, but she was unprepared for the sight of the runway lights through the front windshield stretching out in front of her like a carpet. From a pilot's eye view, the ribbon of lights seemed to go on forever as the dark runway corridor drew ever nearer. Father Jared set the little plane down with hardly a jolt, and Eliza exhaled. She hadn't realized until that instant that she'd been holding her breath throughout their descent.

In less than five minutes, they were parked at the San Luis Airport FBO and Father Jared was fastening the tie-downs to the plane. As they headed inside, another priest met them at the door. He gave Jared a big hug. Eliza thought he looked troubled.

"Eliza Roberts, this is Father Paul Fortis," said Father Jared.

"Very pleased to meet you, Mrs. Roberts," said the young priest. "I've heard from Father Jared how you single-handedly hold Our Lady's parish together."

"Please, Father, call me Eliza."

Paul's smile faded as he turned back to his friend. "Your father isn't doing well today. They took him to the hospital ICU about an hour ago. I was talking to Rosario just before you landed, and they don't know if he'll make it through the night. He goes in and out of consciousness. We should go straight to the hospital."

As they crossed the parking lot, Father Jared was all business. "I hate to drag Eliza through this. The Granada is on our way. Let's drop her off first, then we can go to the hospital. I didn't expect things to get this bad this soon." He threw his suitcase into the trunk and put Eliza's overnight bag in the backseat.

"Nobody did," said Father Paul. "Let's just pray we get there in time."

"Amen," said Father Jared. He signed himself with the sign of the cross as they climbed into the car. But Eliza couldn't help but think there was something less than whole-hearted about it.

Chapter 21

Thursday, April 19, 2012

Jared was impressed by the way Paul navigated his way through the hospital parking lots and brought his car to a stop in one of the empty "Clergy Only" spots. *Of course, Paul must have been here a hundred times by now.* Hospital visits were still a bit new and strange for him. The nearest hospital to him at Our Lady's was in Hollister and the monsignor insisted that if any visiting were to be done, the parishes there would do it. That way, he needn't bother. Jared felt a little awkward following Paul through the sliding glass doors underneath the huge, lighted "EMERGENCY" sign across the front of the entryway.

The candy-striper at the reception desk gave them a cursory glance once she saw their collars. Paul stepped up to the lady (Jared thought she was a little old to be a candy-striper) and told her, "Father Fortis to see Kurt Röhrbach in ICU." Without looking up, she made a note on a pad of pink papers.

"You know your way, Father?"

"Yes, Sheila, thanks."

Paul steered them around a corner where they were standing in front of two elevators side-by-side. Even after Paul pressed the "up" button, it seemed to take forever for the floor indicator light above the door to count down the floors, one by one. At five, the countdown stopped, and Jared couldn't help himself. He started punching the button a few more times. He knew very well that wouldn't accomplish anything, but there was always that secret hope that some kind of sympathetic magic might convince the machine to respond with more consideration.

As if to answer his summons, the countdown resumed, and the doors parted for them. He was thankful the car was empty. Paul reached the controls first and pressed "2." After the initial jolt, a low hum that he could feel as much as hear let him know the car was moving.

When the doors reopened, Paul stepped out and turned left down the hall. Jared followed behind, feeling a little awkward in these alien surroundings. Ahead of them stood a pair of metal doors with a small pane of frosted glass in the center of each. A large sign on one of the doors proclaimed, "ICU. No Admittance. Hospital Personnel Only." In perfect contradiction to that, there was a smaller sign to the side of the doors that read, "Push Button for Admittance," over a red arrow pointing downward to a matching red button. Without hesitating, Paul pressed the button and, a few seconds later came the "click-buzz" indicating that the door was unlatched. Paul pulled the door open, they stepped inside, and the door closed and latched behind them.

A young nurse dressed in blue scrub slacks and a matching blue smock was coming toward them, holding a clipboard. She opened her mouth to speak but, before she could get a word out, Paul said, "Kurt Röhrbach, please. Jared noted an expression that fell somewhere between concern and embarrassment cross her face. "Are you his son?"

"No," he answered, "this is Father Röhrbach," indicating Jared.

"I see." She looked Jared up and down. "Would you wait here a moment, please?" and, without waiting for a response, she turned and ducked out of site in the large room that lay in front of them. Jared scanned the room. It was brightly lit with a large, low-walled enclosure along one wall. At the counters behind the wall various hospital personnel in the same blue scrubs or smocks either stood examining paperwork or sat at one of the computer screens, which cast an eerie green glow on their faces. The room seemed oppressively quiet except for the occasional hum as a printer disgorged yet another page of paperwork, or an annoying beep that originated in some piece of exotic machinery.

Evenly spaced along the three other walls of the room there were ten or twelve sets of double sliding glass doors. Several of the doors were standing open, shedding light on the ends of their hospital beds in otherwise darkened rooms. The other doors were closed, their rooms dark, with hospital curtains drawn across the interiors of the glass doorways. Only one of these rooms had a light on inside. Jared wondered about that one.

"Father?" A woman, somewhat older than the first one to greet them, was standing by his side looking up at him as though expecting an answer.

Where did she come from? "I'm sorry... What was that?"

"Would you step in here for a moment, please?" she repeated, indicating a small sitting room off to his right that he hadn't noticed before. Her sympathetic yet professional demeanor alarmed him. It was the same attitude he assumed when delivering bad news to parishioners. She didn't have to say another word. He knew. They were too late. His father was gone. Feelings of sorrow and anger welled up from within him. But anger at whom? His father who hadn't waited for him? Paul who had driven them there from the airport? Or himself for assuming that there would be time?

Jared followed the woman's lead, stepped into the little room, and sat in one of the leather-upholstered armchairs. "How long ago?" He didn't need to have her go through the motions of breaking the bad news to him. He'd spare her that.

She seemed to have been thrown off-balance by his question. "I'm sorry?... He...uh... Your father passed away about fifteen minutes ago."

He felt somehow pleased with himself that he had thrown her off her game. *Isn't it odd the little games our minds play when we'd rather not face facts?*

"Jared? Are you all right?" It was Paul sitting in the chair next to him holding onto his forearm.

"Yes, of course," he lied, looking first at Paul then at nurse—her badge said "Jane" something—then back again.

"Can I get you something to drink, Father?" She had returned to her script. "Bottled water? Fruit juice?"

"No. Thank you. Nothing."

"...see him now?" Paul was asking him something. He figured out what it was.

"Yes. Sure." Paul patted him on the arm and "Jane" led the two of them to the room with the light on and slid open the glass door and stood there waiting for them to go in. A thought struck him. He did *not* want to see Hannah. "Is my... Is Hannah here?"

"Yes, Father," she said.

He flinched. He had half a mind to turn back around the way they'd come rather than see her. Then he heard Paul's voice in his head mocking him for basing his decisions on whether Hannah would do something or other.

"...but we had to take her to the family room. She was very upset, and we had no choice but to sedate her. Her nurse, Mrs. Alvarez, is with her. I can take you to her, if you wish."

Not on your life, lady. "No, thank you. That won't be necessary." *Ever.* Now that that issue was settled, he was ready to go in. Paul was hanging back, perhaps waiting for him to make the first move. So, he stepped inside the little room, pushing the hospital curtain aside. The hospital bed was right in front of him. His father lay there, like a little gaunt manikin, with his head nestled in the center of a hospital pillow, the thin, white cotton blanket pulled up to his shoulders.

His eyes were closed, his cheeks were sunken, and his face was very pale. There was no makeup and no soft lighting to blunt the sharp reality of his death. There were no flowers flanking the body to make the scene more palatable. The hospital machinery sat still and silent. The room was uncomfortably cold.

Kurt looked tiny, a shadow of the man he'd grown up with. He had always been such a robust man—a force of nature. He could tame any situation. "When did he get so small?" he said aloud. The sound of his own voice startled him.

He felt Paul's hand on his back. "He's been sick quite a while, but just recently he began losing the weight. He didn't want you to know... He didn't want you to worry."

"But why didn't you tell me he was this bad? I would have come to see him a long time ago."

Paul looked down and shook his head. "I haven't seen him in a few weeks myself. I got too busy to visit him. I was surprised, too. I didn't realize he was going down so fast. Rosario told me, of course, but he'd been failing for so long that I didn't think..."

"How could I have been so stupid, Paul? He kept calling me, leaving me phone messages about wanting to talk, and I ignored him...on purpose. I wanted him to feel the way I felt when Hannah would beat me and I'd call him at work and he wouldn't have time to talk to me, or he'd be out of the country and not take my calls. He was always too busy, always gone somewhere taking care of things that were more important to him. More important than me."

"'I'll call you later,' he'd say, but then he never would. So, I made him wait the way he made me wait. I thought I was right doing the same thing to him. I never returned his calls. But who got hurt in the end? Me...again." He turned from staring at his father's lifeless face and looked straight at Paul. "But I loved him. I loved him. All those things wouldn't have hurt so much if I hadn't loved him as much as I did." He could feel the lump rising in his throat as he pointed at his father's remains. "This isn't what I wanted. If he had only said, 'I'm sorry,' then I would have said I'm sorry, too." He looked back at Kurt. "Now, he'll never know how much I loved him."

"He knew," Paul murmured. "He knew very well." He took Jared's hand and led him over to the back corner of the room where there were two chairs identical to the ones in the little office. "Come over here and sit down a minute. There are some things you need to know—that Kurt wanted you to know."

"He talked to you about me?" He followed Paul over to the chairs.

150

"Yes. A lot. Now, come sit down."

Jared sat facing Paul. He felt very tired and drained.

"Your father understood a lot more about you than you give him credit for. Of course, he knew how much you loved him...and how hurt and disappointed you were. You may find this hard to believe, but he never blamed you for being angry at him. Somehow, he didn't take it personally. He knew you were angry at things beyond both of your control, and he believed that you'd see things differently one day. He loved you enough to keep trying to reach you, Despite it all. That's what happened at your ordination. He wouldn't let anyone, or anything keep him away from seeing you ordained. You know that one way or another, Kurt made things happen." Paul gave him a wry smile. "Something like someone else I know."

Jared was starting to feel that everything he'd been doing to punish his father had somehow ricocheted back onto him. "Wasn't he upset that I never answered his calls?"

Paul shook his head. "He was disappointed and sometimes sad. But he knew you heard the voice messages he left for you. He figured if that was the only way he could communicate with you, he'd never give it up."

"And he never did."

"There was one thing he wanted to tell you, but he couldn't do it over the phone. So, he told me what he wanted you to know and made me promise that I'd tell you when I thought the time was right."

"Do you want to tell me now? I want to hear it."

"Are you sure? It's about Hannah."

Jared felt his insides tighten by instinct. *Of course. It's always about Hannah, isn't it?.* He took a deep breath. "Look, I just said I was stupid not to listen to what he had to say. I don't want to be stupid again. Go ahead. What did he want you to tell me?"

Paul fished in his jacket pocket and pulled out the silver locket on a chain that Kurt had given him. "When I heard that Kurt was failing, I grabbed this. He wanted me to give it to you when you were ready to listen." He held it out to him. "He said it's important."

Jared took the locket and pressed the little latch on the side. It swung open, showing two people he didn't recognize in faded shades of gray, a woman on one side and, facing her on the other a man in a Nazi officer's uniform. "Who are they?"

"They're Hannah's mother and father."

"Her father was a Nazi?"

"Uh-huh. They both were. He was Hitler's governor of Salzburg." Paul went on to tell Jared the whole story of Hannah's terrible childhood and the role that Kurt and Lillian had played bringing her back with them to the States.

Jared thought it was odd how gaining a little compassion could start draining the heat out of his fiercest resentments. As the story of Hannah's life unfolded, Jared began to understand where all the hollering, the insults and cursing, the harsh punishments and beatings he endured after his mother died had come from. That didn't excuse them in his mind—there is no excuse for treating a young child like that—but it explained them. As Paul spoke, for the first time in his life, the thought occurred to him that maybe Hannah had done the best she could with what she had. He wondered if he could ever bring himself to forgive her. *Who knows? Maybe someday.*

At least now he could understand why Kurt married her. It wasn't a personal affront to him, and it wasn't romantic love. His parents had done a wonderful thing rescuing Lilly's cousin Hannah from a miserable existence and giving her a life second-to-none. It was now clear that Kurt knew he was dying, and he married Hannah so she would be cared for even after he was gone. His father had done a very unselfish thing, and he had blamed him for it. Jared was starting to feel more than a little bit ashamed of himself. It was a feeling he didn't like. After all, he didn't know anything about all this. "Why didn't he tell me all this sooner?"

Paul gave him an accusing look. "Why do you think?"

That did it. Jared felt his cheeks getting hot and he looked down at the floor. It stung him to the core to realize after all this time that his father wasn't the one at fault for ruining their relationship. He was. Not only was he not used to not getting what he wanted, but he certainly was not used to accepting the blame for it. He wanted to leave. "Paul, lets..." He looked up at Paul and saw him smiling at someone over his shoulder. He spun around. A middle-aged woman with brown eyes and salt-and-pepper gray hair tied back at the nape of her neck stood behind him. She seemed kindly and polite—he guessed that she had been standing there a while waiting for them to finish.

"Rosario," said Paul, "this is Father Jared, Kurt's son."

She smiled at him. "Father, I'm so happy to finally meet you." She glanced at the hospital bed beside her. "And I'm so very sorry about your father. He was a wonderful man, and I will so miss working for him."

Jared wasn't sure what to say. He felt like a stranger to his father's household. He had made himself an outsider and created a vacuum that Rosario—and Paul—had stepped into in his absence. "Rosario," he said, "it's nice to meet you, too." He closed the locket, slipped it into his pocket and stood to shake her hand, but his legs felt wobbly. "You'll have to forgive me. This is all way too sudden."

He could see the compassion in her eyes as she held his hand in both of hers. "I know. We were none of us prepared for this. Poor Ms. Hannah. She yelled and yelled when Mr. Kurt died. We had to give her something to make her sleep. I will take her home a little later." She gave his hand a little squeeze. "Is there anything you need me to do, Father?"

He was tired. He was finding it hard to think clearly, and he wasn't used to feeling so out of control, so vulnerable. "I don't know just yet. I may need your help when I start making the funeral arrangements. I have no idea what he might have wanted."

"Please don't stress yourself over the arrangements, Father. He always said he didn't want you to be worried about him or burdened."

"Burdened?" Jared asked.

"Your father knew he was dying for a long time. He's already made all the arrangements. The hospital has the paperwork, and everything will be taken care of as he requested. He wanted me to assure you."

This was something else he hadn't anticipated. What arrangements had he made? "The arrangements have been taken care of?" asked Jared. "What does that mean?"

"The funeral home will pick him up here, and he'll be cremated. He wanted Ms. Hannah to have his ashes. That's what he told everyone."

What about me? Did he want me to say his funeral Mass? "And what about his service? What arrangements did he make for a funeral?"

Rosario looked concerned. "I'm very sorry, Father, but Mr. Kurt didn't want any kind of service."

He felt his alienation was complete, and it burned. "What about what I want?" he said, withdrawing his hand from hers. "I'm the one left behind."

"Jared." Paul rested his hand on his shoulder.

He was powerless to change his father's mind now. A good son would honor his father's wishes. He could always say a private Mass for his father, maybe with his friends at the parish and Paul. It wouldn't be the same, but it would be something. There was nothing more to be done here. "Thank you, Rosario, for all you've done for him and my family." She smiled back at him.

He walked over to the bed to say farewell to the most important person in his life. If only he had realized it sooner. He leaned over and kissed his father's forehead, stroking his wispy gray hair. "Papa, I'm sorry. I missed so much."

"He was sorry, too," Paul said.

"Goodbye, Papa. I love you." Jared straightened up and turned to the man who'd been with him and supported him through it all. "What have I done, Paul?" Paul embraced him and held him close for a moment. Then, releasing him, he slipped his arm around Jared's waste, ushering him toward the door. Just before they passed through and out into the main room, Jared turned and looked over his shoulder one last time. "G'bye," he whispered.

Chapter 22

Friday, April 20, 2012

Paul awoke to Jared's naked body wrapped around him. The love of his life wasn't exactly snoring—it was more like a series of little snorts. With each breath, Paul could smell hints of last night's cocktails. He had kept Jared moderately inebriated as they reminisced about life with Kurt, sometimes tearfully, sometimes wracked with laughter, until they both wound up emotionally exhausted, too tired for sex, but needing the comfort of each other's bodies.

It was almost seven o'clock in the morning and, not for the first time, Paul realized that even in the midst of personal tragedy, life for the rest of the world would go on. Chances are, Eliza was just waking up at the Granada. She would expect to hear from them, and there was still that meeting with the bishop at ten. Paul would make sure everything happened at the chancery as it should. He untangled himself from Jared's arms and legs so as not to wake him and went into the kitchen to make coffee. After last night, it was the thing Jared would most need when he awoke.

They were supposed to join Eliza at the hotel for breakfast, but he couldn't imagine Jared would be in any condition—physically or emotionally—to keep that appointment. He dialed the number for the Granada Hotel and asked for her room.

When she answered, he broke the news of Kurt's death to her. "Would you mind catching breakfast at the hotel, and I can swing by and pick you up around nine? Would that be all right?"

"Of course, Father," she said. "Please tell Father Jared how very sorry I am." She paused. "I suppose that means that he won't be able to be with me when I talk to the bishop."

Paul could hear the concern in her voice. "Probably not," he murmured.

"Oh, well, that can't be helped. I'll just have to do the best I can. I hope the bishop understands this will be very hard for me."

"Please don't worry about the bishop," Paul said. "You'll have no trouble talking to him."

"Thank you, Father. That helps," she said. "I'll see you at nine. I'll keep Father Jared and his family in my prayers. Oh, yes...and I'll let his friends at the parish know, too."

Paul hung up and was gathering the necessities to make breakfast when Jared appeared naked and bleary-eyed in the kitchen doorway.

"Who was that?"

"Eliza."

"Oh, God!" Jared said. "Breakfast. I forgot all about it."

Paul raised the flipper in his hand. "All taken care of."

"Thank you. I just can't do that today."

"I know, Jar." Paul finished the breakfast preparations and, as he was setting the plates down on the table, the phone rang.

Jared answered it and put it on speaker so Paul could hear.

"...Father, my name is Harold Wright, and I was your father's estate attorney."

"News travels fast," Jared said.

"Not exactly, Father. Mr. Röhrbach left instructions with Rosario Alvarez that I was to be notified immediately after his death. Your father wanted me to answer any questions you might have."

"Do you have a copy of his will, Mr. Wright? I have no idea where it is."

Of course. Kurt's fortune. Paul realized he was holding his breath, anticipating what was coming next.

"Yes, but the will is not much of anything," the attorney said. "You can see it if you want, but it's just what we call a pourover will. A formality. It states that any of your father's assets or possessions not already in his trust will thereby be transferred into it."

"I see," said Jared. "So, all my father's assets are in a trust?"

"That's right."

"Do you know what the value of the assets might be?"

"His accountants will have to do a thorough evaluation for tax purposes, of course, but the best estimate we have right now is somewhere between $850 and $900 million."

It was much more than Paul had imagined.

For a moment, Jared was silent. "Who controls the trust?"

"There's one trustee, Father," said the attorney. "Your stepmother, Hannah Schümer Röhrbach."

"Right," said Jared.

Without saying another word, Jared tossed the phone to him and left the room. "Mr. Wright," he said. "It's Father Paul Fortis. Father Jared asked me to listen in. I'm afraid this comes as a big shock to him on top of his father's death. Couldn't you have waited?"

"I'm sorry, Father, but these were Mr. Röhrbach's instructions. He wanted his son to have no doubts about how the estate was to be handled. He is still sole trustee of what remains of the ten-million-dollar trust his father set up for him."

Paul heard the sound of breaking glass coming from the bedroom. "All right," he said. "I'd better go look after him. I'm concerned about how upset this has made him."

"I understand," said the attorney.

Please tell Father Jared again that I'm sorry for all of this. I regret having to be the bearer of that kind of news."

When Paul returned to the kitchen, Jared's food was untouched. was in the

bedroom sitting on the edge of the bed staring straight ahead, his face pale.

"That bastard," he said. "That fucking bastard."

"I'm so sorry," Paul said. "I didn't know about any of this. I don't know what to say." Paul realized that creating the trust was Kurt's way of making sure his wife was taken care of for the rest of her life, and not an intentional slap at his son. But Kurt had underestimated Jared's hatred for his stepmother.

"What broke?"

The lamp. I threw that goddam locket and knocked the lamp over. You want to clean it up for me?"

I might as well. He's in no mood to do it. The lamp by the window lay in shards on the floor. He grabbed the little wastebasket they kept beside the desk and got down on his hands and knees. So as not to cut himself, he picked up the sharp pieces one by one and dropped them into the trash. When he retrieved the crumpled lampshade, he saw the locket lying open where it had landed. He picked it up and examined it. The force of the impact must have dislodged the back of the case, and it was hanging open, displaying two additional photos. He'd never seen a four-photo locket before.

The photos in the rear compartment were of different woman and man. The woman was a much-younger Hannah. She was wearing her hair in the same braided fashion as her mother in the photo on the front side. Her face was much too lined and care-worn for a woman of her age. The man's picture was opposite Hannah's. He was middle-aged and, although dressed up for the photo, his clothes were ill-fitted. He had dark, wavy hair and a full beard. But it was the man's eyes that captured Paul's attention. They were piercing and expressive. Paul was certain that he'd never seen that man before, yet there was something familiar about him: the eyes, the hair. He wondered if this might be Hannah's ill-fated husband, Max. It made sense. Who else would share the locket with Hannah and her parents?

Paul carried it over to Jared. "Look at this, will you?" He held it out to him.

"What?" he snipped. He glanced at the photos lying open in Paul's hand. Expressions of curiosity, recognition, and contempt passed across Jared's face in rapid succession. He pushed Paul's hand away. "Get rid of it," he said. He scanned the room. He was shaking. "I'm done with this. They can burn in Hell for all I care."

Paul closed the locket and slipped it into his pocket. "What are you going to do?"

Jared shook his head. "I don't know. I have to think. I can't do anything right now." He lay back on the bed. "Why do those two people have to keep messing up my life? Even when he's dead, he can still do this to me." He pounded the mattress with his fists, then he raised himself on his elbows. "There's something you can do for me. I need you to get over to the Granada and pick up Eliza so you can stop Sullivan from fucking me over."

"Are you sure you don't want to handle it yourself?" Paul asked. "It's important."

"Do I look like I'm in any condition to meet with the bishop?"

"True," Paul said. "What will you do in the meantime?"

"I don't know. You take care of Eliza and the bishop, and I'll try to figure out what's next."

Paul went into the bathroom to shower. He was afraid Jared would do something stupid, but nothing he could say to him would help the situation. He had to accept that the man he loved was an adult and would have to take responsibility for his own decisions. He finished dressing and got ready to leave. Jared sat on the bed with his head down. "Will you be all right?"

"I guess so." He looked up. "Don't worry about me. Just do what you can to help Eliza. I'll see you later."

"Okay. Just be careful and remember that I love you." He hugged Jared and gave him a kiss.

Jared hung on to him for a while, then gave him a pat on the rump. "Get going. It's almost nine. She'll be waiting for you. She is nothing if not punctual."

Paul headed out the door and was soon driving up to the hotel. Sure enough, Eliza stood outside, waiting for him as he pulled up to the curb. He got out and opened the passenger door for her. "Good morning," he said.

She gave him a pointed look. "How is he?"

"Not all that well, I'm afraid," Paul said. "He got more bad news this morning, and it almost put him over the edge. He's putting on a brave front, but I know him too well. He's a mess inside. Sorry to be so blunt, but since you seem to be his best friend up in Tres Robles, I thought you should know."

"Thanks for your candor," she said. "I appreciate it."

It took a couple of minutes to drive to the chancery, but Eliza fiddled with her purse and accounting binders the entire way. As they got out of Paul's car, he said, "Hey—there's no need to be nervous. I told you yesterday, the bishop's an easy person to talk to."

"I can't help it," she said. "I've never done anything like this before."

"Why don't we go to my office and review what you're going to tell him, just to put you at ease."

She smiled. "Thank you. I'd appreciate that."

Paul led her into his office, and she sat down, gripping the accounting binders to her chest. He sat opposite. "Now, what will you be showing the bishop?"

She laid the binders open on the desk and went over some of the details.

He questioned her on some points, and the more she concentrated on explaining the data to him, the more relaxed she became.

The hour was up before she knew it. "Time to go," he said. "How do you feel now?"

"Already?" She looked at her watch. "Thank you for that, Father. I feel much more confident now. I think I'm ready."

They stood up, and he helped her gather her papers. She followed him to the bishop's office next door, and Paul rapped at the door and stuck his head inside. The bishop was sitting in one of the side chairs and Roger Spellman was on the sofa.

"Are you ready for us?" Paul asked.

"Yes, of course," said the bishop. "Come in. We were waiting for you."

Paul led Eliza in, and the bishop and Roger stood to greet her.

"It's so nice to meet you, Mrs. Roberts," the bishop said. "Welcome to the chancery office. Please sit down." They settled themselves in the comfortable chairs. "Why don't you put your binders here on the coffee table so we can all have a look at what you've brought."

Eliza sat and spread them out on the little table.

"Now tell us what this is all about." The bishop smiled.

"To be honest with you, Bishop," she began, "I've had a concern about the parish finances for a long time. I took over the books about six years ago. Even then, I saw that the parish receipts were diminishing, but there was no one I could talk to about it."

"What about the monsignor?" asked the bishop. "Did you approach him with your concerns?"

"It has always been difficult to talk with him about anything to do with finances. Whenever I tried, he would get angry with me and tell me it was nobody's business but his. After a while I gave up." The bishop and Roger exchanged knowing looks. "It just seemed like our weekly deposits were getting smaller and smaller as time went on." She looked at Paul, and he gave her a nod of encouragement.

"When Father Jared came to the parish, he noticed the same thing. When he asked about the finances, the monsignor got angry with him, too. There didn't seem to be anything we could do."

"Do you think the parishioners held back on their donations to show dissatisfaction with the parish or the pastor?" asked the bishop. "I know Monsignor Sullivan is not the easiest man to get along with."

"That's just it, Bishop. There was no way to tell. We can't see any of the records. The monsignor allowed only two people to count the collections and then they turned everything over to him. All he ever let me see was the bank receipts after he made the deposits. He wouldn't even let me see the bank statements."

"And you suspected something wasn't right?" he asked.

"Neither Father Jared nor I wanted to believe anything was wrong, but you know how it is: when you're kept from knowing the facts, it's human nature to wonder why."

"So, what happened to bring you here now?"

"One of the two people who counted the collections got sick in January and Father Jared got a friend of ours to replace him. On Sundays, they make a tally sheet of all the money in the collections, and it goes into a bag with the money to be turned over to the monsignor. Our friend secretly made copies of the tally sheets and passed them on to me. Here they are for every week since she started helping with the counting." She passed a small stack of papers to the bishop. "And," she went on, "I've stapled a copy of the deposit receipts to the back. You'll see that the difference between the money they counted, and the money deposited every time is about four hundred and fifty dollars. Since our average weekly deposit is less than two thousand dollars, that represents a large percentage of our receipts."

The bishop scowled as he reviewed week after week of receipts, passing them on to Roger, one at a time. "I don't like the looks of this," he said. "You were right to bring this to my attention."

"There's something else, Bishop," she told him. "You know, we've had a lot of water damage in the church. We're going to have part of the roof replaced, and it's going to cost around ninety thousand dollars."

"Yes," said the bishop. "I've seen the estimates."

"The monsignor took me aside yesterday and told me that all the invoices for the work were to be given to him, and no one else was to see them, especially not Father Jared. He said he would take care of submitting them to the diocese himself and seeing that the contractor was paid."

"Really?" said the bishop.

"Yes. We still don't want to believe that the monsignor is doing anything wrong, but we don't understand why he's so afraid of Father Jared knowing anything."

"What do you think, Roger?" said the bishop.

"There is a strong set of circumstantial evidence here that would suggest something untoward may be going on. Mrs. Roberts is right that we need to have clearer evidence of wrongdoing before we go accusing anyone of anything. Let me ask you, Mrs. Roberts, could you send me copies of your parish books for, say, the last five years, as well as weekly or monthly copies of the books going forward?"

"Why yes, I certainly could," she said.

"How about making copies of the construction invoices before they get to the monsignor?"

"If I can—of course."

"I often use a forensic accounting firm with some of my cases and, with the bishop's permission, I'd like to put them to work reviewing everything. We can also work with our insurers, so we'll have full transparency about the construction costs from this end. If something's not right, we'll be able to find it out with certainty, or at least put everyone's mind at ease. What do you think, Bishop?"

"Let's do it," he said. "If it costs the diocese and we're wrong, it'll still be worth it to settle our suspicions."

Roger Spellman handed Eliza his card. "When you get a chance, please send me your contact information at home. We'll coordinate our approach going forward. Of course, I don't need to tell you we must keep this in strictest confidence among the people in this room—and Father Röhrbach, of course."

"Thank you, Mrs. Roberts, for all your hard work," said the bishop, standing. "Roger will take good care of you. I'll keep close tabs on the situation myself. And, if you need anything else or have any other concerns, please don't hesitate to contact me." He asked Eliza and Roger to wait outside the office so he could speak to Paul alone.

"Just duck into my office," Paul said to Eliza. "I'll be right with you."

"Certainly, Father. No problem." Eliza followed Roger out of the bishop's office and shut the door behind them.

"How's Jared doing?" said the bishop.

"Not too well, I'm afraid," Paul said. "His father died before he got to see him, and then this morning, his father's attorney called to tell him that the bulk of the estate is going to his stepmother whom he despises. He's a wreck."

"Tell him I'm praying for him and to take as much time as he needs to get himself settled. I'll call Terry Sullivan myself and make sure there'll be no problems for him from the parish. Have him call me when he's feeling up to it."

"Thanks very much," he said. Paul left the office and got Eliza. Together, they drove back to the Granada.

"You were right, Father," she said to him. "I think I got my message across to him."

"There's no doubt about it," said Paul. "You were wonderful."

"Will you be able to join me for lunch?" she asked.

"I would love to," he said. "I'll need to drop you at the hotel and go back to the apartment to check on Father Jared. I'll meet you in the hotel restaurant in about an hour."

The apartment was very quiet when Paul arrived home. The breakfast dishes had all been cleared away and the kitchen was spotless. Paul called out for Jared, but there was no response. On the kitchen table, he found a note in Jared's handwriting.

Paul—

I had to get away from here. Couldn't stand it any longer. Please give Eliza a ride back to Tres Robles tomorrow, since you're going to Cambria anyway. Sorry if it's out of your way. Her hotel is taken care of. I'll be in touch later. Thanks.

—Jared

He read the note several times, then crumpled it up.

As usual. When the going gets tough, Jared gets out of town.

Chapter 23

Friday, April 20, 2012

Tony lounged in the back of a cab heading out of West Hollywood. Business was steady—and good. He was on his way to see one of his regular clients, the kind that made doing business easy. When his pocket vibrated, he shifted to one side to pull out his phone. He was surprised to see it was Jared. Fridays were his day off, but Tony hadn't expected to hear from him today.

"Hey, Tony. You busy?"

"Always. Why?"

"Any chance you could blow this one off and meet me at the condo later tonight?"

"You bet!" Tony still got excited at the prospect of spending time with him.

"Thanks, Tony. I owe you."

"For nothing," said Tony. "Anything for my Jared." He hung up and called his client who was disappointed, but Tony knew he'd be back.

"Hey, man," he said to the driver, "change of plans. Take me to 851 North King's Road West Hollywood instead, okay?"

"It's your dime." The cab was just coming up on the 101, so he turned around and headed west. Rush hour was well underway, so it was slow and go all the way to the condo.

Tony had some time before Jared would arrive, so he made the best of it by making sure everything sparkled. The place was spacious and elegant with a Stackstone wall and fireplace down one side of the living room, and sliders opening onto a balcony on the other. He kept everything pretty neat, but he wanted it perfect for his man.

When Jared arrived, his face was haggard and drawn and his eyes were puffy and bloodshot. He looked as though he'd just come off a week-long bender. Tony rushed over to him, throwing his arms around him. "What the hell happened to you?"

"Everything," said Jared. "I'll tell you over a drink."

"Let's get you out of those clothes."

While Jared got comfortable, Tony poured them both vodka tonics. Once they were settled on the couch, Tony said, "Now, lover boy, what's going on with you? You look like hell."

"I don't want to talk about it," said Jared. "It's been two of the worst days of my life."

"That's your choice, man, but you know you're going to tell me sooner or later."

"Oh, damn it. All right." He told Tony about missing his father by fifteen minutes.

"I feel so guilty about it. I didn't find out he was sick until two weeks ago. I thought he'd have a couple of more months. It all happened so suddenly."

"Damn!" said Tony.

"That's not all." Jared took a long drink and told him about the estate. "He left everything to my stepmother, the woman I can't stand. I got nothing. Zip. Zilch."

Tony stared at him. "Man, I don't know what to say." He put his arm around Jared's shoulder and pulled him close. "What are you gonna do?"

"I don't know. I thought I'd come spend a lost weekend with you. You're just the man who can take my mind off everything."

"That's me, all right." Tony laughed. "Escape is my business." He kissed Jared on the forehead. "Tell you what, Baby. Let's just let Tony take care of you for a while."

Tony grabbed Jared by both hands and led him into their bedroom. He eased him down on the bed and said, "Stay there." He went into the bathroom and filled the Jacuzzi tub with hot water. Back in the bedroom, Tony climbed onto the bed. Turning Jared onto his stomach, he climbed on top of him, straddling his thighs, and began kneading the muscles of his shoulders and back.

After a few minutes, Tony pulled Jared into the bathroom. He adjusted the water temperature and said, "Get in." Then he started the jets. Jared slid down into the foaming water until only his face showed. He closed his eyes and sighed. Tony got a washcloth, soaked it in cold water, and laid it across Jared's forehead and eyes. Then he set their sound system to play a smooth jazz station. On his way out, he dimmed the bathroom lights and said, "I'll be right back. Don't go anywhere." Jared just smiled.

Tony went into the kitchen and poured each of them a glass of pinot noir. Jared smiled as soon as he caught scent of the wine and reached a hand out of the water for the glass. Tony handed it to him. "You relax, Babe. Dinner is coming." He went back into the kitchen and, before long, there were two filet mignons broiling in the oven, broccolini and carrots steaming on the stove, and Portobello mushrooms sautéing in a frying pan.

By the time dinner was ready, Jared looked more like his old self. Tony had set an elegant table for them with candles and good china, glassware, and utensils. The broiled meat filled the condo with the irresistible aroma of a fine steakhouse. They sat down and Tony raised his wine glass. "To happier and more prosperous days!" he said.

"I'll drink to that." Jared clinked his glass with Tony's and they both drank. Then Jared raised his glass again. "To my dad—God bless him." His face darkened. "And to Hannah—may she get everything she deserves."

The two men ate and talked about Tony's business. He had turned a nice property deal that had made him a profit and put his real estate company in a good position. It was the biggest deal he had closed so far that year. Then, Jared told him about how he thought his boss was ripping off the company and how he was taking the evidence to the regional manager.

Tony encouraged him to talk about it, if for no other reason than that it took Jared's mind off the family matters. Though after a couple of glasses of wine, his spirits were much less likely to take another tumble. Tony did his best to make certain the touchy topics never came back up.

"How about we do the club?" Jared said. "I'm in the mood to let off some steam."

"That's works for me," said Tony. "I'll clean up here. We can get dressed and head out, have some fun, and still make an early night of it. I don't want to wear you out so you're too tired to give me some of *that*."

Jared laughed. "Too tired? Not a chance."

It wasn't long before a cab had dropped them off at the club where they had first met. The place wasn't crowded yet, but the music was hot and there was already enough eye candy out on the dance floor to keep them both entertained. Half the people there recognized Tony—which was a testament to the success of his business. There were new prospects at the club every time he showed up, and he was there almost every night. He didn't mind coming there with Jared, because Jared had so much fun every time they partied there.

Tony wasn't going to let the music and the crowd go to waste, so he led Jared out into the middle of the dancefloor. They danced furiously, ecstatically. By the time they stopped and looked at each other, panting and dripping with sweat, with that look that said, *"Enough!"* almost two hours had gone by. They clung to each other, half-staggering to the bar, and pulled up a couple of barstools. In seconds, Cody stood across the bar from them. Tonight, he hadn't bothered with the tank top, and his smooth, muscular chest and beefy arms were already showing the bronze effects of the warm spring sunshine.

"The usual, guys?"

"Sure," said Tony. "I'm off tonight, so don't skimp."

"Who, me?" said Cody with a wink. "Never." Their drinks appeared in a flash. Hot and sweaty as they were, the two guys downed their drinks like water. They turned to watch the gyrating mass of man flesh on the dancefloor, and, by the time they had turned back around, there were two fresh drinks in front of them. That was another advantage of coming to this club on his day off: Cody never let them go dry.

Jared grabbed Tony by the arm and dragged him back onto the floor. He pulled off his shirt, and Tony took his cue from his partner and did the same. They got into it, both loving the look and feel of each other's bodies glistening in the laser lights. Before long, Tony was getting tired and, to be honest, a little drunk, so he cut short their dancing and led them back to their stools. No sooner had they sat down but, thanks to Cody, fresh drinks appeared. Tony's head was getting a little fuzzy, but *Fuck it, I'm off tonight.*

Guys on the dancefloor stole glances at Jared and him with obvious envy. And why not? Jared was hot and handsome, and he seemed to enjoy the attention too.

But then something changed. Jared's face went pale, and he stared past the dancefloor to the other side of the room. Tony followed his gaze to a tall, good-looking young man about their age with sandy hair going every-which-way and piercing blue eyes staring straight at them.

Without any warning, Jared raced across the dancefloor. By the time he reached the opposite side, the blond guy had vanished into the crowd. Jared stood there looking all around him, but to no avail. Eventually he gave up and wended his way back across the club to Tony.

"Somebody you know?" Tony asked.

"Yeah." Jared was still scanning the crowd.

"From the church?" Tony dropped the bomb and waited to see if it would explode.

"No. From school." Jared picked up his drink and sipped it absent-mindedly, never taking his eyes off the sea of bodies surrounding him.

Suddenly, he stiffened. He turned back to Tony. "What did you just say?"

"Nothing, why?" said Tony, feigning innocence.

"You *know*?" Jared stared at him.

"Of course, I know." He shrugged. "I have to know my partner. It's good for business."

"How did you find out?" He was looking at him clear-eyed.

Tony tapped the bar with one finger. "I told you: I read the papers. The *Times* thought your father's death was big news. You didn't read the article? And the obituary? You should have. They were so interesting, *Father*."

"I was going to tell you," Jared stammered. "Really, I was."

"Sure," Tony said. "It's not good to keep secrets from your partner, and even worse to lie to him."

"I'm sorry, Tony. I didn't know how you'd take it, me being a priest and all."

"You never gave me the chance, did you?" Tony took another gulp of his drink. "What else haven't you told me?"

"About what?" Jared's whole body looked tense. "I haven't lied to you. I just haven't told you everything about me. What's left that you want to know about? I'll tell you anything."

Will you? I seriously doubt that. "Well, for starters, you never told me there was another you running around out there."

Jared's eyebrows came together. Then he grimaced. "Oh. You mean my twin brother? What did the paper say about him?"

"It said his name is Justin and he's living abroad. Does he look like you?"

"We're identical." He gazed across the room. "Your old table is empty. Can we sit over there out of the noise and talk?"

"Sure," said Tony. They picked up their drinks and sat down at Tony's old office. "So, where's your brother now?"

"I don't know. Nobody in our family does."

"You're telling me he just disappeared?" Tony frowned into his drink. He should have known things were too good to be true with this guy.

"Sort of." Jared took a deep breath. "It's a long story."

Tony set his drink on the table with a little more force than he'd intended. "I got nothing else going on. Talk."

Jared shifted as though the chair was uncomfortable. "Several years ago, there was this late-night party back home in Cambria, and then a bad accident. A hit-and-run. Justin's car was totaled, but he wasn't hurt. An old man was in the other car. He got T-boned, and he was killed." Jared paused. "There was an open vodka bottle in Justin's car."

Tony whistled. "Oh damn."

"Damn is right. The police went looking for him. They were going to charge him with hit-and-run and vehicular manslaughter, but Justin left the country before they could track him down."

"And you expect me to believe he's never contacted anyone in the family to let you know where he is?"

"He hasn't," Jared said. "He's afraid they'll use us to get to him. So, for all practical purposes, I might as well be an only child." He rested his hands on the table. "That's the story of my brother."

"And the fellow you went chasing after just now—he's a friend of yours?"

"Sort of. I didn't want him to see me here with you."

Tony narrowed his eyes at him. "Then why chase him?"

Jared hesitated, taking a long sip of his drink. "To tell him—to ask him—so that he wouldn't..."

"You've got someone up in San Luis who'd be upset if he knew about me." It wasn't a question. It was obvious that was what this was about.

"Yeah." Jared stared down at what was left of the drink cupped in his hands.

"You know, partner, it doesn't matter a rat's ass to me. I'm happy with what you and I have going on here. It's business with benefits; but I gotta tell you, I don't like secrets. Never have. Not good for business. You want to keep secrets, that's your deal, just don't keep them from me. Agreed?" Tony stared at Jared until he raised his eyes and looked directly at him.

"Yeah," said Jared sheepishly.

"Good. Now, let's go home and fuck—*Father.*"

Chapter 24

Jared stood before the altar in Our Lady of Perpetual Help church, looking up at the bright mid-June sky. The sanctuary was a maze of scaffolding, leaving just enough room around the free-standing altar to celebrate Mass. The work had crawled along over the two months the roof had been under construction, but now large beams crossed overhead. Rafters rose above them, and then a wooden skeleton to carry the new half-dome that would extend over the entire sanctuary. For now, the superstructure was open to the sky, so the parish was praying there wouldn't be any unexpected summer rainstorms. Plastic was supposed to be available to cover the opening in case of bad weather, but the area was so large that no covering would be adequate. José and his crew were adding beams to the structure, punctuating their work chatter with unrhythmic bangs from the pneumatic nail gun. When José caught sight of Jared, he stopped what he was doing and slipped handily down the scaffolds.

"Father," he said. "Just the man I want to see. How does it look?"

"Looks great from what I can see. No more problems, I hope."

"No," he said. "None at all. We didn't think we'd have to remove the cross beams, but you saw how rotten they were. Now that we've got the new ones in place, everything's going according to plan. I promise you; this new section will be much stronger than the old superstructure ever was."

"That's amazing," said Jared. "I don't know what we'd do without you."

"I'm sure you'd manage somehow," José said, laughing. "Speaking of getting along without me, I'll be working on another job tomorrow morning. The guys know what to do. There shouldn't be any trouble, but just in case, they've got my cell number. I won't be far away."

"If you say so, José. I trust you."

"I'd better get back to work. We're a man short today, and I don't want to give them any excuse to slow down. The sooner we get a roof on over here, the sooner everybody will breathe easier."

Jared crossed in front of the sanctuary and exited out the side door. As soon as he set foot in the office, Eliza called him.

"Father Jared, can I see you for a moment?"

She had been in the kitchen chatting with Yolanda. She emerged from the Private door into the office. He couldn't tell from the look on her face whether he should be excited or upset. She followed him into his office and shut the door, looking like a committed conspirator.

"José just gave me these invoices for the monsignor." She held up a white business envelope with *Monsignor Sullivan* written across the front in a draftsman's printing. The envelope wasn't sealed, so she opened it and pulled out a wad of pages folded in thirds. It was an invoice from Hernandez Construction Co. made out to the parish. It contained an itemized list of materials, supplies, and labor hours for the work on the church. The heading at the top of the page said, "Second Accounting."

"Let me make copies of them, Father," said Eliza. "I'll make two of everything—one for us that I'll keep at home, and one that we can mail to Mr. Spellman."

She wasn't even out the door before Jared opened a second batch of papers that had been folded separately. "Hold on," he said.

Eliza stopped short and came back to his desk. Unlike the other pages, this set of invoices from Hernandez Construction Co. was made out to Monsignor Sullivan himself. The address was unfamiliar: 5668 Diablo Hills Road. Jared recognized the name. It was a couple of miles outside of Tres Robles, where there were few developed properties.

"What do you make of this?"

"I have no idea, Father," she said. "I can't remember ever seeing that address before."

176

"Look at this list of materials. There's wire and speakers and audio and video components and a big TV. This is high-end stuff." He handed her the second set of papers. "Copy these, too. I'm thinking Roger will find this interesting."

"Absolutely," she said and left the room.

Jared opened his laptop and fired up Google Earth. When it was up and running, he entered the address on Diablo Hills Road. Starting from space, the image on his screen zoomed down to northern California and focused in closer until it pictured a large house under construction. Jared had no idea how long ago that aerial photo had been taken, but if they were installing audio-visual equipment, that meant it was nearer completion than the image suggested. He made out two vehicles parked in that yard. One was a pick-up truck with a rack over the cab—very much like the one that belonged to José Hernandez. The other vehicle was a charcoal-colored compact car—perhaps a Volkswagen Jetta—like the one the monsignor drove.

Eliza finished her copying and brought the paperwork back to Jared.

"Look at this," he said. She came around and looked at the screen. "It's the address on Diablo Hills Road."

"Nice house," she said.

"Do you recognize those cars?"

"Well, I'll be..."

"It looks like the good monsignor is building himself quite a house." Jared refolded the pages precisely the way they had been and put them back into the envelope. He handed it to Eliza. "It'll be interesting to see what he does with these."

She sat down. "This looks very bad for him, doesn't it?"

"It does," Jared replied. "But, as you've reminded me, this is still all circumstantial evidence. It may well give Roger the leads he needs to find some evidence, though. Regardless, I wouldn't bet on the monsignor's innocence."

"That's what I suspected." Eliza looked downcast, as though disappointed the monsignor appeared to be as bad as they'd feared. She was a better person than he was.

"We make terrific conspirators," he said with a smile, unable to conceal his glee.

"I suppose we do at that, Father."

The next morning, Jared watched as Eliza went into the church just ahead of the monsignor. She had promised to keep him busy in there for a while. As soon as the pastor closed the door behind him, Jared jumped into his Porsche and took off for Diablo Hills. It didn't take long to get there. The house on Google Earth had been under construction, but this version looked almost finished. He pulled into the driveway and, too late, spotted José's truck parked off to one side. Beside the truck was José. *Damn.*

"Good morning, Father," he shouted.

Well, there was no going back now. He parked near the pickup and got out. "Good morning yourself."

"What brings you out here? You come to take a look at this place? I didn't think the monsignor wanted anyone to know about it."

José didn't seem to be confronting him. He must have thought the monsignor had changed his mind and told Jared about the house. He decided to play along. "Yes. I was in the neighborhood and thought I'd drive by. I was wondering what it looked like. I see it's nearly finished. It's looking good."

"Thanks, Father." José's chest puffed with obvious pride. "I've done all the work on it myself. I thought I was a perfectionist, but the monsignor has me beat. He knows what he wants and by God, one way or another, he gets it."

"Did it take you long?"

"Almost six years, so far," José said. "It was slow going at times because the monsignor was short on funds."

I bet he was.

"So, we did a little here, a little there. But he's been pushing to get it finished, so I've been spending a lot of time here."

In his head, Jared calculated the dates of the missing funds. The monsignor must have siphoned off church funds to finish his dream home. *We've got him. We've GOT him.* "Is the interior almost done?"

"For sure. And it's nice. Come on, Father, let me show you around."

"I don't have a lot of time today." Jared made a show of glancing at his watch. "But I'd love a quick walk-around."

"Follow me." José unlocked the paneled oak front door and led Jared into an elegant foyer, graced with a curving stairway to the second floor and a large chandelier hanging from the high ceiling in the center of the room. As soon as he saw the interior, Jared knew his suspicions were true. All they would need would be for Roger Spellman and his forensic accounting team to establish the facts. He would give them all the help he could. He slipped his cell phone out of his pocket and, whenever José's back was turned, took pictures of everything he could.

José led Jared from room to room, each one finished in extraordinary detail. Jared snapped photos of the stainless appliances and granite counter tops in the kitchen, the crystal chandelier in the dining room, the oversized fireplace in the living room, and the study's built-in bookcases. Then José took him upstairs. The master suite had a granite-tiled shower in the bathroom and an enormous walk-in closet. There were two guest bedrooms, each with its own ensuite bath.

As they wound their way back to the foyer, Jared slipped his phone back into his pocket. "Thank you so much," he said. "You've been very kind." He leaned in toward José and said, "Can you keep a secret?"

"Of course."

"We're planning a big surprise for the monsignor—a sort of housewarming—and if he knew I'd already seen the house, it would spoil the surprise. Can you maybe not mention it?"

José's forehead crinkled. "You know the monsignor doesn't like surprises, don't you?"

"This is a special surprise. Even the bishop will be involved. It's important that the monsignor doesn't find out."

"Well, if you say so, I won't say a word to anyone. You have my promise."

"I have to say, the workmanship I've seen here today is exceptional. You're quite the craftsman."

"Thank you, Father. I respect a person who can recognize fine workmanship."

While they talked, Jared led them to where his car was parked. He said goodbye to José and headed back to the parish. True to her word, Eliza had kept the monsignor so preoccupied after Mass that he hadn't even noticed Jared's absence—not that he ever paid much attention to Jared. Sometimes, being invisible had its benefits.

Before long, the monsignor hurried to his car and left, telling Eliza he was off to visit a shut-in, but Jared had a pretty good idea where he went on these excursions—especially on days like today when José was working there.

Once the monsignor had driven off, Jared called Eliza into his office.

"Did you see it?" she asked.

Jared was bursting with excitement. "Not only did I see it, but José was there. He assumed I knew all about it. He's been building it for the monsignor for almost six years, and he's very proud of his work, so he was anxious to show it to me. He should be proud of it. It's beautiful."

Her eyes widened. "You got to see inside?"

"He showed me around the whole place. Nothing but the best for our monsignor." He took out his phone and showed her the photos, her mouth falling open in shock.

She looked up at him with an expression of utter disbelief. "It's so much worse than I thought," she said. "How could he do that to us?" There were tears in her eyes. "What's wrong with him that he could be so... so evil?"

For the first time, Jared wondered whether taking her into his confidence had been a good idea. The faith of this sophisticated, yet genuinely good woman had been shaken to the core.

"Eliza." He took her hand. "Priests are human. They have the same limitations as everyone else. The amazing thing is not that he's a bad priest. What's amazing is that God still works through him, and through all his bad priests."

Eliza was silent. The pain and sorrow faded from her face. "'Forgive them, they know not what they do.'" They were the words Jesus had spoken from the Cross.

"Exactly," Jared said. He'd always believed people's faith in God had to be stronger than their faith in His instruments. It was the only way he himself could go on being a priest.

"You're right, of course," she said. "I need to hold onto my sense of compassion, even while I'm trying to fix what's wrong. It's hard."

Jared laughed. "I didn't say it was easy."

She put a gentle hand on his. "Thank you for talking this through with me. You're a wise young man."

When she sighed, Jared knew she'd be all right, and that was important to him.

"What do we do now?" she said.

Jared clasped his hands on his desk. "I think we've done all we can. I'll email these pictures to Roger. That should give him enough to move his investigation forward. At least he'll know where to look to find the money trail—assuming there is one. All we can do is keep our eyes and ears open for anything new until he comes up with something."

Eliza stood up. "Business as usual, then. I'm not sure how I'll pretend there's nothing out of the ordinary going on."

"You can do it," Jared said. "Chances are, it won't be for much longer."

After she left his office, Jared phoned Paul and filled him in on what he'd found out. Just as he was about to close off, Paul said, "I almost forgot. I have news, too."

"Yes?" said Jared.

"Jeff is coming back to stay with us again this summer. He'll be here this weekend."

Jared realized he was scribbling so hard on a piece of paper he had ripped it. He hadn't seen or spoken to Jeff since the near-miss at the club. Despite his misgivings, he forced a positive lilt into his voice. "So, I guess I'll be seeing both of you this weekend."

"That'll be great. Will I pick you up at the airport Thursday night, as usual?"

"Sure. Save some of that hot stuff for me," Jared said, though to his ear it sounded forced.

He hung up the phone and let out a long sigh. He had hoped to avoid a confrontation with Jeff, but he couldn't put it off any longer. He scrolled through his contact list, his finger hesitating over the telephone icon before he pressed it.

"Hey," he said when Jeff answered. "I felt like I needed to call you."

The silence that followed was just long enough to feel awkward. "You mean about seeing me in LA?"

"So, that *was* you in the club." As if he didn't know.

"'Fraid so," said Jeff.

"Listen, whatever you saw there, it was nothing."

"Really?" said Jeff. "That's not what it looked like to me. You and that Tony make quite the couple."

Jared felt trapped. He wanted to hang up but couldn't think of a single thing to say to get off the phone.

"Listen," Jeff said. "I don't care what you do or who you do it with. That's your business. But if I thought you were hurting Paul, I'd make it my business."

"I'm not sure I'm following you," said Jared.

"Paul already knows something's going on, 'cause you're down in LA all the time instead of spending time with him. He hasn't said anything about it, which means he has his reasons. Maybe he's willing to put up with your bullshit just to keep you around. I don't know. That's not what I would do, but you're his business, not mine. I'm not going to make any trouble. Unless you hurt him. Then all bets are off."

"Understood." Jared exhaled. "Thank you, Jeff."

"Don't thank me. Thank Paul for putting up with you. Oh, and one more thing..."

"Yes?"

"I'm not going to lie for you. If Paul asks, I'll tell him what I know."

"Fair enough."

There was another awkward silence on the line. Then Jeff said, "Who the hell are you, dude? You're sure not the man I thought you were."

Jared hung up, Jeff's question echoing in a hollow corner of his heart.

Chapter 25

Friday, August 17, 2012

Monsignor Terrence Sullivan was annoyed. No, he was more than annoyed. He was angry. For one thing, he saw no reason to have to drive all the way down to San Luis Obispo just to talk with the bishop. If it were important, the bishop could phone him. If it wasn't, it could wait until the bishop's next visit to the parish. But what angered him the most was being ordered to come down to the chancery without being told the reason. He was nobody's lackey. To top it off, the bishop hadn't even had the courtesy to call him himself. He had that new young secretary of his do it. The whole thing was downright insulting, and he intended to let Bishop Mickleson know as much.

He pulled his car into an empty space in the chancery parking lot and turned the engine off. It was warm, even for mid-August, and his air conditioning hadn't worked in years. He fastened on his Roman collar and checked his watch. He was already ten minutes late, but it served the bishop right for making him drive all this way. He climbed the chancery steps and went through the double doors. A young priest he didn't recognize was sitting in the waiting area. When he spotted him, the priest stood and came toward him.

"Monsignor Sullivan?"

"Yes. And you are...?"

"Paul Fortis, the bishop's secretary. We spoke on the phone."

"Oh, yes, so we did. You know, young man, the next time you order someone to drive two hours, you might have the decency to tell him why."

"Monsignor, please take a seat," Paul said, with what the monsignor considered icy civility. "The bishop will see you shortly."

Without waiting for the monsignor to reply, he turned and headed down the hall, leaving the monsignor alone and fuming.

The monsignor checked his watch, becoming more outraged by the minute. He couldn't stand to be treated so disrespectfully. He had given his whole life to this diocese and, bishop or not, Mickleson was a newcomer from some poverty-stricken slum in Ohio. Sullivan had been suspicious of the man from the beginning. The first time he'd encountered the bishop, he had determined to have as little to do with him as possible. Since then, he'd managed to avoid all the clergy gatherings—the meetings, the retreats, and especially, the Chrism Mass dinner for priests of the diocese on Wednesday of Holy Week.

He heard footsteps and looked up. The bishop's secretary was back.

"The bishop will see you now," the young upstart said. "Please follow me." Again, without waiting for an answer, the fellow turned and started back down the hall.

The monsignor struggled to keep up with him. "You could at least wait for me."

When they reached the door to the bishop's office, the young priest rapped a couple of times, opened the door, and ushered the monsignor in, closing the door behind him. What the monsignor saw made him stop short.

The bishop stood by his chair at the head of the conference table. Sitting side by side at the back of the table were Monsignor Yates, Sister Margaret Thompson, Roger Spellman, and a young man he didn't recognize. No one smiled. In fact, they were all staring at him. A warning light flashed in his mind. He was so used to operating in his own domain that he had ignored the question of accountability. *What do they know?*

As he stood there fielding their cold looks, facing what looked for all the world like a jury of his peers, he began to feel like the newly ordained priest he'd once been. The memories of those first years came flooding back—how he'd been made to feel like an unsophisticated country boy by his fellow clergy. With them came the feelings of helplessness and shame that marked his first years in the ministry. Once again, he experienced his struggle with the poverty he'd brought with him to the ministry, the dependence on the generosity of others to drive him around for years before he could afford his own car. He felt the isolation of being stuck at the rectory while his peers took days off and went on vacation. His stomach churned as he felt the sting of being laughed at and made fun of behind his back. Every slight, every insult he had endured through his entire career, came rushing back to him.

With all those feelings came something else he hadn't experienced in a long time: the memory of an idealistic young man committed to overcoming all obstacles in his way, answering the call to be of service to God and mankind like the first disciples. There remained traces of the vision he'd once held so close, of leaving everything behind to follow the Lord who would someday say to him, "Well done, good and faithful servant." But as he looked at the people in that room, he realized that dream would never come true, and the bravado that had kept him so unassailable for so many years melted away.

"Please, Monsignor," said the bishop, "sit down."

Sullivan took a seat at the table opposite the others, while the bishop sat at the head.

"I know you know Monsignor Yates and Sister Margaret," said the bishop. "I think you remember Roger Spellman, our attorney. You probably don't know Jeffrey Hensen. He's Roger's paralegal." Jeff nodded at the monsignor. "Do you have any idea why I called you here this morning?"

"No, Bishop, I don't," he lied.

The bishop sighed and shook his head. "Terry, we've all known for a long time that the finances at your parish are a mess. The diocese has been subsidizing you for years."

"We are a poor parish, Bishop," he said. "You knew that when you came to this diocese."

"Yes," said the bishop. "I did. All this time, the diocese has been trying to help you, not only by giving you assistance to meet your expenses, but also by providing you with programs to build your parish community. Instead of developing your resources, the parish situation has gotten worse over time."

"It takes money to run programs—money we haven't got."

"That's been your excuse for as long as I've known you," said the bishop in a sad tone.

"It's not an excuse," he said with a huff. "It's the truth."

"Is it?" said the bishop. "We thought for some time now that the problems at Our Lady of Perpetual Help ran deeper than just the poverty of its parishioners. That's why I insisted you take an associate against your wishes. I've tried sending someone to you—what, four times?—and I was fortunate this time that Father Röhrbach is a strong young man who will not be bullied. I asked him to report back to me regarding the situation at your parish."

Any thought he had of controlling himself blew up in a wave of anger. "You sent that snot-nosed kid to spy on me? How dare you?"

"How dare I?" said the bishop. "I think you better calm down and remember where you are and whom you're talking to."

The monsignor felt his face getting red, but he said nothing.

"Up until recently, you've been successful at keeping the details of the parish finances secret from everyone. But Father Röhrbach has found some serious discrepancies."

"Discrepancies?" the monsignor almost shouted in indignation. "You're taking the word of that sissy priest over mine?"

The bishop's eyebrows rose, and the monsignor noticed that the paralegal, some flunky or other, got a strange look on his face. Sullivan smiled; he'd hit gold.

"That's right," he said. "Your precious little spy is carrying on with a male prostitute in Los Angeles. I overheard their phone calls."

The bishop didn't flinch. "The discrepancies were serious enough that I turned them over to Roger for investigation." He nodded at the attorney, who opened a thick manila folder in front of him. The monsignor looked at him in stunned silence as his world collapsed around him.

"Monsignor," said Roger, "what we have here are the actual offertory tally sheets from January eighth of this year until this past weekend." He held up the slips of paper. "We also have the bank deposit receipts for the same period. The discrepancies over that entire period are consistent. Every week, there is evidence that four hundred and fifty dollars of the money collected was not deposited, and we know that all of the deposits were made by you personally."

"I always hold back some petty cash for unexpected expenses," said the monsignor. "There's nothing wrong with that."

The attorney folded his hands over the folder. "We have your parish books, and none of that money was ever recorded. That's a violation of federal law. In any case, up to that point, we had decided to give you the benefit of the doubt that this was an inadvertent omission. However, we did ask Father Röhrbach to continue being observant."

"Continue spying, you mean," said the monsignor.

"I said what I meant, Monsignor," Roger said. "By chance, Father Röhrbach came upon this invoice for work you're having done on a property outside of town." Roger held up a piece of paper.

The monsignor's throat tightened. He felt the trap closing in on him. "So, what?" he said with a bravado he no longer felt. "A lot of priests have their own houses. I'm getting old. I need somewhere to retire. There's no crime in that."

"Maybe not," said Roger, "but the level of work we've seen at that house seems inconsistent with the salary of the pastor of the poorest parish in the diocese."

"Seen?" said the monsignor. "What have you seen?"

"This." Roger pulled out several photographs and spread them out on the table. The monsignor felt the blood drain from his face.

"This is your house, isn't it?"

The monsignor didn't say a word.

"Based on this circumstantial evidence, we asked the court to subpoena your bank statements for the last six years. We've been able to trace the cash deposits and disbursements to Hernandez Construction Company for that entire period. We can now show conclusively that you have embezzled a total of $132,616 to date."

The monsignor's mouth felt like it was stuck together. He couldn't have spoken even if he wanted to—but he didn't want to.

"When the water damage to the church occurred," Roger went on, "we decided to wait before confronting you about the collections to see what you would do. We were informed that you gave instructions that Father Röhrbach was not to see the invoices. He was nonetheless able to forward us copies of the originals. We also alerted our insurers who provided us with the invoices you submitted for payment. We've determined that you embezzled a further ten thousand dollars from fraudulent and doctored invoices, and that is insurance fraud. The total we've arrived at that you've taken from the parish and the diocese comes to $143,000."

"I...I..." The monsignor's hands were shaking so badly that he held them beneath the table.

"Terry, I'm going to give you a choice," the bishop said. "You can resign from the parish and deed the property to the diocese. We'll sell it and return the money you stole to the parish. Any money that's leftover you can keep."

"Or...?" said the monsignor.

"Or I will remove you as pastor, you can keep the house, the diocese will press charges, and you will go to prison."

"That's not much of a choice," the monsignor demurred. "I'll give you the property."

Roger pulled out two sets of papers. "Here are two documents you need to read and sign." He slid one across the table. "This one is the quit claim deed I had drawn up on the property and the contents. Sign there, and the property will be transferred to the diocese. You will receive the proceeds less the amount owing to the parish and the diocese within thirty days of the sale. You will agree not to visit the property between now and the registration of the deed. Any clothing or other personal items you've left there will be returned to you after we take possession of the property. Appliances and furniture will convey with the property."

He held up the second document. "This, Monsignor, is your letter of resignation as pastor of Our Lady of Perpetual Help parish."

Sister Margaret leaned across the table. "This is a serious offense you have committed, not only against the people of your parish, but against the diocese as a whole. You have violated the trust of the people you were ordained to serve. The bishop and I are agreed that your faculties for saying Mass, preaching, and hearing confessions are removed as of now. You are no longer permitted to function as a priest. Are we clear on this?"

"Yes, Sister, I understand." The monsignor's voice was as weak as milk. He reached into his breast pocket, pulled out his glasses, and put them on. With a shaking hand, he took the first document and signed it. Then he read the resignation letter. The full impact of what he'd done fell upon him like a crushing blow. The last of his bravado crumbled, and he began to weep. He had lost everything he had worked for these many years. But it was more than that. He wept for the innocent boy who had presented himself for ordination so long ago with dreams of heroic goodness. He put his signature on the bottom of the letter, and he was done.

"Thank you for making this easier on all of us, Terry," said the bishop. "I accept your resignation effective immediately, and I hereby appoint

Monsignor Yates as pastor in your place. When you're ready to return to Tres Robles, please let Monsignor Yates know. He'll follow you up there and help you move your things out. I've also asked him on behalf of the diocese to help you find a place to stay for tonight, and to help you arrange for something more permanent until you receive the proceeds from the sale of the property. Do you have the parish keys with you?"

"Yes, Bishop," he almost whispered.

"Then give them to Monsignor Yates now, and we'll be finished here."

Monsignor Sullivan stood and struggled to take the keys from his pants pocket. His hands were still shaking, and tears blurred his eyes. Then, snapping the keys off the ring, he handed them across the table to Monsignor Yates.

"I'm so sorry it had to end this way," said Monsignor Yates.

"Me, too."

Disappointment was reflected in the eyes of every person sitting around the table. But when he looked at the bishop, he saw not so much disappointment but rather compassion for another human being who had taken a wrong turn—who had "missed the mark" in the Hebrew sense of the word 'sin.'

He took off his clerical collar and laid it on the table. Then, without a word, he turned and left the room.

Chapter 26

Friday, August 17, 2012

Jared sat in Paul's office, shifting in his seat across the desk from him. Paul was fidgeting with the pens and papers on his desk, arranging and rearranging them. On the other side of the wall, the scenario that Jared and Eliza had set in motion was playing itself out. The bishop had been quiet about his intentions—sharing them only with Monsignor Yates, Sister Margaret, and Roger Spellman—except to say that Jared and Paul should stay nearby. Still, Jeff had gotten wind of the plans and had filled them in on the fate that awaited Monsignor Sullivan. At times, they heard raised voices in the next room, but they couldn't make out what was being said. Now, they waited for the bishop to summon them into his office.

Jared couldn't help wondering what lay in store for him. He wouldn't mind if the bishop chose to leave him at Our Lady of Perpetual Help—under new management, of course. He'd grown to like and appreciate the people there: Eliza and Yolanda, Frank, Paula and Lupe. Every one of them had been dedicated to their parish and had been his loyal supporters. If he had to leave, he would miss it. Although he was also hoping for some kind of reward for the service he'd performed.

The intercom buzzed. "Let's go," Paul said.

Everyone in the bishop's office was relaxed and smiling. The bishop invited Jared and Paul to sit at the conference table. Monsignor Sullivan was nowhere to be seen, but a clerical collar sat on the table. Jared knew what it meant: they would not be seeing the monsignor again. He wanted to feel sorry for the man, but he couldn't. He could find it in his heart to forgive the monsignor's dishonesty, but the man lacked basic human compassion. People—himself included—had suffered from his avarice and pride, and it hadn't seemed to bother him at all. The monsignor had gotten what he deserved, and in public for everyone to see.

The bishop took his seat. "Fathers, this unfortunate chapter in the history of this diocese is closed. Monsignor Sullivan has resigned his position and has deeded his property to the diocese to repay what was taken. He will not be reassigned."

Jared smiled at Paul.

"Jared," the bishop said, "we owe you a huge debt of gratitude. I gave you the most difficult assignment possible—one that three other priests with a lot more experience than you failed at—and you held fast and delivered more than we could ever have expected. I can't tell you how proud I am of you, and I know I speak for everyone in this room. I am so thankful you're a priest of this diocese." Everyone around the table applauded and Jared was overcome by joy. He felt like a different person: no longer a newly ordained boy, but now, somehow, a mature and seasoned priest.

"As of now, the only people who know about this outside of the people in this room are Eliza Roberts and Lupe Vargas and I'd like it to stay that way. No one else needs to know what happened. So, I'm asking you all to maintain a strict silence regarding this matter. Is that agreed?" Everyone at the table gave their assent. The bishop then turned to Jared. "I want you to speak to your friends at the parish and impress upon them how important it is that this situation remain confidential. Will you take care of that for me?"

"Certainly, Bishop," Jared said.

"Now, on to happier matters," said the bishop with a smile. "Monsignor Yates has served this diocese well for a long time. He was already vicar general when I came here six years ago. How long have you held that office, Dave?"

"Nine years," said Monsignor Yates.

"He's been after me for a while now to give him a parish of his own, and when it seemed probable that Our Lady of Perpetual Help would be vacant, I asked him if he'd like to take it on. He gave me an enthusiastic yes, so today I appointed him pastor. I know the people there will love you."

Again, everyone at the table applauded.

"Thank you, Bishop," said Monsignor Yates. "I'm excited about the possibility of turning this parish around, now that it will have substantial funds to work with." He turned to Jared. "I hope you won't mind staying on a week or so to help me get situated."

"Of course, Monsignor," Jared said. "I'd be happy to help in any way I can." Jared realized his time in Tres Robles was about over. His stomach jittered with nerves: what was coming next?

"That means, of course, that Monsignor Yates is resigning his position as vicar general. Dave, there's no way we can adequately thank you for your service here to the diocese. You've provided the foundation on which to build this diocese into something we can all be proud of. Choosing your successor has not been easy. There are several qualified candidates who could step into this number two position. I considered my choices, and frankly, I can't think of anyone who could fill that position better than you, Paul."

Paul's eyes grew large. "But, Bishop," he said, "I haven't even been ordained two years."

"I've taken that into consideration," Bishop Mickleson said. "All the same, I've watched you work with Monsignor Yates and Sister Margaret. I've been so impressed by how quickly you've picked up what they've had to teach you. And I've never given you a task that you haven't excelled at. There's no question in my mind that you'll grow into the position, so there's nobody I'd rather have as our vicar general than you. Will you accept the position?"

Paul smiled at him. "If you think I'm up to the challenge, who am I to disagree?"

"It's settled then," said the bishop. "The appointment can be effective today, and I'll leave it to you and Monsignor Yates to work out your transition. Does that work for you, Dave?"

"Absolutely," said Monsignor Yates.

Jared turned to Paul and gave him a big hug. "Congratulations. This is so awesome for you." Monsignor Yates came around the table to shake Paul's hand, followed by Sister Margaret and then Roger and Jeff, who also hugged him. As the congratulations were being showered on his friend, Jared wasn't quite sure how he felt. Of course, he was happy for Paul, but at the same time, he was envious that the bishop was promoting Paul faster and farther than he. After all, they'd been side by side in everything right through until their ordination. He resented playing second fiddle to Paul now, considering what it could mean for his determination to be ordained a bishop.

"Ladies and gentlemen," said the bishop in a loud voice, "we're not finished here."

Jared moved back to his seat along with everyone else.

"Paul's promotion leaves us with yet another vacancy. After several years without a secretary, I have to admit that Paul has spoiled me. I want to thank him in front of you all for taking such good care of me." The table once again broke out in applause.

"I don't intend to leave myself without a secretary this time. So, my next appointment is not only the fulfillment of a promise I made almost two years ago to bring one of our priests into the chancery to work, it's also a reward for his exceptional work on behalf of the diocese."

Jared hoped the bishop was talking about him.

The bishop turned to him and said, "Jared, I'd like to offer you the position of bishop's secretary. Would you accept it?"

Once again, Jared felt a surge of joy. This would make it possible for him to live full-time in San Luis Obispo. No more long weekend trips back and forth from Tres Robles just to catch a few hours with Paul. What was more, he would be working shoulder to shoulder with Paul and the bishop. At last, he'd be inside the bishop's circle instead of out in the boonies. He'd be that much closer to his goal of having a diocese of his own. There was no question this was the next step.

"I would be honored to accept the position," he said. "Thank you so very much."

"No, Jared," said the bishop, "thank *you* for all you've done for us over the past months, and welcome to the chancery."

The mood in the room was jovial—a vast contrast to earlier that morning. Paul seemed happy, more so than Jared had seen in a long while. But Jared had little time to pay attention to his friend. Everyone was shaking his hand, patting him on the back, and giving him warm hugs.

"Okay, ladies and gentlemen," said the bishop. "Let's take this out in the hallway, if you don't mind. There's still work to be done today." Everyone moved toward the door. Paul broke away to thank the bishop, while Jared was still surrounded by well-wishers.

"Jared," the bishop called across the room. Jared stopped and turned. "Could I speak with you in private for a moment, please?" Jared excused himself and returned to the bishop. Paul and the others left the office, closing the door behind them.

As soon as they were gone, the bishop said, "Sit down for just a minute, if you don't mind." He pulled out a chair for Jared, then seated himself.

"Of course," Jared said. "What can I do for you?" He was surprised by a sudden burst of nerves.

"You are an amazing person, Jared Röhrbach, and I consider myself blessed to have you in my diocese."

"Thank you, Bishop. I feel the same way about you."

"I hope you're satisfied with your assignment. Your friend, Paul, will help you learn the ropes."

"I'm very satisfied. It's awesome to be called to work here with you."

"Good. Do you think you'll be wanting to share the apartment with Paul?"

"I haven't spoken with him about it yet, but I'm sure that will work out well for both of us." *If you only knew.*

"Excellent," said the bishop. "I want you to be happy, and that's why I wanted to talk with you."

"Okay. What's on your mind?"

"When we were interviewing Monsignor Sullivan, he made an accusation about you."

Jared tried to think of what the monsignor could have had on him.

"He said you were involved with a fellow in LA."

Crap. He was listening.

"I might have dismissed the accusation as something the monsignor made up to discredit you, but I saw Jeff Hensen's reaction. He was upset. That told me Monsignor Sullivan wasn't just blowing smoke."

Jared's pulse raced. He avoided meeting the bishop's gaze.

"You're an adult, Jared," the bishop said, "and you have to do as your conscience dictates. For all I know, you were preaching the Gospel to that young man. I don't need to make a determination now. But it's up to you to stay out of trouble. I'm not your mother, and I'm not here to discipline you. I *am* going to remind you again that you have great potential. You've shown that these past few months. But if you're not careful, temptations can lead you down the garden path without your even being conscious of it. You know what I mean?"

"Yes, Bishop," Jared murmured.

"And then," said the bishop, "when you least expect it, there are consequences." He picked up the monsignor's clerical collar and rapped the table with it a couple of times.

"I understand."

"Good," said the bishop. "Now you and Paul get out of here and go do something fun for the afternoon." He stood up, and Jared stood as well.

"Thanks, Bishop," Jared said. "For everything." He shook the bishop's hand and left the office.

Paul and Jeff were waiting for him. "What did he say?" asked Paul.

"Nothing important. He just wanted to give me some tips." He caught Jeff's eye and glared at him. Jeff gave him a confused look. "Let's go get some lunch," Jared said. "How about Urbane Café? It's right around the corner."

"Fine with me," said Paul. "I'm up for anything." They set out on foot and within five minutes were seated at an outdoor table by the sidewalk. "I need a restroom break," said Paul. Order me a diet Coke, please." He made his way around the other tables and disappeared into the back of the restaurant.

"What's up?" asked Jeff, when Paul was out of earshot. "Why the evil eye back there?"

"You tipped off the bishop that something was going on in LA."

"Absolutely not," said Jeff. "I didn't say a word."

"It wasn't what you said," said Jared. "It was your reaction to something the monsignor said."

"Well, maybe, but it wasn't deliberate. I had no idea the monsignor knew about Tony."

"Yeah. My second or third day there, he listened in to my phone call with Tony outside my door. Now the bishop knows there's something going on."

"What's he going to do about it?" asked Jeff.

"Nothing, I guess. He just warned me to stay out of trouble."

Jeff sighed. "You are one lucky son of a bitch. That's all I can say."

"Why is he so lucky?" Paul had appeared behind Jared, and he started and gave Jeff a look.

"Just all the stuff he went through in Tres Robles," Jeff lied. "He was lucky that everything worked out so well."

"You were amazing." Paul put an arm around Jared and gave him a hug. "Isn't it funny," he said, "you go along with your routine, feeling like nothing will ever be any different, and then—*wham!*—everything changes."

"And the more it changes, the more it stays the same." Jeff stared at Jared.

Jared's jaw tightened with a flash of anger, but all he said was, "You know, Jeff, I do believe you're right."

Chapter 27

Paul lay on his back panting and covered in sweat. There was just enough breeze from the ceiling fan to make the surface of his skin feel cool. Jared lay close to him, his breathing in perfect sync, his fingers intertwined with Paul's. *This is what a life together feels like.* Hours and days of routine—separately and together—punctuated by moments of pure transcendent ecstasy: the boundaries between them collapsing into a sense of oneness more profound than Paul had yet experienced. He hadn't guessed that Jared's moving in with him would make such a difference to how he experienced their lovemaking. How was it possible to feel so exhausted and so exhilarated at the same time?

"That was amazing," he said.

"Mmm-hmm," Jared said, squeezing Paul's hand.

Jared was the love of Paul's life. Paul had realized that almost from the beginning. He was everything Paul could have wished for in a partner: handsome, bright, self-assured, and bold. At the same time, Jared didn't make it easy for Paul to love him. Paul, who was introspective almost to a fault, kept trying to discover the same depth of self-knowledge in Jared, but in vain. Jared said he loved him often enough, yet Paul always felt like their intimacy was incomplete, that he was chasing the real Jared in the dark. He knew the one thing that would sever the thread of intimacy between them would be jealousy. So, Paul dismissed any suspicions he might have had to avoid going down that road.

Jared's eyes were closed in pure contentment and a half-smile played on his lips, his chest rising and falling. Paul felt sad. What was it the philosopher Galen was quoted as saying? *Post coitum omne animal triste est?* Was it just post-coital sadness he was feeling like every animal? Or was it something else? Here he was, as close as he'd ever be to the man

200

he loved, and yet he felt—what?—loneliness? He was troubled. He had what he had been seeking his entire adult life, and yet he felt unsatisfied. In that instant he realized the truth: he had surrendered to Jared, but Jared had not—could not?—surrender to him. Jared always held part of himself back, and so part of him was always a stranger. Doubtless, it was elemental to the mysterious allure of the man. But, at the same time, it was his tragic flaw. Paul saw himself at last as he existed: suspended in uncertainty somewhere between the Jared he loved and the unknown Jared. It was the life he had chosen, but he wondered: could he—could anyone—sustain the suspense, or would something in him fail in the end? Neither God nor the man lying beside him seemed willing or able to answer.

"What are you thinking about?" asked Jared.

"Just thinking about what we're going to do tomorrow," Paul said. "I'm going to be busy most weekends. I hope you won't mind taking over for me at Saint Theresa's helping Father Richard."

"Hadn't thought much about it," said Jared. "I guess I should do that."

"You haven't met Father Richard, have you?"

"No, I haven't," said Jared.

"I'm going up there tomorrow for the night. You want to come?" asked Paul.

Jared was silent for a long while. "I don't know. I'll have to think about it. Ask me tomorrow."

"Okay," said Paul, though he found Jared's uncertainty unsettling. What was behind his hesitation? "You ready to pack it in?" he said.

"Yup," said Jared. "Good night."

Paul hoisted himself up on his elbow and leaned over to kiss his partner. Jared met his lips, and they held a long, passionate embrace. When Paul came up for air, he said, "Good night, love," then he lay back down, shoulder to shoulder with Jared. In no time at all, he fell into a deep, dreamless sleep.

He awoke to the sound of his cell phone ringing. When he opened his eyes, the room was filled with sunlight. Neither one of them had set an alarm. He stretched, doing his best to avoid waking Jared, and the ringing stopped. Paul climbed out of bed and grabbed the phone off the dresser. *Kurt Röhrbach, missed call* was displayed on his screen. He ought to change the name in his contact list.

He went to the kitchen to make coffee, then returned the call. Rosario answered immediately.

"Are you coming up to Cambria this weekend?" she asked.

"I was planning on it. Why?"

"Ms. Hannah wants to talk with you. She's very insistent. Could you stop by the house?"

"Of course. I'll drive up a little early today and drop by before I go to the parish. I should be ready to leave in about an hour."

"Perfect," said Rosario. "Hannah's strudel should be out of the oven by the time you get here."

Paul hung up just as Jared walked into the kitchen—naked as usual. "Who was that?"

"Rosario." He told Jared about his plans to visit Hannah. "You're coming with me to meet Father Richard, aren't you?"

"I don't think so," said Jared. "I want to spend the weekend with my friends in LA."

Paul's heart sank. "Who are these friends of yours? How come you've never introduced me? Is there something I need to be worried about?"

Jared laughed him off. "Of course not. What could you possibly have to be worried about?" He pinched Paul's cheek. "Are we getting jealous?"

"No," said Paul, trying to sound more convincing than he felt.

"Look, dear heart: I'm with you. I live with you. My stuff is here with you. Please don't nag me just because I need to get away and visit some friends from time to time. You never used to mind. What's changed?"

"Nothing." Paul looked away, feeling chastised. "I guess it's just part of getting used to living together. When you're away, I miss you."

"Well then, don't worry," said Jared. "You're my guy. Don't forget that." He came over to Paul and kissed him. "I can meet Richard Loring next weekend, okay?"

"Okay." Though it wasn't. But once again, he chose to accept his lover on his terms; having part of Jared was better than having none of him at all.

The drive to Cambria seemed longer than ever. Paul could feel the empty seat next to him in the car. He tried to fill the emptiness with music from the radio—even singing along—but he was one voice short.

He forced himself to focus on his destination. He had not been a regular visitor to Hannah since Kurt's death. When he did visit, half the time she was confused, and the rest of the time she seemed merely to endure his presence, so he had spaced his visits farther and farther apart. This was the first time she had asked to see him. There was no question as to whether he would go. He had promised Kurt to care for Hannah, and he felt a profound duty to be responsive where her stepsons would not be.

Maybe it was his experience with Jared and the ache of loneliness he was bearing that morning, but as he walked up to the door, the property seemed haunted by the ghosts of three teenage boys running, shouting, wrestling, and playing: the two identical Röhrbach boys and himself alive with carefree abandon. He followed the phantoms of his youth until they disappeared around the side of the house, voices still echoing in his mind. Hannah stood in the doorway looking in the same direction with a wistful smile on her face. Perhaps in the gathering fog of her illness, she was seeing most clearly of all.

"Paul?" she called out. "Is that you?"

"Yes."

"Oh, good," she said. "I was just enjoying the morning. Please come in."

Paul followed her into the kitchen. The room was filled with the aroma of fresh-baked pastry and apples. His mouth began watering even before he spotted the baking dish cooling on the counter. Rosario served up the steaming hot strudel onto fresh plates.

"Good morning, Rosario," he said. "How are we doing this morning?"

"*We* are fine," said Hannah, eyeing Paul with a critical stare. "I'm losing my memory, not my mind."

Rosario rolled her eyes at Paul and smiled as she set a plate before him.

Hannah sat down across the table from him while Rosario brought mugs of coffee. "Now, Paul," said Hannah, "I want to have a talk with you. My husband trusted you and you've never let us down—not like our boys."

Paul didn't dare say anything. Agreeing or disagreeing to a comment like that would cause trouble.

"You know my husband left me his entire fortune in a trust," Hannah said. "I have no family left. My drunk husband, Max was killed by a train. I have one cousin, Franz, who is a priest in Austria. I've never met him. Besides him, there are just the twins, and they want nothing to do with me." She folded her arms across her ample chest. "So, you see, I am alone."

"I wish things were different with your stepsons," Paul said.

"Yes, but they are not. So, here we are." She set a folder on the table and pushed it toward Paul.

Paul took out a small stack of papers. Even with no legal training, he could see that he was holding an amended set of trust documents. Hannah took them out of his hands and leafed through them. Then she spread the pages out in front of him and pointed to a section about halfway down the page entitled Successor Trustees.

The sight of his name there was like a knife in his heart. "What does this mean? You're making me a trustee?"

"In a way," she said. "On my death, you will become the sole trustee. You'll be able to dispose of the assets as you see fit."

"But what about your stepsons? Don't you want them to have a share in their father's estate?" Paul had no trouble imagining Jared's fury when he discovered that his father's wealth had gone to Paul instead of to him.

"That will be up to you when the time comes. As I said, when I'm gone, you can do whatever you like with it. It will be no concern of mine."

"I don't know what to say."

"Say nothing," she said. "Eat your strudel. It's getting cold."

Hannah's life might have been fading into the oblivion of Alzheimer's, but her cooking skills were undimmed. Her strudel was as good today as it had been the first time he'd tasted it as a timid schoolboy—sitting at the same table, flanked by his best friends, Jared and Justin. They had always made him feel like a member of the family, never guessing that one day he would be the family's sole heir. None of this was playing out as he thought it would, but then again, *Man proposes; God disposes.*

He drove the short distance back to Saint Theresa's as though on autopilot. He couldn't stop thinking about all the inevitable complications that would arise upon Hannah's death. There was no way he could keep all that wealth. He'd never been poor, but he had never handled accounts of any real size, either. And what would Jared do when he found out? It would be the end of the road for them as a couple. And what about Justin? Money made hiding so much easier, but it could also create a direct trail for the police to find him.

In any case, Paul worried less about how his two friends would manage the news than how he would manage his two friends. He understood why Hannah had chosen him as her heir, yet he wished she hadn't.

Chapter 28

Sunday, August 23, 2015

Jared was laughing so hard his sides ached. He hadn't had this much fun in the three years he'd been working in the chancery as the bishop's secretary. Who knew a lawyer could be so funny? Okay, so he was a little drunk, but then so was Roger. And between them, hanging on their shoulders, was Jeff, who was a *whole lot* drunk. Roger and he took turns shushing each other because they didn't want Jeff's law career to begin with an arrest for public drunkenness. Yet, every few steps, one or the other of them burst out laughing. Jared checked the time on his phone, but the number it displayed looked like 6:66 and he knew *that* couldn't be right, so he announced to his companions that they'd have to be quiet because it was "oh-dark-thirty" in the morning—but that just got Roger laughing again.

"Why've you got one eye closed, man?" Jared asked Jeff.

"Helps me figure out which sidewalk I'm supposed to be on." He walked with his head down, focused on his feet.

All night, people they didn't even know bought Jeff drinks to celebrate his passing the bar exam, but he had just left most of it in a shrub along the roadway several blocks back.

Jeff looked up and grinned. "Jeffrey Hensen, Attorney at Law."

Jared and Roger laughed all over again.

They half-walked, half-stumbled the remaining blocks to Paul and Jared's apartment. The walk and the fresh air seemed to do Jeff some good.

"Do you think you can make it up the stairs without us carrying you?" Jared asked.

"I think so," said Jeff, "as long as I can hold onto you to keep my balance."

"You want to get him upstairs yourself?" Roger asked.

"I can try," Jared said. "If he passes out on the way, I'll just cover him up with a blanket and leave him wherever he lands." That started them laughing again.

"If you're sure you'll be all right, I'll call an Uber and head home," Roger said.

"No, Uncle Roger," said Jeff. "You have to come up with us for a drink."

"'Fraid not," he said. "I think we've all done enough celebrating for one night."

"Speak for yourself," Jeff told him. "I'm not done yet."

Jared started laughing again. "We'll see about that." Then he said to Roger, "Go ahead and call your ride. I'm sure I can manage him from here."

"Good night, Uncle Roger." Jeff gave him a big hug and a kiss. "Thanks so much for everything. You know I couldn't have done any of this without you. You've been so good to me…" and he started blubbering.

"Oh, Lord," said Roger. "Get him to bed, Jared, will you?"

"Sure thing," Jared said. "Thanks for a fun night." He hugged him and Roger climbed into the car.

"Okay, baby boy," said Jared. "Let's get you upstairs."

"Applesolutely."

Jeff climbed the stairs, hanging on to Jared's shoulder to steady himself. When they got to the elevator, he braced himself against the wall as a precaution against falling over. He made it to the second floor and to the apartment door without another mishap.

"Now, Jeff," said Jared, "you have to be quiet. We don't want to wake Paul." Paul had left the bar hours ago because he had a morning appointment.

Jeff put his index finger up to his lips and said, "Shhh!" loud enough to be heard on the next floor.

"Behave yourself." Jared tried to sound stern, but that made Jeff start giggling. "We're not going in there until you're quiet," he said. "Even if we have to stand out here the rest of the night." When he was sure Jeff could control himself, he opened the door and helped navigate Jeff into his bedroom, closing the door behind them.

"Let's get you into bed," Jared whispered. He pulled Jeff's shirt over his head and tossed it onto a chair. Jeff's slender but muscular frame had grown more attractive over the last four years since Rome. Drunk though he was, Jared forced himself not to think about things like that and to concentrate on what he was doing. He helped Jeff sit down on the side of the bed, then squatted down in front of him to take off his shoes and socks. As he worked, Jeff ran his fingers through Jared's hair, and when he looked up at him, Jeff was grinning at him. Alarm bells sounded in Jared's brain, though they were muffled by the alcohol. Jared stood up. Jeff wouldn't be able to finish undressing by himself. Jared could always put him to bed as he was, but curiosity got the better of him. *I can handle this.*

"Up you go." He helped Jeff stand, then loosened his belt, unbuttoned his slacks, and let them drop to the floor around Jeff's ankles. Jeff was commando, and when his slacks had fallen away, his rigid erection sprang up in front of him. Jared had never seen Jeff in that state before, and it caught—and held—his attention. It took all the restraint he could muster not to reach out and grab hold of what Jeff was shamelessly presenting to him.

"Jared, thank you," Jeff said. "I'm sorry I was mean to you. I was wrong about you. You are a great guy, and I love you. I do." With that, Jeff threw his arms around Jared's neck and pulled him close so that Jared felt Jeff's erection pressing hard against his crotch. That was all it took. He managed to pull his own shirt off. He had never touched Jeff's naked flesh, and he started fondling his way down Jeff's chest, while Jeff nuzzled his ear and neck. The sensations overwhelmed his already weak resolutions. Jared dropped to one knee and swallowed half of Jeff's erection.

"Wait! What? Nooo!" Jeff grunted, pushing Jared off him so hard he landed on the floor on his backside. "What are you doing?" he cried. "Why did you do that? I didn't mean... I was only... I can't do that! Get out of here! Leave me alone!" Jeff backed up until he was against the far wall, looking at Jared with panic in his eye.

"Whoa, Buddy," Jared said. "I was just trying to help."

"Get out," said Jeff.

"I'm going. I'm going," Jared panted, crawling backward on the floor toward the door. "Calm down. It's okay."

Jared opened the door and backed into the hallway, closing it again after him. He could hear Paul's regular breathing coming uninterrupted from their bedroom. *Thank God.* He hadn't woken up. In no time, Jared was stripped and lying beside Paul, waiting for the grogginess of the alcohol to take him. He hadn't been wrong: deep down, Jeff wanted him. It was Jeff's loyalty to Paul that had stopped him, even in his drunken state. Whatever it was, it was a crappy ending to a joyful night, and he realized that it was his fault. He kicked himself for having let himself go like that.

Even in his drunken sleep, Jared was startled by the dream. He was standing there again in an unfamiliar place facing very familiar faces. His mother and father stood to his left and right, flanking his brother and Tony, but this time Bishop Mickleson and Paul stood in the center. They were all looking at him, but he couldn't read their blank expressions. They weren't disapproving, but they weren't approving, either. Why were they all there, staring at him? And who was standing in the shadows behind them? He tried speaking, but no words came. He tried reaching out to them, but they faded away.

When Jared opened his eyes, he knew it would be a four-Advil morning. He tried to put the dream out of his mind and focus on the day ahead. He had no idea what time it had been when he'd crawled into bed next to Paul. He hoped he'd gotten his minimum four hours of sleep, but it sure as hell didn't feel like it. He looked over to where Paul had been, but there wasn't even a dent in the pillow to mark his place. He must have gone to his appointment. Jared dragged himself into the bathroom. He hoped that a pee and four little blue-green capsules would help him feel better. They didn't—at least not at once. After a couple of shots of fresh-brewed espresso, the fog began to lift. That was the price for yesterday's fun. And it had been fun. Regardless of the sour note it ended with, it had been a blast.

Today, Jeff would start his career as a full-fledged attorney with Roger's firm. Jared hoped to God Roger was giving him the day off. *The boy's still asleep.* Even though Jeff was a year younger, Jared always thought of him as *the boy*.

Jared's phone buzzed with a text from Paul. The bishop wanted to meet with them in the chancery at ten o'clock. *Ugh, figures.* In no time at all, he had himself looking clerical, if a little haggard.

When he got to the chancery, he went straight to Paul's office.

"My God, look at you," said Paul, laughing.

"A little too much celebrating, I think."

"Good thing I left when I did," Paul said. "I can't imagine what Jeff looks like."

"I have no idea. By the time I left he still wasn't up. I had to pour him into bed last night."

"How late were you? I didn't hear you come in."

"To be honest, I couldn't tell you," Jared said, stifling a sigh of relief. "The numbers on the clock wouldn't stand still long enough for me to read them."

The phone on Paul's desk buzzed. The bishop was ready for them.

Bishop Mickleson was sitting behind his desk when Paul and Jared entered his office. He got up and ushered them over to his sofa. He took one of the comfortable armchairs for himself. When he had a look at Jared's face, he said, "Oh dear. What happened?"

Jared and Paul both laughed. "Jeff Hensen passed his bar exam," said Jared, "and we were out celebrating. I may have overdone it a bit."

"Maybe quite a bit," added Paul.

Jared tried not to flinch. *That was unnecessary.*

"The two of you may need to learn how to tone down your celebrating, if that's the case," said the bishop. "You might have quite a lot to celebrate if things work out."

Jared's pulse quickened. "Why? What's going on?"

"I was talking with the cardinal over the weekend. Of course, he asked how you both were doing, and I told him in some detail what you've been up to. He's delighted to hear you're doing so well."

"Thanks for the good report, Bishop," said Paul. "We appreciate your support."

"I only told him the truth." The bishop leaned forward in his chair. "He gave me some interesting news. Archbishop Baker of the Mobile archdiocese is retiring next year. They're already starting the search process for his successor. The cardinal has some influence down there, and he has assured me that my name will be put forward as a candidate for that position. If all goes well, I may be selected as the next archbishop."

"Congratulations," said Jared. "That's great news."

"We'll miss you, Bishop," said Paul. "I can't imagine working with anyone else. You've spoiled us both."

"Maybe so, but that's where my conversation with the cardinal gets interesting."

"How so?" asked Paul.

"He's working to have one of you two succeed me here as bishop of San Luis."

Paul and Jared looked at each other in shock. "But we're not even five years ordained," said Paul. "Nobody's going to be in favor of ordaining men with so little experience."

"By the time the selection is announced, you'll have your five years—both of you. It has happened that men as young as you have become bishops and have done well. Besides, except for Monsignor Yates, no one here has more experience in running the diocese than you two, and both of you have had good pastoral experience."

"What about Monsignor Yates?" said Paul. "Why not select him?"

"He doesn't want it," said the bishop. "He's told me so in no uncertain terms every time I've brought it up to him."

"So, you believe that the choice will be between the two of us?" Jared asked. His mind was already racing with calculations.

"That's what it looks like to me," said the bishop.

"What should we do to prepare?" asked Paul.

"I'm afraid there's not a lot we can do—yet," said the bishop. "The final selection for the Mobile Archdiocese hasn't been made yet. I'll have to fly down there several times over the next few weeks and months, so you'll have to cover for me as usual when I'm gone."

"Okay," said Paul.

"Once the final selection has been made, we'll know a few weeks in advance of it going public. That's when things will start getting busy here. That's also when we can start working to make sure both of your names are on the list that goes to Rome. In the meantime, I want to help you prepare for the life of a bishop. It may be quite different from what you're expecting."

"Thank you, Bishop," said Jared. "That would be awesome."

"This is scary," said Paul. "I hope I'm ready for this."

"Why don't you hold that off until you've actually been selected?" The bishop chuckled.

"Nervous Nellie," Jared whispered to him. Paul elbowed him in the ribs.

"Do you have any questions?" asked the bishop.

"When will you know about Mobile?" asked Jared.

"Archbishop Baker will be retiring at the end of January of next year. I assume I'll be notified sometime in mid-December if I am the archbishop elect. Then, there will be three or four months for the transition and to prepare for the installation. Assuming I'm selected, it will be spring of next year at the earliest when I'd be leaving here."

"We have some time, then," said Paul.

"Yes, but if the choice is made in January, you can assume that the two of you and Sister Margaret will be making the decisions for the diocese after that. I would have to spend a lot more time in Mobile, and when I'm here I'll have other priorities. So, if the cardinal is right—and he almost always is—you guys will have a diocese to run for a while, regardless of whether you're made a bishop."

"I'm excited." Jared's eye was fixed on the purple tab that peeked out from below the opening in the bishop's collar. "I always hoped someday we might get the opportunity to serve as a bishop, but I never thought it would happen so soon."

"How do you feel about this, Paul?" asked the bishop.

"I've been afraid this might happen before I was ready for it," said Paul. "And now, here it is, staring me right in the face."

"Stop worrying." The bishop pushed his wireframe glasses up his nose. "People are never ready to assume responsibility. If you waited until you felt ready, it'd never happen. You're the oldest in your family, right?"

"Yes," said Paul.

"Do you think your parents felt ready to take on the responsibility of a family when you were born? No, we don't wait until we're ready to assume responsibility; we assume the responsibility and then grow into it as best we're able. If you are chosen as bishop, I don't want you to let fear stand in your way. I want you to accept. Is that clear?"

"Yes, Bishop," said Paul.

"And you, Jared." The bishop turned to him. "You'll say yes?"

"Absolutely," Jared answered without hesitation.

A look passed across the bishop's face, though maybe Jared was mistaken.

"I don't have to remind you both to pray about this. This will be a sacred undertaking, not a political appointment. Understood?"

"Yes, Bishop," Jared and Paul said.

"Good." The bishop stood up to signal that their meeting was ending. "Congratulations. Think about what I said and get back to work. Nothing's happened yet."

Jared followed Paul out of the bishop's office. Once the door was closed behind them, they stood in the hallway and looked at each other. Jared felt energized. His deepest desire was coming true. He would have to work hard to eclipse Paul, though. Paul always seemed to be a half-step ahead of him. Every time since they'd been ordained, it had been Paul who'd gotten the higher appointment.

"What are we going to do?" Paul still looked shell-shocked.

"I don't know about you," said Jared, "but I'm going to have a drink."

Chapter 29

Saturday, December 19, 2015

Jared approached a large Spanish-style building with a sign over the front door announcing it as the Sunday Room. He opened the big, wooden double doors and walked into an expansive hall with its high raftered ceiling, large hanging Craftsman-style lights, and a highly polished herringbone-pattern wood floor that seemed almost to glow under his feet. The room had been transformed since he'd been there last. The ceiling rafters were festooned with massive garlands of white, red, and gold that ended at each wall in enormous red velvet bows with gold accents. The garlands were alive with brilliant dots of twinkling colored lights that left splotches of dancing color across the floor. A pair of extravagantly decorated Christmas trees flanked the stage at the far end of the hall. Tables with white and gold coverings lined the side walls.

A dozen or so young men in black tuxedos with vests and bowties in a variety of colors scurried about the room carrying trays of hors d'oeuvres or pastries. One of them was Tony. He sauntered over to Jared and smiled.

"Well…how does it look?" He was so excited and bursting with pride, he almost stood on his toes.

"Amazing," Jared said. "Like a Christmas fairy land." They both laughed. He was somewhat awestruck by it all. Though this was the result of his careful planning, seeing it in real life was something else again. "Where did you get the wait staff?"

"Some are friends, some are clients…"

"You didn't." Jared laughed.

"Why not? You're offering them good money. They jumped at the chance to do this."

Jared grew serious. "Remember what I told you: no playing around. This is a serious reception. There's a lot on the line for me. I can't have anything go sideways."

"I know, boss. You can always count on Tony for a good time."

"Hey." Jared tapped him on the shoulder. "Stop that." He looked around the room again. "We only have about a half hour before the archbishop and the guests start to arrive. Where's the banner?"

"I've got a couple of stepladders coming so we can pin it up to the curtain. It'll be up in just a minute. Let me go see what's holding them up." He headed off in the direction of the stage, but Jared stopped him.

"Where's Cody?"

"Behind the bar." He pointed to the other side of the room. "See him?"

"Oh yeah," Jared said. "And Tony...no offense but make yourself scarce when the guests get here. I don't want anyone to recognize you."

"Got it covered, boss." Tony grinned at him and took off toward the stage.

"And quit calling me that!"

He headed for the bar. He'd never seen Cody in formal wear before. He always looked good enough to eat when he was working in shorts and tank top in the club in LA, but here he looked like he'd stepped out of the pages of GQ. "Cody!" he called out.

Cody looked up and his eyes widened. "Well, look at you." He'd never seen Jared in his *work clothes* either.

"Come here a minute, would you?" Jared led Cody through a doorway into a small side room.

"Whatcha need, Jared?"

"Like I told you before: tonight's going to be a big, fancy affair, and I need to keep it low-key. Have your guys mix the drinks kind of weak—not like at the club. We don't want any of the guests to get out of hand."

"No problem."

"Except one guy." Jared pulled up a picture of Paul on his phone. "Keep him drinking and make them nice and strong, but don't overdo it. I want him to enjoy himself but not pass out." He raised his eyebrows. "Can you remember his face?"

"Sure. It's my job to remember faces." He thought for a second. "What's his name?"

"It's Paul, but just call him Father. Don't let on that you've seen him before."

"Who says I haven't?"

Jared recoiled for a second. *Interesting.* "Thanks, Cody," he said. "Enjoy yourself tonight."

Jared returned to the main hall. Across the stage was a huge banner that read, *Congratulations and Farewell Archbishop Mickleson!*

He scanned the room once more with a feeling of satisfaction. *This will be a reception to remember.*

A young man approached him and said, "I'm with the quartet. Where do you want us to set up?"

Jared pointed out the place near the stage they had left clear of tables. "You've been told to play only soft jazz this evening, right? Nothing that would drown out conversation."

"Yes, sir," he said. "If we get too loud or something, just give me a high sign and we'll quiet down."

Jared checked his watch. It was nearing seven. The main doors opened, and in came Paul with Archbishop Mickleson, Sister Margaret, and Monsignor Yates who must have come down for the occasion. Jared rushed over to greet them. "Archbishop, welcome. Paul, Sister, Monsignor, come in, come in." He turned to Mickleson. "I'm so excited about this reception. It's been in the planning for months. I hope you enjoy it."

The archbishop looked around at all the decorations and the tables full of food. When he caught sight of the banner, he broke into a broad grin. "Oh, my goodness," he said. "This is quite the display."

As the archbishop and his retinue moved deeper into the room, talking excitedly, Paul pulled Jared aside. "In the planning for months? We only got confirmation of the appointment two weeks ago."

Jared just smiled.

Paul shook his head. "And how were you able to book this place the Saturday before Christmas?"

Jared turned up his hands, as though catching a gift from Heaven. "Well...the bishop told us the choice would be made in mid-December, so back in August I rented this space for the first three Saturdays of the month and took a chance." Paul looked stunned. "Everything else was pre-planned; I just had to tell them when."

"You're nuts," Paul said. How much did this cost?"

"It doesn't matter." Even without Papa's inheritance, the trust he'd set up for Jared was still way more money than he needed.

As they chatted, more guests arrived. The space was filling up. Although he had put together the guest list, he had never met the majority of the attendees. He did recognize some people, though. There were the heads of all his diocesan agencies and many of his fellow priests. There was the mayor of San Luis Obispo and his wife and one of the state senators. There was the rector of Saint Stephen's Episcopal parish in town with the bishop of the diocese of El Camino Real and his wife. There were also other clergy of various flavors, most of whom he didn't recognize. The ambient noise level kept growing, but true to their promise, the quartet provided an elegant and sophisticated background.

He walked around the room introducing himself to dozens of guests whose names he wouldn't remember ten minutes later. All the while, he kept an eye on the tables of food and the young men who were keeping them well stocked, as well as those passing among the guests with trays laden with goodies. Through it all, the archbishop was thronged with well-wishers, and he was beaming.

Jared scanned the crowd for Paul and found him leaning over the bar, having a tête-à-tête with Cody. *That's what comes from hiring a professional.*

It was almost an hour into the event when he caught sight of a man in the crowd with a big camera. *Yes. The press is here.* It would be the biggest social event of the season. As they moved around the room, the cameraman filmed an attractive reporter. Jared edged his way into their path until the reporter spotted him.

"Hi, Father," she said. "I'm Sally Cook from KSBY News. Would you mind if I asked you some questions?"

"No, not at all. I'd be pleased. Jared Röhrbach." He offered her his hand.

"Congratulations for putting together a spectacular evening."

He tried to mutter a quick, "You're welcome," but she kept on without missing a beat. "What will losing Archbishop Mickleson mean to you and to this community?"

He took his time explaining some of the more significant impacts the archbishop had made during his years in San Luis. He wasn't nervous. He'd been pretty sure of the questions he'd be asked, so he had prepared himself well.

Then came the question he was hoping for. "Do you know who the next bishop will be?"

"No one but the Pope knows that yet."

"How about you? Would you accept the position?"

"That's not likely to happen," he chuckled. "I'm too young. The church prefers men with more experience as their leaders." A minute later, Sally Cook and her camera set off to corner another dignitary. Jared was amazed that everything was going so well. Cody made the rounds, filling up people's glasses, paying special attention to Paul.

By eight-thirty, Jared wove his way through the crowd and squeezed in beside the archbishop. "We have a little program planned in your honor tonight," he said, "if you wouldn't mind making your way to the stage."

He found Paul a few steps away in a small group, listening to their conversation. "It's time," he said. "You're on." Paul turned to him with a puzzled look. "The archbishop is on his way to the stage. You're introducing him, right?"

Paul's face lit up. "Oh. Right." He fished around in his jacket pocket. "I have some notes right here." He was swaying a little.

"Here," Jared said. "I'll take that," and he grabbed the half-empty drink out of Paul's other hand. "Go on up to the stage with the archbishop. You can find your notes when you get up there. The guests are waiting for you."

"Oh. Yes," said Paul, and he set out for the stage. As he was going up the steps, he tripped and lurched forward. It was the archbishop himself who was there to grab him before he fell. Paul giggled and blushed and made his way to the podium. Clinging to it with one hand, he went back to searching his jacket pocket with the other. The hall went quiet. It took a minute or two until he pulled out the papers with a little flourish as if to say *Ta-dah!* He spread the papers out in front of him and tapped the microphone a couple of times, sending a series of nerve-wracking booms through the hall. Then he began. "Ladiesh and genleman..."

As Paul spoke, Jared scanned the room. The expressions on the guests' faces ran the gamut from curiosity to mirth to disgust. Sally and her camera were standing right in front of him at the head of the crowd. *Exactly as planned.* Part of him felt embarrassed and sorry for Paul as he watched him on the dais trying to keep it together. *Still, all's fair in love and war.* Paul had a big lead on him in their race to be the next bishop. Now the playing field would be a little more level.

The score for this period: Jared one, Paul nothing.

Chapter 30

The late morning sun threw shadows across the furniture in Paul's office as he volleyed back and forth between the notes on his desk and the calendar on his computer screen. He was putting together another draft of the archbishop's schedule for Confirmations around the diocese. In the months since Clarence Mickleson's selection as the archbishop-elect of the archdiocese of Mobile, the schedule changed every other day. It was the archbishop's custom to give Confirmation to the young people himself, but Paul was delegated to fill in whenever he wasn't available, and that was increasingly often.

There was a knock on his door.

"Come in," he said, still absorbed in the task at hand.

"Hey, Paul." Jeff's voice pulled his attention away from his work.

"What are you doing here?"

"Yeah," said Jeff, "Nice to see you, too."

"I'm sorry." Paul sat back in his chair. "It's always nice to see you, Jeff. What business brings you to the chancery today?"

"Playing errand boy," he said. "I had to deliver some papers to the archbishop and thought I'd grab the chance to see you." He sat down uninvited in the chair opposite Paul. "There are big doings afoot."

"Really? What kind of doings are we talking about?"

"I can't tell you," Jeff said, with his boyish grin.

Paul was beginning to feel annoyed at this interruption. "Then why bring it up?"

"Because I wanted to let you know I did something that's going to help you out—a lot. You can thank me now or later."

"Jeff, really." Paul sat forward again and picked up some of the papers from his desk. "Another time, I'd enjoy playing 'Riddle Me This' with you, but I'm trying to get this schedule to the archbishop when I have no idea what he's going to be doing over the next few weeks. You're not helping."

"If it were me," Jeff said, still grinning, "I'd set that aside for a few minutes. Who knows? Your problems could clear themselves up with one phone call."

"What are you talking about? Don't be such a wise-ass."

"You'll see," Jeff said.

The phone on Paul's desk buzzed. Jeff stood up. "Have I ever mentioned I'm clairvoyant?"

Paul frowned as he picked up the phone. The archbishop wanted to see him. He hung up and looked askance at Jeff. "What's going on?"

"See you later," Jeff said, grinning from ear to ear. "Good luck," and he headed out the door.

"Wait!" Paul called after him. "Aren't you going to tell me what this is about?" But by the time he reached his door, Jeff was out of sight.

Paul headed down the hallway toward the archbishop's office. He was about to knock when he heard Jared's voice inside. "Come in," said the archbishop as Paul opened the door. The archbishop and Jared were sitting in what was becoming their usual spot: the furniture grouping in the corner with the sofa and armchairs. Paul took his place beside Jared on the couch.

"Well, gentlemen," said the archbishop, "the moment has arrived. I was talking to the cardinal about two hours ago, and the selection has been made. One of you will be my successor."

Paul went pale.

"I know it's a little premature," the archbishop continued, "but the cardinal wanted to give you plenty of time to prepare before the official announcement is made. He's coming over for my installation in Mobile, and he wants to make your announcement himself while he's here."

"Which one of us is it?" Jared looked like he was sitting on an anthill.

Barely breathing, Paul said nothing.

"As I told you before, this was a very difficult decision. The cardinal wants the two of you in responsible positions, and he's been pushing both of you hard. It came down to considering the prudence and maturity of your judgment. You're both mature for men who are barely thirty, but the cardinal and I felt that one of you would benefit from a little more experience before being given the responsibility of a diocese.

He turned to Jared. A big smile came across Jared's face. "Jared," said the archbishop, "facts have come to our attention that made us think Paul would be the better choice at this time."

The smile vanished. Paul felt as though the floor had dropped out from underneath him.

"But why?" Jared asked.

"You have very close ties to some friends in Los Angeles."

Paul flinched.

"Yes, but..." Jared stammered. "Since when was that a problem?"

"Remember Monsignor Sullivan? You and I had a talk about your seeing someone down there."

"He's just a friend," Jared said. But the guilt was all over his face no matter how hard he tried to hide it. Paul's fears had been justified after all.

"Is it true you staffed my reception at Christmas with men from an LA gay club?"

What? Paul's eyes widened. So, that was how Jared had organized such a lavish affair so quickly.

"They're all professionals," Jared was saying. "They're the best in the business. And nothing inappropriate happened."

Except that I got horribly drunk. He stared at the carpet. Could Jared have set him up? He looked over at him. *No.* He refused to believe that about the man he loved—and the man who said he loved him.

The bishop shook his head. "How would that have looked if it had been made public?" He paused. "You even invited the press. Of course, that was wonderful and most fitting, but what if it had gone wrong?"

"But it didn't, Bishop. Everything went as I'd planned."

"Did it?"

Paul leaned forward. He was wondering the same thing.

Jared looked confused.

"If everything went exactly as planned, how did I find out about it? Obviously, someone else knew."

"But Bishop...," Jared started to say.

"Please," the archbishop interrupted him. "It's behind us now. It was an error in judgment that could have had serious consequences for me and for this diocese. That didn't happen, but frankly, it was just dumb luck. It doesn't disqualify you from consideration at another time. The cardinal just wants to be convinced that this was merely a lapse and not a pattern of behavior. If it's any consolation, he will make sure that you will be among the next candidates to be considered."

Although Jared said nothing, Paul could see by the tension in his jaw that he was livid. This must have been what Jeff had been talking about. Somehow, he'd found out about this selection. Did he know about the LA business, too?

"Paul, congratulations on your selection. I'm assuming you will accept?"

"Yes, Bishop, I accept." Paul spoke more out of a sense of duty to Archbishop Mickleson and Cardinal Romero than from the conviction that he was capable of assuming the responsibility.

"Excellent," said the archbishop. "Jared, I'm sorry it wasn't you this time but trust me: there *will* be a next time." He stood up and shook Jared's hand. "You've served me and the diocese well, and I hope you'll put your considerable talents to work helping your friend Paul as he takes on the leadership of this diocese."

"I will, Bishop," said Jared, though he wouldn't look at Paul.

Paul realized the cost of his good fortune. Jared was not accustomed to being number two ever—to anyone. Had Jared been selected, Paul knew that not only would he have been happy for his friend, but he would also have been happy to serve under him. But that was him, not Jared.

Jared stood in front of the archbishop like a scolded puppy. The resentment on his face gave Paul chills. Paul realized their entire relationship was dependent on his remaining submissive to Jared. He had always been the one to apologize or give in, even when the fault wasn't his. As he studied Jared, he knew their relationship— the love he had counted on to sustain him into the future—was over.

"I can see you're upset," said the archbishop. "If you can, try to focus on the fact that you're still on the list and that your best friend is being recognized for his service. Can you do that?"

"I'll do my best," Jared said, though he didn't sound at all convincing.

"Why don't the two of you take the next couple of days off to celebrate. I don't think we'll be needing you for anything special, at least until Monday. You can head out now, if you want, Jared." He turned to Paul. "Would you mind staying to go over a few things with me before you leave?"

"Thanks, Bishop," said Jared. "I could use the time away. I'll see you on Monday." He shook hands with the archbishop, turned, and left the room without so much as a glance at Paul.

It was all Paul could do to hold back his tears. There was no use running after him. He told himself they could talk this out and preserve their relationship, but he knew Jared too well. When Jared felt wronged, his capacity for blame was boundless, whether it was deserved or not. His hatred for Hannah was ample proof of that. Paul wasn't ready to give up on him, but the realist in him was preparing for the worst.

The meeting with the archbishop to go over a myriad of details concerning both of their transitions lasted much longer than he'd expected. He struggled to focus on the business at hand. At the same time, working on the plans for the future helped take his mind off other concerns. It was almost three o'clock by the time he left the chancery. He sat in his car with his hands on the steering wheel, overcome by fear. What would Jared be like when he got to the apartment? When Jared was upset, he could be vicious—and he knew exactly what to say to hurt Paul the most.

Paul parked and took the elevator to the second floor. The closer he got to their front door, the harder his heart pounded. He unlocked the door and stepped inside.

"Jared?" he called out.

There was no response.

He walked through the apartment. "Jared?" he called again.

He went into their bedroom. No Jared. At first, everything looked as it always did. Then he noticed Jared's hairbrush wasn't in the bathroom; his bathrobe wasn't hanging on the back of the bedroom door. Panic mounting, he threw open the closet door. Jared's side of the closet was empty. His worst fears rushed in. He hurried to their dresser and opened Jared's drawers, already knowing what he'd find. The drawers, too, were empty.

"Jared!" shouted Paul as the tears he had tried so hard to hold back burst through. He sat down hard in the middle of the floor, buried his face in his hands, and sobbed.

He had no idea how long he'd been sitting there when he heard a key in the lock and the front door opening. "Jared?" he called out.

"Paul?" It was Jeff. He rushed into the bedroom and dropped to his knees, putting his arm around Paul's shoulders. "What's the matter? What happened?"

"Jared's gone," Paul managed to get out between sobs. "He left me."

"Why?" asked Jeff. "What happened?"

"He didn't get chosen as bishop, and he's blaming me."

"Oh God," said Jeff.

"I don't care," said Paul. "Really. I don't. He can have the position if he wants it. I just want him back."

"Paul." Jeff held him tighter. "Pull yourself together, man. Think this through."

"What do you mean?"

"Jared always does this. Think back. Whenever things haven't gone his way, he takes off. He even ran out of his own ordination. It's not you, Paul. It's him. He's always been a spoiled child. He's never grown out of it."

Paul became aware that his face was wet, along with his hands and arms and the front of his shirt. His chest hurt. But Jeff was right. Jared always ran away. Maybe that was what he had feared when he'd seen that look on Jared's face in the archbishop's office. Deep down he'd known Jared had already abandoned him. Not only would their apartment be empty, but so would Jared's heart. Jared, whose life and love he had shared for the last seventeen years, was gone for good.

As Paul embraced the reality of what had happened, his sobbing slowed and stopped. He reached out and embraced Jeff, burying his face in Jeff's neck.

"You're gonna be okay," Jeff murmured to him. "This isn't about you. Jared did this to himself. He's fucking himself over, and he doesn't even realize it. He thinks he can get away with anything and still come out on top. You're going to hate me for saying this, but Jared doesn't deserve you. He never did."

Paul lifted his head off Jeff's shoulder and pushed himself just far enough away, so Jeff's face came into focus. "What do you mean?"

"I've known things about Jared that I've kept quiet about for a long time. I could never tell you about them. I knew how much it would hurt you if you knew, and I couldn't bear to hurt you. I still can't."

"Tell me," Paul said.

"I don't know how to say it."

Paul fixed Jeff with his eyes but Jeff wouldn't look at him. "You've got to tell me. I need to know."

Jeff took a deep breath. "Jared hasn't been faithful to you."

"You mean his whoring around?" Paul dismissed it with a wave. "That's been obvious for as long as I've known him. That doesn't mean anything."

"No, I mean his relationship with Tony Keating in LA. They share a condo together."

"What? Who?" Paul's head swirled with the news. "How do you know about this?"

He took another deep breath. "While I was at UCLA, I used to go to the bar where Tony works as a rent boy. Everybody in the bar knows Tony, and they all know about Tony's boyfriend, Jared. He's pretty famous around West Hollywood."

Paul stared at Jeff. "It was you!" Jeff had gotten him the position of bishop...and had destroyed his relationship with Jared. "You told the archbishop."

"No," said Jeff. "I never spoke about any of this with the archbishop. My uncle, Roger, already had the information from the Sullivan affair, and there were hints from some of the people at the reception. It wasn't hard for him to connect the dots. When he asked me about it, I didn't lie."

"I want to hate you right now," said Paul.

"Go ahead if that's what you need to do. I just want you to know that your

228

Jared is incapable of being faithful to anyone or anything."

Paul narrowed his eyes. From the look on Jeff's face, there was more. "Tell me."

He bit his lip. "The night we were celebrating my passing the bar exam..."

"You mean just a few months ago?"

"Yes. He tried to seduce me in my bedroom while you were sleeping."

"And?"

"And I threw him out on his ass, drunk as I was. He climbed right into bed with you and, the next day, acted as if nothing had happened."

"You weren't tempted?" he asked. "I've seen how you look at him."

"No. I couldn't do that to you. I care about you too much for that."

Paul looked at Jeff and saw, for the first time in years, the man he'd had such a crush on back in Rome. It was sobering to realize that all this time, Jeff had been standing in the wings watching while he made a fool of himself with Jared. "I don't know whether I love you or hate you right now."

"I don't have that problem," said Jeff. He pulled Paul close to him and held him tightly.

Chapter 31

Archbishop-elect Mickleson sat in his tiny private chapel, as he did every morning, for his time of prayer and meditation. As usual, he was trying to pray the rosary, but his mind was distracted by random thoughts, so he kept losing his place. He knew better than to let distractions annoy him, having learned the technique of watching his thoughts drift by without reacting—but this morning, he kept hopping on board with them. He thought back to those mornings over the past few years when Paul would come by the residence and they would celebrate Mass together, then Paul would join him for breakfast, and they would share thoughts on the state of the diocese and the world. He would miss those times. Paul had a sensitivity he very much appreciated.

Several times, he had invited Jared to pray with him and share his breakfast. But he always felt something was missing. Jared was sharp and a skilled administrator, but his practicality never made up for a certain spiritual acumen that just wasn't there. In every sense, the archbishop was delighted with the cardinal's choice of Paul. He understood that Paul's sensitivity would endear him to the people of the diocese. That could go a long way toward making up for whatever might be lacking on account of his youth and inexperience. He knew the people would be predisposed to welcome a new bishop, but they could turn critical toward him in no time. And the clergy were another question altogether.

He thought about the welcome he had received as a new bishop arriving in California from the Midwest rust belt, and how easy his transition had been. California—even northern California—was an area of wide diversity. The Latino culture had been a vital element of life here ever since it had been settled as part of Spanish Mexico. Most people were used to accommodating differences, and he felt at home here, even where a majority of the population didn't look like him as an African American.

His experience with the Archdiocese of Mobile was already proving to be quite different. Every one of his trips down there had provided him with the same experience. The people he met were polite, almost to a fault. They smiled at him and exuded graciousness. There was never a hint of rancor, nor could he fault them on their willingness to help. What he experienced, however, was a lack of genuine warmth. He did not feel welcomed—despite their speeches—but rather tolerated. It felt to him as though they were dealing with him because they had no other choice, rather than because they wanted him to be there. He knew Alabama was a conservative state—even metropolitan Mobile—but the conservatism he felt there was a different species from that of northern California. Southern conservatives could be very stand-offish. Even their warmth could feel cold.

He was glad he'd had the experience of serving in San Luis Obispo to mature him. Still, he understood that the challenges facing him in his next position would be more complex. It was wise of the cardinal to help Paul ease into the next phase of his clerical career by letting him take over this diocese. Despite Paul's fears, the archbishop knew he was ready, and there was a strong base here whom he could always count on for support. He hoped that he was as ready for his coming assignment as the cardinal thought he was.

He looked down at the rosary in his hands; once again, he'd lost his place. With so many changes disrupting the flow of his life, distractions were becoming the rule rather than the exception. "Hail Mary, full of grace…" he started over.

The door to his chapel opened. "Bishop, I'm sorry to disturb you." It was Maria, his housekeeper. "You're wanted on the phone. It's Rome."

Resigned to leaving his morning prayer unfinished, the archbishop got up and went into his study. He sat himself at his desk and picked up the phone.

"Clarence? It's Cardinal Romero. I know it's early there. I hope I'm not disturbing you."

"Your call could never be a disturbance, Cardinal. I'm always at your service."

"Good," said the cardinal. "I have several things to go over with you this morning, and my time is very limited today."

"It's good you caught me at home because the chancery office is closed today. It's a national holiday in the US—Memorial Day."

"Then, I hope I'm not interrupting your holiday."

"Not at all, Cardinal," said the archbishop. "What do you need?"

"I'm flying into Los Angeles, staying with you for two weeks, and leaving to go back to Rome from Mobile. I will be arriving on Sunday, the twelfth of June. Could you arrange to have a car at the airport to drive me up to San Luis Obispo?"

"Of course. It's rather a long ride, though. Wouldn't you prefer a closer airport?"

"No," said the cardinal. "This flight to Los Angeles works best for me. I can nap in the car on the way up."

"You know Father Jared is a pilot. It's possible he could fly you up here if you'd prefer."

"Yes, that might be better," said the cardinal. "He and I need to have a long talk."

"I'll speak to him," said the archbishop, "and we'll set something up."

"The installation is scheduled for Saturday, correct?"

"Yes, Cardinal. It's June twenty-fifth."

"Then I'll make the announcement regarding your successor that week, before we leave for Mobile."

The archbishop was jotting down notes as they spoke. He'd have Jared contact the press tomorrow.

"Now, about your successor. That's the real reason for my call."

"Yes?" said the archbishop. "What is it?"

"I'm afraid there's been a change of plans."

"How so?" The archbishop didn't like the sound of this at all.

"I'm afraid that your Paul Fortis cannot be ordained a bishop."

The archbishop's throat went dry. "I don't understand. What's the problem?"

"I received a small parcel this morning containing a love letter from Paul Fortis to a man named Jeff Hensen. It was written a number of years ago on seminary stationery while Paul was in Rome. It seems they were carrying on a homosexual affair. The letter is very graphic and explicitly sexual. My English is quite good, I think, but I had to look some things up to understand what they were saying."

The archbishop felt sick to his stomach. "Oh, my God." His voice came out in a whisper. "Who sent it to you?"

"It came anonymously but from somewhere in California. Someone over there wanted to make sure Father Fortis would not be appointed bishop. Who is this Jeff Hensen?"

"He's an attorney," replied the archbishop. "His uncle has been our diocesan attorney for years. He lives with Paul and Jared. I can't imagine he would do something like this to Paul. Is it possible the letter is a forgery?"

"I asked myself the same thing and examined it closely to make sure it wasn't. I have in my personal files several letters Paul Fortis wrote to me while he was at the seminary in Rome. This letter is on the same stationery and in the same handwriting as the ones in my files. I'm satisfied that, regardless of who sent it to me, it was written by Paul."

"What have you decided to do?"

"You know the troubles we have had over the past few years, particularly in your country, with priests and sexual misconduct. The Holy See will not accept the ordination of a known homosexual as a priest, let alone as a bishop. Obviously, Paul's condition cannot be a secret, because someone over there had that letter before I got it. Perhaps it was Jeff Hensen."

"I understand."

"It's still your diocese, Clarence, and I won't tell you what to do; but if I were you, I would consider it most inappropriate to keep that priest on as your vicar general. Do you agree?"

"Yes, Cardinal. Under the circumstances, I will have to dismiss him."

"That's what I would do in your position."

"What about my successor?"

"I've decided to allow Jared Röhrbach to take your place as bishop of the diocese. He was always my second choice anyway. The Holy See agrees, and the necessary paperwork is being drawn up. I will bring it with me when I arrive in two weeks."

"I understand. Jared will be very pleased. He was quite upset when I told him he hadn't been chosen."

There was a moment of silence on the line. "That is not a good sign. I'm uncomfortable with a man who wants too much to be a bishop. As you well know, humility is an essential attribute. That's also one of the reasons why Father Röhrbach was not my first choice. Pride is a sin and a liability, but not a disqualifier. If it were, none of us could ever be bishops."

"You're quite right." The archbishop was uneasy with the cardinal's decision but had no provable reasons to dissuade him from the choice he had made—only hearsay. His hope was that the difficulties of the office would help Jared mature. Still, he was even more unhappy about what he had to do next: deliver the message to Paul and Jared. "Is there anything else you needed to discuss?"

"No, Clarence, I think that's all for the moment. Please give Jared my congratulations."

The archbishop hung up the phone and sat with his elbows propped on his desk and his face in his hands. Hadn't he warned the boys over and over to behave themselves? Hadn't he told them how easy it was for the cardinal to turn from an ardent supporter to an opponent if there was even a hint of impropriety? There was no going back now. The decisions were out of his hands. He picked up the phone and called both men to come over right away.

He paced across his office as he waited for them to arrive. Something felt odd about the situation, but he couldn't define what it was. Besides, there was nothing to be done. The cardinal had made his decision, and Clarence Mickleson was not about to circumvent it. Second-guessing him would be worse than useless.

Maria appeared at his study door. "Father Fortis is here, Bishop," she said.

"Thank you. Please show him in," he said.

Paul entered looking very worried and took a seat facing the archbishop's desk.

"We have a serious problem," said the archbishop as gently as he could. "It seems someone sent the cardinal a letter you wrote to Jeff Hensen while you were in school in Rome."

Paul's eyes grew large, and his jaw dropped.

"From what the cardinal tells me," the archbishop went on, "the letter was explicitly sexual in nature."

Paul stared at his hands in his lap.

"Of course, the cardinal won't tolerate even a whiff of scandal, so he has rescinded your selection as bishop."

"Oh, my God," said Paul.

"I'm afraid it gets worse," said the archbishop.

"How could it? My reputation is ruined."

"The cardinal wants me to remove you as vicar general. I have little practical choice but to do what he suggests. I'm so sorry, Paul. If it were up to me, we'd work something out, but it isn't. It looks like you have a very clever enemy out there somewhere. Whoever it is knew how to inflict the most damage on you. Do you have any idea who would do this to you?"

"It had to be Jeff. He's the only one who's seen those letters." Paul struggled to maintain his composure. "What will you do with me now?"

"I don't know," said the archbishop. "You'll have to give me a few days to figure something out. You're not suspended. I'll do my best to find a good assignment for you. This couldn't have happened at a worse time. The cardinal will be here in less than two weeks, and I was counting on your help. But that's my problem. You have enough to worry about. Just stay home for the next few days, and I'll give you a call as soon as I have something for you." He paused, his chest feeling tight. "Are you going to be okay?" There was no question—Paul was not okay.

"I don't know. I guess so, as long as they don't convict me of Jeff Hensen's murder."

"Try to be patient, Paul. I promise I'll do the best I can for you."

It broke the archbishop's heart to see Paul looking so crushed. He gave him a warm embrace and walked him out of his study. They ran into Jared, who was sitting in the living room by himself. He noticed that Jared avoided looking at Paul as he passed by him.

The archbishop ushered Jared into his study. "Sit down, please." Jared seemed calm and composed. Under the circumstances, the archbishop had expected him to look more anxious.

"Jared, we've had an issue come up with Cardinal Romero. For reasons I can't go into, the cardinal has changed his mind about my successor. He has now recommended you to succeed me. The final papers are being drawn up. The cardinal will be here in two weeks and will want to meet with you. Your appointment as bishop of San Luis will be made public the following week. Congratulations."

236

"Thank you very much, Bishop," said Jared. "I'm overwhelmed. I don't know what to say."

Though Jared didn't look overwhelmed. In fact, Mickleson didn't think he looked the least bit surprised.

"What happened to Paul?" Jared asked.

"He's being reassigned. I'm afraid, under the circumstances, we can't have him working in the chancery."

"Why on earth not?"

"I can't talk about it," said the archbishop. "It's confidential."

"I feel so sorry for him." Jared glanced around the room and then smiled. "Would you have time to meet with me tomorrow to go over the plans? Time is getting pretty short."

"Yes, of course," said the archbishop.

Nothing about this situation seemed right. Not only did Jared's emotions not match his words, but he should have been shocked to hear the news— and he wasn't. Either the archbishop was missing something, or there was something going on that he wasn't aware of. Regardless, he was sensing some manipulation of the situation. "Jared, just remember that my reasons for not recommending you were based on hearsay, but you did not deny them. If there are any other situations I should be aware of or secrets you're holding that could compromise you, me, or this diocese, I want you to tell me now so we can avoid any future difficulties. Are there any?"

"No, Bishop. On my honor."

"All right, then." He looked into Jared's eyes but couldn't interpret what he was seeing. Compared to Paul, Jared was nearly impossible to read.

"Is that all for now?" Jared asked, standing.

"Yes, I suppose," he replied. "Will you be talking to Paul?"

"Why? Did he ask you to have me come by?"

"I thought you two shared an apartment."

"No." Jared looked away. "I moved out a couple of weeks ago."

"Paul never said anything to me about it." Come to think of it, neither had Jared. "What happened?"

"Nothing much," said Jared. "We had a disagreement, and I thought it best to live somewhere else."

The archbishop was overwhelmed by a feeling of disappointment that bordered on disgust. "Maybe the cardinal and I were wrong about the two of you."

"What do you mean?" Jared looked taken aback.

"We've been grooming you both for years to be ordained bishops, and you're behaving like high-schoolers." He shook his head. "Get out of here, will you?"

Chapter 32

Monday, May 30, 2016

Paul drove into the apartment parking garage in a blind rage. When he spotted Jeff's car still parked in its space, he could scarcely control himself from ramming into it. He was shaking so badly, it took him three tries to park his car, and with every try, his anger grew. He got out of the car and slammed the door so hard he triggered the car alarm on the vehicle parked next to him. When the elevator door opened, he charged in, almost knocking Mrs. McNulty off her feet. She moved out of his way as nimbly as her arthritic legs would allow, and Paul mumbled something that he hoped would pass as an apology.

When he got inside the elevator, he hammered on the "2" button until the poor machine started moving. The door reopened on the second floor and the elevator spit Paul out into the hallway. He pulled his keys out of his pocket, but his hands shook, and he fumbled with the ring and dropped the keys on the floor. It took him several stabs to get the key into the lock. He pushed the door open with all his force. It crashed against the inside wall so hard that the pictures on the wall jumped.

Jeff stood in the middle of the living room, eyes and mouth agape. "What the...?"

"You goddamned fucking son of a bitch!" Paul charged across the room but brought himself up short with enough presence of mind not to assault the man. "What the fuck did I ever do to you, scumbag?"

"Oh, God, Paul! What happened?" Jeff stammered, backing away.

"You know goddamned well what you did, motherfucker! What I want to know is why?" Paul shouted.

"I don't know what you mean. I didn't do anything. Please, tell me what happened."

"My letters, you asshole. What did I do that was so horrible that you'd send one of them to Romero?"

Jeff went pale. "That wasn't me. I still have your letters. They're right here in my room. Stay there, I'll show you." He scrambled by Paul and ducked into his room. In less than a minute, he returned with the package of letters in his hand. "Look. They're all here." He handed Paul the little pile secured by a rubber band so dried up that it stuck to the envelopes.

Hands shaking, Paul leafed through the pile. What remained of the elastic crumbled and fell in pieces on the floor. "Why did you keep these?"

"Because they meant something to me. But I swear I haven't even looked at them since Rome." His voice was panicked.

The elastic and the condition of the letters suggested Jeff was telling the truth. "Are they all here?"

"I don't know. There were eleven."

Paul counted the envelopes. Ten. "There's one missing. Where is it?"

"I have no idea. They were all together in my briefcase the day I left Rome. I counted them and put them in there myself."

Even through his blind rage, the reality of what Jeff was telling him sank in. If a letter was missing, it must have been lost in Rome. There had only been four of them left in the residence that morning. If Jeff didn't have it—and, of course, Paul didn't—then it could only have been old Father Rinaldi...or Jared.

He stood in the center of the room shaking, but at last he allowed himself to breathe. All at once, the reason for Jared's moving out became obvious. The man he thought he loved so faithfully had thrown him under the bus for the sake of his own career. He felt dizzy. He sank into the nearest chair, his anger now mixed with the grief of betrayal. It was as though a light had come on, and Paul saw for the first time the man Jared was in all his ugly shallowness. The image of Jared he had created in his own mind, and all the excuses he'd invented to avoid seeing the truth, dissolved. He had come to understand that Jared was a shell of a man, incapable of fidelity, incapable of even rudimentary honesty.

Paul looked up. Jeff stood across the room, back to the wall, staring at him. "Forgive me," he murmured. "It was Jared."

"Jared? Why would he do that to you? I thought he loved you. "

"He did it because he wants to be bishop. I'm such a fool. In his mind, the rules don't apply to him. I never saw until just now that the only person Jared loves is himself. He abandoned his father, he sacrificed his brother, and now he sacrificed me so he could get ahead." He put his head down. "I've been such an idiot."

Jeff crossed the room and knelt next to Paul. "I'm so sorry he did this to you. Now I wish I had warned you about him earlier. Maybe things would have been different."

"No," said Paul, "I wouldn't have listened." You can't make someone listen when their mind is closed to the truth.

They sat in silence for a minute, until Jeff nodded to the framed photograph that sat on the bookshelf. "I don't know why I'm surprised someone that good-looking could be such a jerk."

Paul swiveled around to look and then laughed. "That's not Jared."

"Huh? Of course, it is."

"No. That's Justin, Jared's identical twin."

"You're joking," he said. "I get it. Jared's the evil twin."

"Maybe so." Paul sat back in his chair.

Jeff looked dumbfounded. He leaned in toward the photo for a closer look. "He has a twin? How do I not know that? Why doesn't anyone ever talk about him?"

It had been a secret for so long that Paul looked around the room before he spoke. "Because I'm the only one who knows what happened to him and where he is. Justin didn't want anyone in the family to know so that if the police questioned them, they wouldn't have to lie or be forced into telling them his whereabouts."

"The police?" Jeff sat down next to Paul. "Why would the police be interested in him?"

Paul told him about the accident.

"Jared was the one who killed the guy?" Jeff asked.

Paul nodded. "In Justin's car. He was blind drunk, and speeding. When Justin and I got to the crash site, it was a mess. The car was totaled, and there were broken booze bottles all over the front seat. Justin insisted we get Jared out of there before the police came. He didn't want Jared's career in the priesthood to be ruined. So, we drove Jared back to my place and put him to bed. Then we went back to Justin's parents' house, and he packed some things. He took the fall for it. I dropped him off at the bus station, and he caught the first bus out of town that morning."

"Where is he now?" asked Jeff.

"Austria."

"Why did he leave the country?"

"The police figured Justin was driving because it was his car. When they interviewed Jared, I lied and told them he'd been at my house all evening. We never told their father the truth, and he never forgave Justin for the crash and for running away."

Jeff sat back in his chair. "So, all along, people have been covering up Jared's messes. No wonder he feels entitled to do anything he wants."

"Yeah," said Paul. "I saved his ass and look where it got me."

"Has Justin been back to the States since then?"

"No," said Paul. "He's afraid he'll be stopped at immigration and have to stand trial."

"How long ago did you say this was?"

"Let's see," said Paul. "We've been ordained almost five years, and it was four years before that, so I'd say eight or nine years."

"I'm assuming they'd charge him with vehicular manslaughter. The statute of limitations on that is only six years. He'd be safe to come back, even if he had done it."

Paul's eyes widened. "Really?"

"Really." said Jeff. "If he wants to. Call him. I'll talk to him."

Paul got his phone and dialed the number.

"Justin Röhrbach, *guten abend*," said the voice on the line.

"Justin? It's Paul."

"How are you, Your Excellency? Am I right that some heavy congratulations are in order? The selection has been made, right?"

"Not exactly. Your brother ruined my chances of that." Paul proceeded to tell him what Jared had done and why.

"That's it, man," said Justin. "This shit has gone on long enough. We've turned our lives inside out for that fucker, and this is how he repays us? I'm done with it."

"There's nothing we can do," said Paul. "The damage is done. It's over."

"Not by a long shot. My brother will never be bishop once the authorities find out what I know about him. Who do I go see with my story? Don't you guys know some cardinal in Rome?"

"Yes," said Paul. "Cardinal Romero. He's in the office of the Congregation for Bishops just outside Saint Peter's square. I'll email you the exact address if you want." Paul glanced at Jeff, whose eyes were wide as he listened to Paul's side of the conversation. "What are you going to do?"

"Head down there for a little chat."

"Whatever you plan to say, you'll have to get him to see you before you can tell him anything. He's the prefect of the Congregation. He's not easy to reach. I wish I could help, but it's a little late for that."

"I'll talk to him. I can be very persuasive. Can you send me a picture of him?"

"Sure, but..." Paul hesitated. "You're not going to put on a collar and pretend to be your brother, are you? You can get arrested in the Vatican for impersonating a priest."

Justin laughed. "No. I'm not going to pretend to be Jared. Besides, he's the one who's impersonating a priest. He's a miserable excuse for a human being, let alone a man of God."

"Okay, well whatever you do, I just hope you're successful. It won't restore me to the cardinal's good graces, but maybe it'll stop Jared."

"Don't worry," said Justin. "It'll stop him." He was silent for a minute. "How's Hannah doing?"

Paul swallowed hard. "I'm sorry, Justin. She's gotten worse since we last talked. Rosario can't handle her anymore. I had her brought to a nursing home here in San Luis, so I could be closer to her. I gave Jared the address..."

Justin made a rude noise with his mouth. "He'll never go there. He hates her too much."

"No," said Paul. "I think you're right. I visit her when I can. She's getting good care, but most of the time she doesn't recognize me. For a while, she kept calling me Justin." He heard Justin's intake of breath. "It seemed to make her happy that I was there. If you could see her, she might rally a little. I don't know how much longer she'll be with us."

"I'd love to see her one more time," Justin said. "I feel horrible that I missed out on saying goodbye to my father, but I never would have made it out of the airport without getting arrested."

"Oh my God," Paul said. "That's the real reason I was calling you. You can come home."

"What? What are you talking about?"

"I've got my friend Jeff Hensen here. He's an attorney. I told him the truth about the accident—I mean, I hope you don't mind—and he said you're beyond the statute of limitations. They can't arrest you."

"Are you sure? I don't want to risk anything more because of my worthless brother."

"Here," Paul said. "Jeff will tell you himself." He handed the phone to Jeff.

Jeff introduced himself and explained about the statute of limitations. "You are home free." There was a pause, and then he said, "Thanks for helping Paul out. He doesn't deserve what he's being put through. I'll give you back to him. See you soon, I hope." He handed the phone back to Paul who said a few words before hanging up.

"I can't believe how much he sounds like Jared," Jeff said.

Paul hung his head. "I'm sorry for screaming at you. I don't think I've ever been that upset at anyone in my life."

"It's okay," said Jeff. "You couldn't have known."

Jeff came over and put his arms around Paul and held him. Paul relaxed in his arms and, for a moment, let go of the tension that had wracked his body ever since his interview with the bishop that morning. He felt Jeff's gift of himself—a gift that had nothing to do with sex. It was affection, pure and simple, so different from anything he had experienced with Jared. It was an expression of love, free of any conflict with his conscience or dedication to his ministry.

For that moment, at least, he understood that the two of them wanted nothing more than to be there for each other.

Chapter 33

Sunday, June 12, 2016

Jared was scared. His dream was becoming more like a nightmare. Each time it happened, he was aware that he was dreaming but felt helpless to make it stop. Here it was again. The same people were spread out in a line in front of him. Each pair parted to allow another pair to come forward: his parents, and between them Justin and Tony, and between them, Bishop Mickleson and Paul. They were all the people he loved who had cared for him. The line of characters in front of him moved aside again, making room for someone new coming into the middle between the bishop and Paul. At first indistinct, the figure came forward into the light. It was Hannah, and she was angry. She stepped out of the formation and moved toward him. He tried to yell, but nothing came out. He tried to run, but his legs wouldn't move. When she wrapped her ghostly arms around him, a chill spread through his entire body.

He woke up shivering, angry and upset. It was bad enough that the woman had haunted his life; now she was haunting his dreams. He looked at the clock. It was almost three in the afternoon, and he was in the guestroom of the priests' residence at Saint Theresa's church in Cambria. He had finished his weekend assignment helping Father Dick Loring and had stretched out for a nap. He was still in his clerical clothes. He sat up and rubbed his eyes as if that would somehow erase the memory of Hannah coming for him.

Everything was going so perfectly for him. The only sour note was Hannah—his last bit of unfinished business. *Why am I worried?* She'd lost her mind and was in a home where she couldn't bother anyone. He was annoyed that he kept obsessing about her. Maybe it was because she had the inheritance that should have been his.

He stood up and undid his clerical shirt, folded it, and laid it in the overnight case he used for his weekend assignment. He slipped on a dark blue polo shirt and tucked it in. He was off for the rest of the day, and there was something he wanted to do before he left Cambria. He snapped the case shut, straightened up the bed, and went out into the hallway. Father Dick's bedroom was empty. The TV was on in the living room, but Dick had nodded off in his favorite easy chair, breathing heavily. Jared crept to the front door and, as silently as he could, eased himself out.

His red Porsche was parked in the driveway, looking incongruous in front of the rectory. Now that he was about to be named bishop, he'd have to exchange it for something more appropriate. He threw his overnight bag in the trunk and drove off. Since Hannah was now in San Luis in a nursing home, he knew the house would be empty. They had gardeners and a caretaker visit the house regularly, but it was Sunday, and no one would be there. He pulled up in front of it and got out. Every time he came here, it felt weird. The place felt empty—not of furniture, but of people, empty of life.

He took out his old key, unlocked the front door, and went inside. It was still broad daylight. In the turret room that had been Papa's study and office, nothing had changed. Not a book had been moved. There wasn't even any dust on the furniture. He opened a panel in the wainscoting to reveal Papa's safe. As a kid, he'd watched his father open it countless times and had committed the combination to memory, though he never let on to his father that he knew it. He opened the safe and removed the papers that were inside. He was looking for the trust papers. Roger Spellman had told him what was in them, but he'd never seen them himself. He sat cross-legged on the carpeted floor and sorted through page after page of paperwork until he found it. Sure enough, his father had named Hannah as sole trustee. He and Justin were named as beneficiaries. That meant they'd split the inheritance if Hannah were to die. From what he understood, that wouldn't be long now. He felt more secure now that he knew for certain he and Justin were next in line. Without a doubt, there was more than enough there, and he had no problem sharing it with his brother.

So, there it was, at long last: everything he had worked for. He would be bishop and, of course, he'd make Paul his vicar general again. Paul would be upset for a while about losing the episcopacy, but he'd get over it. In fact, Paul would be in his debt for restoring him to a position of importance. There were many advantages to that. Having the kind of power and prestige that awaited him would open several doors. In fact, if he was astute and played up to the cardinal, he might even land himself a position in the curia in Rome. The cardinal would always be looking for cash to fund his projects. Even with the money he had now, it wouldn't be that hard to help out. And the inheritance—his birthright—was on the horizon.

He folded the documents and tucked them into his back pocket, then replaced the other paperwork in the safe. As he twisted the dial to make sure it had locked securely, the thought came to him that maybe he should wipe it clean of his fingerprints. That made him laugh out loud. He was no thief. The paperwork was his. He closed up the house and made sure nothing had been left out of place. Minutes later, he was on his way to San Luis. Hannah still haunted the back of his mind, though he had an idea about how to fix that, too.

Instead of going straight to where he was staying, he looked up the address of the nursing home Paul had given him: the Village at Sydney Creek. It was on Laurel Lane, a thoroughfare just south of the center of town. By the time he had parked, it was early evening. Some people were leaving from one of the side doors, and he walked over to have a look around. Just inside the doors, there was a well-marked diagram of the complex. It took him a minute to locate Hannah's room on the map, in the hospice ward. He navigated through the building with little difficulty. On the way, he passed a few of the staff dressed in green scrubs or blue cotton jackets. They smiled at him and nodded, and he returned their greetings. It wasn't long before he stood in front of room D106. The name "Hannah Röhrbach" was on a small plaque beside the door. He pushed the door open and went in.

The light was fading outside the window, but it was still bright enough in the room to see his stepmother in a lone hospital bed against one of the side walls. Her head peeked out from the covers, propped up on several pillows. A curtain with mesh at the top was pushed back against the wall on one side. There was a hospital tray table near the bed on the other side. A sterile-looking metal bedside table and an upholstered armchair completed the furnishings. He closed the door and went over to her. As fierce and powerful as she had always appeared to him in years past, today she looked like a shriveled caricature of herself. Her eyes were closed, and she was breathing slowly, probably asleep. He couldn't get over how he had let this woman dominate him for his entire life. So many of his choices over the years had been made to keep her at bay. That was nearly over now. Soon he could exorcise her out of his mind and out of his dreams— he hoped.

She opened one eye. It startled him for a second. With her condition, he expected her gaze to be unfixed and wandering. Instead, she stared right at him. Did she recognize him? Now both eyes were open, and her head was turned toward him. Some of the old Hannah was still there: he could feel it.

"Hi, Hannah," he said. "It's Jared."

Her face hardened, and her stare became more intense and threatening, but she didn't speak.

"Do you remember me?"

As her facial expression shifted to one of contempt, his initial bravado ebbed away. He had the distinct impression that she wasn't as far gone as he'd been led to believe. But he was determined not to let this shell of a woman intimidate him. He pulled out the trust papers from his pants pocket. "Do you recognize these?"

Her eyes drifted to the pages in his hand. Her lips curled into an unmistakable smirk.

"You do, don't you?"

Her eyes drifted back to his face, but the smirk remained.

"You know what's going to happen next, don't you? You're going to die, and all that money will be mine. You can't do anything about it."

Her eyes grew wide. He couldn't read her expression. Then, she started to laugh.

"What's so funny? You're going to die."

She laughed louder.

"Shhhh!" What if somebody in the hallway heard? He didn't want anyone to know he was there.

She only laughed louder. Her mind was gone, but she was still mocking him. His annoyance with her was growing into something more. He was afraid of what was happening and angry at the same time, and he needed it to stop. "Be quiet," he said a little too loudly, but it made no difference to her. "If you don't stop, I'll make you stop."

She paused for a second and looked into his eyes with a fierce expression that said, *I dare you.* The laughter grew louder and more challenging. The old Hannah was still there, and she was still powerful.

He'd had enough. He grabbed one of the pillows from under her head and held it over her face. The laughter continued, though muffled. He pressed harder. He'd show her. She'd never do this to him again. Gradually, the laughter changed into something that sounded like hiccups. Tears of rage rolled down his cheeks as he pressed even harder. "Stop!" he hissed though clenched teeth. The hiccups became weaker and farther apart until, at last, she was quiet.

He yanked the pillow away from her face. *What did I do?* "Hannah!" he said in a hoarse whisper. "Hannah! Don't do this!"

Her eyes were open but no longer staring at him. Her face was contorted in a sardonic grin, but she wasn't moving. He grabbed for her wrist. Her arm was limp, and there was no pulse. *Oh God!* He couldn't stop looking at her face. It was seared into his memory. *I didn't mean it,* but even then, he knew it was a lie. *Gotta get outta here*. He stuffed the pillow back under her head and closed her eyes so that she looked like she was sleeping.

His mind was racing. Only those two orderlies had seen him come in. If he could get out of there without anyone else seeing him, maybe he'd be okay. He opened the door a crack. The corridor was empty. There were voices at the nurses' station around the corner, but the nurses couldn't see him. Two doors down, an exit sign was mounted on the ceiling. *Must be a fire exit*. He slipped out into the hall and hurried to the door. *What if there's an alarm?* He had to take the chance. He pushed the crash bar on the door, bracing himself for a loud alarm, but it swung open noiselessly. He stepped out and closed the door behind him.

Don't run. Don't draw attention. He walked briskly around the side of the building. His Porsche was right there in front of him. He looked around. Evening gloom had already descended. He was wearing dark clothing. Maybe no one would notice him. In fact, there was no one in the parking lot. Within a minute, he was driving away from the building. He glanced back in the rearview mirror. The building was cloaked in darkness, but the row of windows across the front was alive with glowing lights.

It took him no time to drive to the furnished apartment he'd been renting since he'd left Paul. Once inside, he went straight to the liquor cabinet and fixed himself a tall strong drink. The first couple of swallows sent a warm glow travelling down his insides. He took a deep breath and exhaled. He was still shaking. Standing at the counter, he finished his drink and poured himself another. His mind started to slow down. There was no undoing what he'd done. Two realities dawned on him: first, that Hannah would now be seared into his consciousness. He would never, for the rest of his life, be rid of her. The second was that in just a few days, half his father's huge fortune would be his. He carried his drink over to the easy chair and plopped himself into it.

He needed to think this through. When the nursing home discovered Hannah's body, they'd call the person responsible for her. That would be Paul. So, logically, Paul would be the one to give him the news. He needed to be prepared to talk to him, but he started to feel a little woozy. When had he last eaten? That would have been lunch at Saint Theresa's, and it hadn't been much, just a sandwich and a soda. No wonder the booze was hitting him so hard. *Better slow down.* He made his way back to the kitchen. The remains of a deli-cooked chicken he'd had for dinner Friday night was still in the refrigerator. It would be better than nothing. He didn't even bother heating it up in the microwave. He stood at the counter and gnawed at it until most of it was bones.

It had been over an hour since he'd left the nursing home. *Why isn't he calling?* He couldn't call Paul. He'd have to wait, but his anxiety was thrumming. It made him think of how he'd felt after that accident years ago. The image of that old man lying limp in the crushed seat of his car bleeding all over came back to him. At least then, he'd been so drunk he had felt mostly sick to his stomach. The anxiety hadn't started until the next morning when he'd awakened at Paul's and had realized where he was and why. It was the waiting, and his inability to do anything else, that had gotten to him then—and it was getting to him now. Going to bed was not an option. He felt in the pit of his stomach that Hannah would be there in his dreams, waiting for him.

He fixed himself another drink. And another. He drank until the blackness arrived.

Chapter 34

Monday, June 13, 2016

Paul sat on the couch in his apartment, massaging his temples. It was after five P.M., but the bright California sun was still high in the sky. He had a headache that had been aggravating him all day and most of last night. He blamed the phone call that had come in the middle of the night from the nursing home. Of course, they had to call him. He had Hannah's medical power of attorney. Nonetheless, it was an odd call. As a priest, he was accustomed to getting the occasional sick call in the middle of the night. For some reason, more sick people died at night than during the day. Yet never before had he been asked—no, almost ordered—not to come.

Since all the arrangements for Hannah's death had been made long ago, everything should have gone as planned. There was to be a cremation but no service—she had been adamant about that—but he should have had the opportunity to come by before the funeral home picked up her body. It didn't make sense. He decided to call the Reise Mortuary. He had done services there before and knew the Reises well enough.

"I didn't get the chance to bless her body at the nursing home," he explained to the receptionist. "Would it be all right if I came down there in a few minutes? I would appreciate it."

"Of course, normally there would be no problem, Father," the receptionist said, "only we don't have the body yet."

It took Paul a second to process what she was saying. "What do you mean?"

"They haven't released it to us. I'd be happy to give you a call as soon as it's here."

Paul was stunned. "Who has the body, then?"

"I'm sorry, Father, but I don't know. The nursing home told us they had no further information. That's all they said."

He thanked her and hung up. *Something strange is going on*. He looked at his watch. It was closing in on suppertime. He thought of calling Jeff, when his phone rang. It was a number he didn't recognize. *Maybe its news*. It was Justin.

"Where are you?"

"I'm at the chancery. You need to come down here right away. The archbishop needs to see you.

"What's all this about? I know there's something going on. Does it have something to do with your stepmother?

"Yes, but that's all I can tell you right now."

"But you have to tell me something. I called the funeral home just a few minutes ago and they don't even know where Hannah's body is. And I've been trying to reach you since you and the cardinal arrived this morning. "What gives?"

"Don't worry. We'll explain everything when you get here...and park in the back where you won't be seen. I'll meet you there."

"This is all too cloak-and-dagger for me," he sighed. "I'll be right down. I can't wait to see you. It's been too long."

Justin was standing by the back steps of the chancery, leaning on the railing. *Life in Europe has been good to him*. He was even a bit trimmer than Jared and was more tanned. Paul jumped out of the car to greet him. "You look amazing, man!" he called out and rushed to wrap his arms around him. "It's so good to see you. It's been, what? Seven or eight years? Welcome home. I couldn't wait to see you."

"Me, too. You've been my lifeline back home. I owe you big-time." He broke their embrace. "We'll have to talk later. Come on. We have to hurry. They want to talk to you.

"Who wants to talk to me? Paul's stomach tightened. *This is not good.* Justin opened the door and ushered him in. "They told me we have to be quiet. No one's supposed to know you're even here."

When Paul entered the office, the archbishop was sitting on the sofa in his little seating area. Jeff and his uncle Roger were sitting at the conference table opposite the door. Five chairs were arranged in front of the archbishop. Two men in suits sat to his right, and there were three empty chairs to his left.

"Come over here, Paul." The archbishop indicated one of the empty chairs to his left. Justin sat down next to him.

As he took his place, the archbishop said, "This is Inspector Peterson from the Cambria police department." He indicated the older of the two gentlemen who was thin, with angular features and receding hair. Paul was stunned. "And this is police Sergeant McGarvey from San Luis Obispo."

Paul nodded to each of them. What could possibly be going on?

"They want to ask you a few questions, and I told them you'd be happy to talk to them."

Paul nodded again.

"What do you know about a fatal automobile accident in Cambria in August of 2007?" the inspector asked.

Paul took a deep breath and related the whole story, from Jared borrowing Justin's car for a party, to Justin's phone call in the middle of the night, to picking up Jared at the accident scene and being questioned by the police the next morning.

"I see," said the inspector. "I think I have a fairly good idea of what happened." He fixed Paul with his gaze. "You realize you could have been arrested and sent to prison for accessory after the fact and interfering with a police investigation?"

"Yes, sir," Paul said. "I've thought about it often."

"I don't think we need to pursue your reasons for helping a felon evade prosecution just now. We'll leave it at that for the present."

"Yes, sir."

"Now, Father, it's my turn," said the sergeant. "When was the last time you saw Hannah Röhrbach?"

Paul wasn't expecting that question, and it threw him off balance. "Uh...this past Saturday? Yes. It was Saturday afternoon." Perspiration dripped down his spine.

"What was her condition when you last saw her?"

"She was doing all right, under the circumstances. She was having rather a good day. She even smiled at me and said a few words. I was quite surprised to learn she had passed away last night."

"Mmm-hmm." He looked up from the file folder in his lap. "Thank you very much for your help."

Paul looked over at the archbishop for explanation, but his expression was blank.

"One more question, Father," the sergeant said. "When was the last time you saw Jared Röhrbach?"

"About two weeks ago, I think. At the archbishop's residence."

"Thank you. That'll be all."

Paul was relieved, though he wondered why they were asking about Jared. "May I go?"

"I think it would be best if you stay where you are for the moment," said the archbishop.

"Mr. Spellman?" said the sergeant, "Would you bring Father Röhrbach in now?"

Roger left the room, returning a moment later with Jared in tow.

Jared was smiling as he came through the door. "I thought you'd forgotten me," he kidded Roger. But his expression darkened as soon as he saw Paul and Justin sitting with their backs to him and the two men sitting across from the archbishop facing him. Paul turned around to look at him. Jared gave him a *What's going on here?* look as though nothing had happened between them. Paul ignored it.

"Come in, please," said the archbishop. "Take a seat here, next to Paul, if you would."

Jared hesitated for a few seconds and looked around the room. When his gaze landed on Justin sitting next to Paul, his eyes grew wide. He was beginning to act like a cornered animal. He sat down in the chair next to Paul. For the first time since they'd been together at the archbishop's house, he looked Paul straight in the eyes. Paul had no trouble reading that look. It said, *Help me!*

Paul looked away.

When the archbishop introduced the officers, Jared bristled. Every sinew of his body showed *fight or flight.*

The inspector began with questions about the accident. At every turn, Jared lied outright.

"No, Paul and I stayed in at his place and got drunk together."

"No, I couldn't drive because my car had been mothballed before I left for Rome."

"No, I knew nothing about the accident until I woke up the next morning."

"Mmhmm," the inspector said. "As a priest, doesn't it bother you that both your brother and your best friend just swore independently you were the one driving that car—and that they both lied at the time to protect you?"

Jared glared first at Justin, then at Paul. There was panic in his eyes.

"Doesn't it bother you at all that your brother took the rap for what you did?"

"It wasn't my fault," Jared growled. "That guy pulled in front of me.

Besides, it happened a long time ago. You can't do anything to me now."

"Doesn't it bother you," asked the archbishop, "that you have lied to and hurt every person in your life who cared about you?"

Jared stared at him in stunned silence.

The sergeant then asked Jared about Hannah. Jared told him the last time he'd seen her was at his ordination in Rome and that she'd seemed perfectly healthy. Had he seen her in the Sydney Creek facility in San Luis? No, he told him he didn't even know where she was.

"You do know that she died yesterday, right?"

"Did she? That's too bad."

"Let me fill you in on a few details, Father," he said. "Did you know that when someone dies unexpectedly, medical personnel are trained to look for signs of abuse?"

Jared shrugged. "Makes sense." But there was something in his voice that told Paul he wasn't quite as nonchalant as he pretended to be.

"Were you aware that one of the tell-tale signs of smothering is bloodshot eyes?"

Jared shook his head. "I'm not sure why you're telling me this."

"Aren't you? Did you know that, when there's suspicion of foul play, the coroner can order an autopsy?"

Jared didn't move. Neither did Paul. The reason for all the mystery around Hannah's death was becoming clear. He could hardly believe where this was all leading.

"Do you know what the coroner discovered? Your stepmother had excess carbon dioxide in her bloodstream—another sign of smothering. He also found fibers around her nose and inside her mouth that matched one of her pillows. That same pillow had bloodstains on the underside that matched her blood type, and she had blood inside her lower lip from having it forced against her teeth. The coroner has concluded that her death was a homicide. She was smothered."

The sergeant paused. "Two nursing home employees have identified you from your picture as someone they had passed in the corridor about the same time as the murder."

"It wasn't me!" Jared cried.

Paul felt sick to his stomach.

Sergeant McGarvey then pulled some papers out of the folder on his lap. "Father, do you recognize these?"

Paul recognized them as the trust papers from Kurt's estate.

Jared barely glanced at them. "They look like legal documents."

"Very good. They're the trust documents that name you and your brother as beneficiaries, should anything happen to Mrs. Röhrbach. Have you seen these before?"

"No," Jared said. "Never."

"May I see the documents, please?" Paul asked. "I was involved in drawing them up."

Jared's face grew red. The sergeant handed Paul the papers.

Paul glanced at them. "These are the old trust papers that Kurt kept in his safe. After his death, Hannah—Mrs. Röhrbach—as sole trustee had a new set drawn up, naming me as the successor. These trust documents have been superseded. I now have full control of the trust."

Jared gripped the arms of his chair so hard that his knuckles turned white. He started at Paul in utter rage.

"Interesting," the sergeant continued. "Would you care to speculate as to how these found their way to the floor under Hannah Röhrbach's hospital bed?" He didn't wait for an answer. "And were you aware that the nursing home has security cameras all over their property? We have videos of you exiting the side entrance of the nursing home, going to your parked car—

a red Porsche isn't it?—and driving away."

The stubborn arrogance left Jared's body and he sunk back into the chair.

"Were you aware," the sergeant said, "that Hannah Röhrbach was your biological mother?"

Jared sat bolt upright. "No. It's not possible. I don't believe you."

Paul looked over at Justin in disbelief.

The sergeant drew a couple more documents out of his folder. "Your brother was kind enough to supply me with these documents. I have here copies of the adoption paperwork for both you and your brother. You were both born in Salzburg, Austria, weren't you? Apparently, your adoptive parents wanted to get you into this country easily. If you want more details, you can always ask your brother." He cocked his head. "Are you ready to come with me now, Father?" Jared said nothing, so he continued. "Jared Röhrbach, you are under arrest for the murder of Hannah Rainer Röhrbach. You have the right to remain silent..."

Paul's mind raced as the sergeant read Jared his Miranda rights and fastened handcuffs on him. Everything he thought he knew about Jared, about Jared's family, about his priesthood, about their relationship, was a lie. Jared looked at him with panic in his eyes. Paul shook his head. *You're on your own, buddy.* He remained silent and unmoved as the two officers led Jared out of the room yelling, "No! Wait! I didn't mean it! It was an accident! Paul, help me!"

The door closed behind them. When the archbishop stood, Paul, Justin and the two attorneys at the back of the room stood as well. He looked sad and worn. "Thank you, Justin for coming forward. You helped save us all from making a terrible mistake," he said. "And Roger and Jeff, thank you for your help and guidance. I'm glad I had you to rely on to guide me through this."

"May I go now, Bishop?" said Paul.

"Yes. Sure. It's been a long day." He turned to Paul. "Please come see me first thing in the morning. We should go over what you'll need to handle. I'm leaving for Mobile with the cardinal in a couple of days, so you'll take over here until my successor is selected."

"Take over? What do you mean?"

"As vicar general—if you'll accept.

"But...I thought..." Paul was stunned.

"That the cardinal wouldn't allow it? No, he only recommended that I replace you. However, you're still the best one for the job, and the most experienced, especially considering all this. You'll have your old office back, of course."

"Of course, Bishop. Thank you. I don't know what to say."

"All right, everyone. The cardinal has been waiting all day for news. He's anxious to know the outcome of this little gathering. I have to rest and collect my thoughts before I meet with him in a little while." He broke into a wan smile. "So, get out of here."

As Paul joined the others on the way out, the archbishop said, "Roger, can I talk to you for a minute?"

As the door closed behind them, Paul said, "Let's go back to the apartment and rest. I've had about all the stress I can take for one day."

Chapter 35

Monday, June 13, 2016

When they arrived at the apartment, Justin sat on the couch and Jeff took one of the easy chairs. Paul was still reeling from everything that had gone on in the archbishop's office and went off to the kitchen to make them all vodka tonics—without thinking, because that's what Jared always drank. When he returned to the living room, Jeff and Justin were whispering together but fell silent. Paul handed them their drinks and plopped himself down on the couch next to Justin.

"Okay. What's going on with you two?"

Jeff looked at him with obvious concern. "We're worried about you, that's all. How're you doing?"

"Peachy, thanks," he said with more bitterness than he had intended. "How do you think I'm doing?" He knew they hadn't meant to offend him; it just felt like they had jabbed a finger into an open wound. "Sorry. I don't know what I'm feeling right now. I never expected any of this."

Jeff shook his head. "I know what you mean. The last few weeks...who could have imagined he was capable of all that?"

"I feel like such an idiot." Paul took a gulp of his drink. "How could I not have seen it after all these years? He was closer to me than my own family, for God's sake."

"Don't be so hard on yourself," Justin said. "He took advantage of all of us."

Paul rested his elbows on his knees, looked down at the floor and let out a heavy sigh. "You don't understand. I bailed him out of one scrape after another for year after year, each time swearing to myself it would be the last...until the next time." He looked at Justin. "You'd think I would have caught on."

Justin put his hand on Paul's shoulder.

Jeff scowled. "You may not like to hear this—especially from me—but love is blind. I know how deeply you loved him. We all knew."

Paul met his concerned gaze. He could feel his lip tremble, but he clenched his jaw instead. *Enough. No more wasted tears.* Jeff may have understood, but that just made his sense of shame burn the hotter. From their time together in Rome, it was obvious Jeff cared for him—so much so that he'd backed away from him rather than compromise his principles. He himself had done the opposite with Jared: he'd given in to him every single time regardless of what his conscience told him was right. "I didn't do him any favors by letting him take advantage of me, did I?"

Jeff shrugged. "Probably not."

"Listen," said Justin, "we all thought we were doing the right thing. Maybe we could have done better—differently, at least—but second-guessing ourselves now won't do any of us any good."

Both Paul and Jeff murmured their agreement.

"Regardless of whatever we did or didn't do," Justin said, "the final responsibility for everything was still Jared's. The consequences are on him alone. We never forced him to do anything."

"You're both right," Paul said. "It's only now I'm realizing that no matter how close I thought we were, Jared never confided in me. He always held back, kept secrets. Every time I thought I understood what he was thinking, I'd get shocked by something he did—right up to the end." He shook his head. "It's not going to be easy putting all this behind me, but I've got bigger worries than what Jared Röhrbach did or didn't do. My whole ministry is on the line. He's made his choices; now I have to make mine."

"He's going to need legal counsel," Jeff said. "I'll talk to my uncle tomorrow morning and see about who'll represent him. Between the two of us, we'll make sure he has help getting through the legal system."

"Who's going to pay for that?" Justin asked.

Paul turned to him. "It should come out of his share of the individual trust funds your father gave you. I'm sure he still has plenty to cover his legal expenses. Assuming he gets out of prison in ten or twenty years, he'll have more than enough to live on. He'll never be destitute."

Justin scowled and took a gulp of his drink. "What he lives on is no concern of mine. I just don't want to be on the hook for any of his expenses." The late evening sun cast long shadows across the room. "I understand Hannah was my father's sole heir. I wonder where the fortune goes now. Who was her attorney?"

"Harold Wright was," said Paul. "On Hannah's death, I became the sole trustee."

"Oh?" Justin straightened. "I thought maybe she might have thought of me."

"She did," Paul replied with a broad smile. "She made me trustee to make sure you received what was yours." He turned to Jeff. "Could you do something for me?"

"Sure. Anything."

"Would you draw up the paperwork to add Justin as a trustee?"

"Of course. I'll take care of it tomorrow."

Justin took hold of Paul's arm. "You don't have to do that, you know."

"It's what Hannah wanted, and it's only right. I insist." He turned back to Jeff. "One more thing. Once Justin is trustee, would you draw up the paperwork to take me off the trust?"

Justin looked up at Paul and frowned. "Ignore that request," he said. Then, he broke out in a grin. "No one has been a more loyal friend to the Röhrbach family than you, Paul. I've trusted you with my life. How could I not trust you with this fortune? You're the most deserving of it of anyone."

Paul was stunned. He only thought of himself as a caretaker. It felt as though Justin was adopting him in place of the brother he'd lost. "I don't know what to say."

"Don't say anything," Justin said.

"Thank you," Paul said and threw his arms around Justin.

"No, Paul," said Justin. "Thank you for all you've done. I'm so sorry for all we've put you through. I'm doing my best to make it up to you."

"What about everything you've been through?" Jeff said.

Justin shrugged. "That's water over the dam. At first, when I was in Europe, I was very homesick and felt sorry for myself, even if it was my choice to leave. But after a while, my nursing career took off and I started to enjoy myself. I can't lie; I had a great life over there."

"How did you find out all that stuff about Hannah and your father and mother?" Paul asked.

"That was one of the advantages of living in Europe. I knew a bit about the family history, and I knew we still had some relatives over there."

Jeff gave a slow nod. "So, you asked around."

"Yup. On my vacations. My Mama had a brother, Johann, who was a priest in Austria. I found him a couple of years ago, and he told me the whole family story and helped me find the adoption papers."

Paul leaned forward in anticipation.

"Hannah was a mess after she left her husband. He was a real jerk, and I'm glad I never got to meet him, even if he was my real father. She was homeless and pregnant with twins. My mom rushed over there to help out any way she could. That's when she and Kurt decided to adopt us boys. And that's why Hannah was so strict with us growing up and why she stepped in to raise us when Mom died. I had to forgive her for her mistakes. She had a horrible childhood and had no clue how to raise boys in America, but she tried. I'll give her that much."

"Jared never knew about this," Paul said. Would it have made any difference if he had?

Justin's hands rested in his lap, palms up. "I wasn't in touch with him, so I never got to tell him."

That triggered Paul's memory. Kurt wanted his sons to have that locket. "Just a minute," he said, and went into the bedroom to find it. It was right where he had stashed it in a little drawer at the top of his dresser where he kept his cufflinks and watch. He carefully took it out and brought it back to Justin in the living room.

"Kurt gave me this to give to Jared. I don't think he believed that he'd ever see you again. It was Hannah's, and when Jared found out that she was the sole trustee of your father's estate, he threw it away, but I kept it. I'm sure that Kurt would have wanted you to have it." Paul handed him the locket.

Justin popped open the catch and looked at the two photos inside. "That's Friedrich Rainer, Hannah's father—and my grandfather, unfortunately. I've seen his picture before many times. And this," he said, pointing to the woman in the facing glass oval, "must be Ada, my grandmother. I haven't seen her picture before." He examined it more closely. "She was very attractive, wasn't she?"

Paul nodded. "There's more," he said. "Open the back cover."

Jared used his thumbnail to pry open the back side of the locket. When he saw the contents, he sat in stunned silence.

"What is it?" asked Jeff.

"It's Hannah," he said, turning it so that Jeff could see the two photos, "...and my father. I've never seen him before." He turned to Paul. "No wonder Papa told you this was important. Max Schümer was a laborer—a handyman—and not someone who'd have his picture taken. This may be the only photograph of him that exists." He looked down at the images lying in the palm of his hand. "Max wasn't a good man. He was a tortured man who made Hannah's life Hell. I'll never know why. But even so, he

266

was our biological father. I can at least acknowledge him for that."

There was a knock at the door. "Are we expecting anyone?" Paul asked.

Jeff went to open it. "Uncle Roger? What brings you here?"

Roger laughed. "I couldn't leave you guys alone without adult supervision. No telling what mischief you'll get yourselves into." He grabbed one of the chairs and sat down. "Gentlemen, I've been sent here on a mission of mercy."

Paul's eyebrows came together. He wasn't sure if he was more curious or more concerned. Both.

"Archbishop Mickleson and I sat down for a long meeting with the cardinal after you left. We had quite the talk. The upshot was that the archbishop changed his mind about your going back to your job at the chancery tomorrow."

Paul's spirit plummeted. He realized he'd still been holding out hope for forgiveness. "He doesn't want to see me after all?"

"Not exactly. He wants you to come to his residence tomorrow morning instead."

Paul was confused. "Why?"

"The cardinal wants to talk to you about your next appointment, and the archbishop would like to show you around your new home."

Paul caught his breath. "What are you saying?"

"The cardinal has changed his mind about you. The archbishop and I can be very persuasive when we want to be. We all agreed that the infamous letter was the unfortunate mistake of a young man, and no one outside of this group ever needs to know about it. Congratulations, Paul. We know you'll make a fine bishop."

Paul stared at Roger, not comprehending what he just heard. "You mean...?"

"Holy crap!" said Jeff. "Congratulations, man." He jumped up and threw himself on Paul, knocking them both sideways into Justin's lap. Justin struggled to stand up but only succeeded in bringing the three of them down in a heap on the floor like little kids, laughing hysterically.

"Oh, my God," said Jeff, when he had caught his breath, "What next?"

Paul pulled himself up, hanging on their shoulders. "God only knows, my friends. God only knows."

Epilogue

Tuesday, June 14, 2016, 3:00 AM

Jared sat cross-legged on a thin slab of foam that served as a mattress, the finely defined musculature of his back pressed against the cold concrete block wall beside the little cot that was provided for a bed. His eyes were closed, not because he was at all sleepy, but because there was nothing to see. The wall opposite was empty, cold and gray, but the lights were out and what little light there was in the hallway outside his cell came through a grimy little wire-latticed window in the steel door. There wasn't enough light to matter. He had no idea what time it was or how long he'd been there. His arrest, transport to the lockup and booking were all a blur. He felt dissociated from the person who been checked in here a while ago. People there had been asking him questions, but he had no recollection of what they were or how he had answered them.

In fact, he had no idea where he was. The sun had still been up when they drove him here, but his mind had checked out. The streets and buildings they had passed were all meaningless landmarks as far as he was concerned. His disorientation just added to the unreality of the entire experience. He was unable to locate himself in time or space.

At first, what had been most real for him were his emotions. He could remember entering the archbishop's office. He could still recall the excitement he felt coming into the office that would soon be his. He was so caught up in it that he had almost missed the cold formality that Roger Spellman had shown him as he was ushered in. The whole scene replayed for him in his mind's eye, only in excruciatingly slow motion. Of all the things that went on in that room earlier this evening, the one thing he most remembered was meeting Archbishop Mickleson's gaze. He wasn't sure what it was he saw in that kindly man's eyes – was it disappointment? Sorrow? Compassion? Pain? Maybe it was all those things, but whatever it was, it was enough to drain every ounce of joy from him and to make his blood run cold.

Seeing Paul there, then Jeff, then his brother had triggered an explosion of rage within him. Their eyes, too, were seared into his memory. All of them had fixed their accusing stares at him; but behind the ferocity of their anger, he had seen something else. Each one of their faces wordlessly testified to his betrayal. Once he had seen them, he began to feel cornered, trapped in the web of lies that he had so meticulously woven for himself. His rage evaporated as quickly as it had arisen and, in its place, he felt only panic.

Yet, of all these feelings, the one he remembered most clearly was the sensation like an electric jolt that went through him when he turned to Paul in silent desperation. Paul—his high school buddy. Paul—the first person he had come out to in adolescent angst. Paul—the boy who had offered himself willingly to him as they first awkwardly explored their sexuality together. Paul—his constant support and encouragement through all the ups and downs of their studies and priestly training. Paul—in everything, his confidant and...protector. It was only when he looked into Paul's eyes and saw *nothing* that his whole flimsy edifice of bravado had come crashing down. He didn't have to think it, he *felt* it: Paul was gone. Not since the day he had stood by his mother's bed holding her limp, lifeless hand in his had he felt such despair.

He tried to keep up appearances in front of everyone. His pride wouldn't let him back down. He tried with all that was left in him to maintain the illusion of innocence, but his lies sounded hollow even to him. By the time the police had escorted him from the archbishop's office, his last ounce of rebelliousness was gone. They hadn't bothered to handcuff him, but it hadn't mattered. There was nowhere left for him to go. And, though he hadn't looked back at the people he left behind in the room, he could nonetheless feel the intensity of their stares as they watched him go. That was the last thing he remembered.

He opened his eyes again to the dim light in the cell. His hands were resting in his lap above his crossed legs. Seeing them, he managed a bitter smile.

He was still wearing the black clerical pants he had put on this morning—tailor-made, of course. They looked a little incongruous with his white t-shirt and bare feet. He turned his hands over, palm up and stared at them. Seeing them made him think back to his ordination. He remembered kneeling in front of the cardinal with his hands outstretched before him. The prelate had anointed theses hands with sacred aromatic oils, consecrating them for the ministry. He tried to recall what he was thinking and feeling at that moment, but he could not. He had been too preoccupied with his imagined future to pay much attention to what was happening to him—and within him—at that moment.

He thought about all the places those consecrated hands had been since that day, and he closed his eyes again trying to block out the images that came to his mind. But those images were too stark and disturbing, and he had to open his eyes again before he imagined in too much detail those hands snuffing the life out of the woman who had given him life. An enormous shiver ran thought his entire body as he stared at those hands lying limp and empty in his lap.

Try as he might, he couldn't turn his thoughts away from that night. He replayed the scene in every disturbing detail. That look in her eyes was as clear as if it had happened only moments ago. She had stared at him as though somehow, she knew that his face would be the last thing she'd ever see. He marveled at how, looking back, he could now see how what he thought was a momentary impulse born of rage was much more than that. It was, in fact, the culmination of a lifetime of self-delusion. He had thought he was the master of that moment when, all along, she had known his weakness. That was what was behind her uncompromising look and her mocking laughter at him. In the end, she had known him better than he had known himself. It had been her final challenge and, despite all appearances, her final victory.

He squirmed in his place. His legs folded under him were growing numb. An ache gripped his lower back and made its way up his spine and spread across his shoulders. He couldn't stand to see those hands anymore. He didn't want to remember with such clarity what that pillow felt like in his clenched fists. He tried once again shutting his eyes to block it all out, but, instead, a new memory emerged. It played across the screen of his eyelids as though projected on them. It was *that* dream.

Now, he realized that the dream was a creation of his troubled subconscious mind, but it still disturbed him to the core to realize how pervasive the lies that he had told himself had been. He had made himself believe that he was master of his own destiny, alone and on his own against a hostile world, but he was beginning to see things differently. They were all there in the dream: the people in his life who knew the truth about him. He could recall the look in each person's eyes—looks that had disturbed and frightened him at the time but had now come to mean something entirely different.

There was Lilly, his mother—his *adoptive* mother—looking at him with fear for his weakness, unsure how he would fare growing up without her. There was Kurt, his adoptive father, looking longingly after him, as though his beloved boy was beyond his reach. There was Justin, his twin, with a look of solid determination in his eyes, committed to doing for him what he couldn't do for himself. Then Tony, a man who lived every moment of his life without a shred of pretense and who had put up with his shallow arrogance because he genuinely cared about him.

It was only when he got down to the last pair of specters—Archbishop Mickleson and Paul—that he reached the core. Here were the only two people who had recognized in him a spiritual depth that he had been unable to see in himself. Beyond his wealth, his looks, and his intellect, they saw spiritual potential. From the look in their eyes, he could now see that they were desperate for him to find it in himself. The archbishop never stopped believing in him and promoting his cause right up until the end. And Paul...oh, God, Paul! How much had he compromised and what degree of integrity had he sacrificed just to be in love with him? And this was the man he most envied and resented? Jared's chest tightened and his jaw clenched as, piece by piece, the reality of his life unfolded in front of him.

He was overwhelmed with shame, not even so much for the things he had done, but for the person he had become.

He didn't want his thoughts to pursue that nightmare any farther. After what he had seen about himself reflected in the faces of those who loved him, he was most afraid of the last one...the one who brought his thoughts full circle: Hannah. At the time, he had seen her in the dream as he had always thought of her: an angry, vengeful woman. He had recoiled from her image. Now, he was starting to see something else. After all, she had loved both of her boys so much that she had been willing to give them up for adoption so that they could have what she was unable to give them. So, what was behind the fire he saw in her eyes? What was behind her uncompromising discipline and her attempts to block him at every move? What could it have been, but *fear*? All along, even to the end, she had tried to keep him from making the choices in life that would bring him inescapable pain. In the end, had she seen that his only way out was *through* the pain? Is that why she was laughing? Is that why she seemed to accept death at his hands so willingly? Perhaps, all along, she had been the only one who truly knew him.

Once again, he opened his eyes. His racing heart had quieted. The ghosts of his past had receded, each one taking its place on the shelves of his memory like decorative figurines. They would remain there, but they had lost their usefulness. Each one bore testimony to the life he had been living, but from now on they could only be silent and passive observers of his way forward.

Tomorrow...tomorrow he would face arraignment on the charges against him, he would be asked to plead, and bail would be set. He hoped the charges would be voluntary manslaughter and not second-degree murder. Roger Spellman had already committed to represent him. He could certainly afford Roger, and, for that matter, he could also well afford whatever bail was set. He could be free from the lockup and home by tomorrow afternoon. But the words "free" and "home" stung him. What's the use of freedom if there's nowhere to go? Where's home if there's no one there for you? What's the use? Wasn't he sitting alone in a cell sinking in shame *because* he'd always been able to manipulate his way through everything?

That's enough. Sometimes facing the consequences is the easier, softer way. He had betrayed the people who loved him and killed the woman who gave birth to him. How much more guilty could he be? *No, for once I'm not running away from this one.* There was no escape from the man he had become. He would plead guilty. He would not post bail. He'd see it through, regardless of where it took him. He'd have to start his life over from scratch anyway. He had no idea what could be salvaged. His priesthood? Maybe. The important people in his life? Some of those who loved him *might* accept his apology. To ask for their forgiveness would be out of the question. But, how about God? He could find forgiveness there, couldn't he?

He needed so badly to do something right then, but he was at a loss as to what to do. He wanted to pray. He wanted to pray the way Paul prayed, getting lost in prayer. But he just couldn't. It had been so long since he prayed like that, that he didn't remember how to do it—if he'd ever known how. All he'd ever remembered doing was going through the motions and mouthing the words. It was something, as a priest, that he was expected to know how to do. Maybe his spiritual bankruptcy was worse than he had imagined. He had prayed, hadn't he? He remembered soaking his pillow with his tears night after night praying God to make his mommy better. But that was out of desperation and grief. This is very different. This is a deeper isolation than he'd never felt before. He was utterly alone, and he had no idea how to pray into the void.

Biography

H. Les Brown has master's degrees in philosophy and theology from the University of Ottawa, Ontario, Canada. He has worn many hats over the course of his careers: minister and spiritual director, computer programmer and tech writer, Chief Information Officer and Quality Systems Auditor, Management and Program Analyst, and Certified Life Coach. He is now retired and living with his husband Craig Gibson in Palm Springs, California.

Glossary

Alb – a long, white garment worn at religious rites by persons having a role in the ceremonies. It symbolizes the white garment given and worn at baptism as a sign of new life. It may be fastened around the waist with a **cincture**.

Archbishop – a **bishop** who heads an **archdiocese**, which is the principal **diocese** in a **province**, or collection of dioceses. The archbishop has a primacy of honor and presides in meetings of the provincial bishops.

Archdiocese – the principal **diocese** in a **province** or collection of dioceses (usually contiguous). An archdiocese is headed by an **archbishop** who has a primacy of honor over the other bishops in the province.

Bishop – an ordained **cleric** who has received the "fullness of the priesthood" and is empowered to ordain **priests** and, with other bishops and the permission of the Pope, can ordain other bishops. The **order** of bishop (also called the Episcopacy) is conferred by the **ordination** (laying-on of hands) by an ordaining bishop and his fellow bishops. In the Catholic Church, a **priest** may not be ordained bishop without the permission of the Pope. A bishop may be the **ordinary** of a **diocese** or **archdiocese** (as **archbishop**) or may serve as an auxiliary to a diocesan **ordinary**. Bishops who have been selected to be electors of the pope are called **cardinals**. Bishops are generally addressed to as "bishop" or, more formally, "your excellency"; cardinals are addressed as "your eminence."

Cardinal – an honorary title given to a cleric chosen by the Pope as papal elector. On the death of a pope, the cardinals meet in consistory to elect a successor. They also serve as advisors to the pope as well as heads of the Vatican **congregations**.

Cassock – a plain, long-sleeved garment including a Roman collar at the neck, covering to the ankles, either closed with a row of buttons down the front or secured with a wide sash of the same material around the waist and hanging down beside the left leg, often ending in a tassel.

Celebrant – a person authorized and empowered to celebrate a religious rite or ceremony.

Chasuble – the outer garment worn by **celebrants** exclusively for **Eucharistic liturgies** and rites performed as part of the **Eucharistic liturgy** (for example, weddings, funerals, confirmations, or **ordinations** held as part of a **Eucharistic liturgy**). The chasuble was originally worn as an outer garment (similar to a poncho).

Cincture – a rope that ties around the waist of an **alb**. It symbolizes chastity.

Cleric – a person who has publicly committed his life to serve the church. In Catholic churches, clergy are exclusively male. Canon (Church) Law requires that every cleric must be incardinated (enrolled) in a **diocese** or its equivalent. The formal Rite of Admission to Candidacy for the Diaconate or Priesthood is a symbolic enrollment for secular clergy (those who are not members of religious orders or communities). Secular **deacons** and **priests** must be incardinated.

Clerical clothes – street clothes indicating the clerical office of the wearer. Permanent **deacons** generally do not wear clerical clothes. Transitory **deacons** may wear clerical garb similar to **priests. Priests** generally wear black or dark blue trousers and shirts and jackets with an attached black or dark blue outer collar with a small opening in the front showing the white inner collar. In addition, western Catholic **bishops** wear a pectoral cross on a chain around their necks. Generally, the pectoral cross is worn in an inner breast pocket so that only the chain is visible.

Congregation – 1. a gathering of church members for worship; 2. offices centered in Rome, generally in Vatican City, that serve as papal secretariats governing the various aspects of the Catholic Church worldwide. Each congregation is headed by a secretary who is usually a

cardinal.

Crosier – a metal staff with a curved top carried by a presiding **bishop** in processions (generally only within his own **diocese**). It derives from a (stylized) shepherd's crook and symbolizes the **bishop's** service as shepherd of the flock (the **diocese**).

Deacon – an ordained **cleric** who has been granted the privilege of reading the Gospel during the **liturgy**, preaching, distributing Communion, presiding at weddings and funerals (when celebrated without the Eucharist), and Baptizing. Permanent deacons may be married (prior to **ordination**); transitory deacons (those who hold the office temporarily as part of their preparation for **ordination** to the priesthood) generally are unmarried and promise celibacy prior to **ordination** as deacons. The deaconate is conferred by **ordination** (laying-on of hands) by a **bishop**.

Diocese – a geographical region or territory administered by a **bishop** that is composed of several **parishes**, each administered by a **pastor**. The principal diocese in a **province** is called an **archdiocese** and is administered by a **bishop** with the honorary title of **archbishop**.

Episcopacy – the state or condition of being ordained a **bishop**. The word comes from the Greek *episkopos* meaning 'overseer.'

Eucharist – the celebration of Jesus's Last Supper, consisting of Scripture readings and the Eucharistic Prayer which culminates in the Words of Institution ("This is my body" and "This is my blood") and the distribution of Holy Communion. In the western Church, communion is given in the form of consecrated (blessed) unleavened bread and, in some cases, wine. Also called the *Mass*.

Holy Week – the week of the year beginning with Palm Sunday and continuing to (and including) Easter Sunday.

Liturgy – (literally 'people's work') any formal religious rite or celebration led by a **cleric**.

Mitre – a double-pointed hat worn by a **bishop** during formal **liturgical**

celebrations indicating the powers of his episcopal office.

Monsignor – a title of honor given to a **priest** in recognition of special accomplishments or length of service. It entitles the **priest** to wear some of the trappings of a **bishop** but confers no special power or authority.

Ordinary – the presiding **bishop** of a diocese who has the authority to manage all the affairs of the diocese. All **clerics** promise obedience to their ordinary (and his successors). A **bishop** becomes an ordinary by the rite of *installation* as **bishop** of the **diocese**. The ordinary may be assisted by one or more auxiliary **bishops**.

Order – an official clerical office in the Church: **deacon, priest,** or **bishop**. Each **order** is conferred by a rite of **ordination**.

Ordination – the rite of conferring the powers and authority of clerical office (**diaconate, priesthood,** or the **episcopacy**) upon a person by the laying-on of hands by one or more **bishops**.

Parish – a geographical region or territory containing a parish church (and possibly one or more secondary sites called "missions") and administered by a **priest** with the title of *pastor*. In areas where there is a shortage of **priests**, the parish may be headed by an ordained **deacon** or a **religious** man or woman. These substitutes for a pastor are called *parish administrators*.

Priest – an ordained **cleric** who has all the powers and authority of a **deacon** and, in addition, is empowered to celebrate the **Eucharist**, hear confessions, and grant absolution in the name of the Church, celebrate the sacrament of the Anointing of the Sick and, in extraordinary circumstances, give the sacrament of Confirmation. Priesthood is conferred by **ordination** (laying-on of hands) by a **bishop** together with other fellow priests. Priests are generally addressed as "Father."

Province – a collection of several **dioceses**, each headed by a **bishop**. The principal **diocese** in a province is called the **archdiocese** and is headed by a **bishop** with the honorary title of **archbishop**.

Religious – a man or woman who has consecrated his or her life to the service of God and the community within the context of a religious order or community. Religious men who are not clerics are most often referred to as "brothers" or "monks" whereas religious women are referred to as "sisters" or "nuns." Religious men may be ordained **deacons** or **priests** (in which case they are referred to as "father"). When they are ordained **bishop**, they are generally no longer directly associated with their religious community.

Sacristy – an area of a church outside of the main worship space where clergy and their assistants vest before liturgical ceremonies. It also contains storage space for vestments, sacred vessels, and implements used in liturgical rites. In older, larger churches, sacristies can be very large and ornate, serving as chapels in their own right.

Stole – a strip of cloth in the appropriate **liturgical color** worn around the neck to symbolize clerical power and authority. **Deacons** wear the stole over the left shoulder, diagonally across the chest and back and fastened by a clip or **cincture** on the right hip. **Priests** and **bishops** wear the stole over the neck and hanging over the shoulders and chest. It may hang free or be fastened in front with the **cincture**. The stole was originally the symbol of office within the eastern and western Roman empires.

Surplice – a white vestment with a wide square or circular neck opening, worn over the head, reaching to the knees and often with wide full-length sleeves. The surplices are worn over the **cassock** by altar servers and is often worn with a **stole** of appropriate color by **deacons** or **priests** during liturgical ceremonies when the **alb** is not worn.

Vestment – a garment worn for liturgical rites, such as alb, cincture, stole, chasuble, and mitre and crosier (for bishops).

Vicar General –the principal deputy of the bishop of a diocese in matters of jurisdiction or the exercise of administrative authority. He possesses the title of local **ordinary**.

Made in the USA
Middletown, DE
01 November 2021

51489220R00166